EVIL NEVER

DIES

EVIL NEVER DIES

T.R. RAGAN

f THOMAS & MERCER

Text copyright © 2015 T.R. Ragan

Published by Thomas & Mercer, Seattle

www.apub.com

Amazon, the Amazon logo, and Thomas & Mercer are trademarks of Amazon.com, Inc., or its affiliates.

ISBN-13: 9781477827703
ISBN-10: 1477827706

Cover design by Cyanotype Book Architects

Printed in the United States of America

DEDICATION

To my best friends who also happen to be the most wonderful
sisters in the world: Cathy, Patty, Sally, and Lorry.
Love you all.

I am a natural born killer. I have been killing since I was a child. These people were simply in the wrong place at the wrong time. You can lock me up and throw away the key, but it won't make a difference because evil never dies.

—The Sacramento Strangler

CHAPTER ONE

Lizzy Gardner Investigations had gone rogue.

While handling the usual skip-traces, missing persons searches, and workmen's compensation cases, Hayley, Kitally, and Lizzy had handpicked six criminals who needed to be punished. The worst of the repeat offenders. The list included five men and one woman, all of whom had committed numerous crimes, including rape, stabbings, muggings, and assault and battery.

At the moment, Hayley stood over one of the men on their list. He couldn't see her through the thick duct tape she'd wound around his head to cover his eyes.

But she could see him.

Owen Dunham was naked and blindfolded, and his hands and feet were each tied to a separate bedpost. He was a rapist. He was the number two man on their list of creepers living right here in Sacramento. The number one guy on their list was Wayne Bennett, but Lizzy was handling him.

Divide and conquer. That was the plan for now.

Following Owen around all night, watching him stagger from club to club, Hayley and Kitally had waited patiently before making their move. It was well past midnight when they followed him onto the freeway, then watched him weave through traffic and somehow make it back home without killing anyone.

By the time he stumbled through the door to his apartment, he was an easy target. They pushed him inside and sent him crashing to the floor. Kitally locked the door, and then they were both upon him, riding him as he thrashed about like a slimy beached fish until Hayley succeeded in injecting him with etorphine hydrochloride. Hopefully not enough to kill him, although Hayley wasn't too worried either way.

Lucky for him, the drug appeared to be wearing off fast, which meant he wasn't dead from an overdose. Dragging him through the apartment and getting him onto the bed had taken some work, but they'd managed.

"What's going on? What are you doing?" he asked as he came to, wriggling beneath the tape and ties.

Ignoring him, Hayley told Kitally to get the knife ready. She could have done that ten minutes ago, but she wanted him to hear every word. She wanted him to sweat, to know what it was like to have zero control. And mostly she wanted him to know that something bad was about to happen.

Kitally began sharpening the blade, making certain he could hear the sound of metal scraping against metal.

Owen Dunham had raped twin girls. Eight years old. Open-and-shut case. He was linked to the sexual assault of five others, but for some reason prosecutors had only concentrated on the twins. Unlike most rapists, Owen spent ten years in prison. He was released two years early for good behavior.

It wasn't long before he met a woman who happened to be the mother of a blonde, curly-haired six-year-old. She and her daughter lived in a trailer park. The woman could not believe her good fortune in finding such a wonderful man, and she swallowed his story about the reason for his prison sentence (unjustly accused by a vindictive ex-girlfriend after he broke up with her) hook, line, and sinker. Not only was he handsome, he helped her around the house and even did things for her, like change the oil in her car. For her birthday, he bought her an entire year of yoga classes because he knew how difficult raising a child could be for a single mother. He also offered to babysit. He wanted her to relax and have some time to herself.

But two months later, class was canceled unexpectedly and the woman came home to find her wonderful, too-good-to-be-true boyfriend raping her daughter.

The police were called.

The rapist took off before the sirens sounded in the distance. Investigators gathered facts and DNA samples. They took pictures and interviewed the child's mother. The woman's six-year-old daughter was subjected to all sorts of tests, lots of probing and prodding. Owen Dunham was ultimately arrested, but something happened along the way, and he was released on a technicality.

This time, he'd gotten away with his crime. Or so he thought.

"If you don't let me go," Owen growled, "I will hunt you down and make you wish you were never born."

"I don't think so," Hayley told him. "After I'm done with you, you're the one who's going to wish you were never released from prison."

"Wait a second. Is this some sort of birthday prank? Did my brother set this up? This is Larry's doing, isn't it?" Nervous laughter erupted. "I don't know how much he paid you to do this, but undo the ties and I'll double it. I'm asking nicely. The money is in my wallet, across the room in my top drawer."

"I don't want your money."

His voice deepened. "What do you want, then?"

"We're here to make sure justice is served."

"What are you talking about?"

3

"Prison time didn't teach you a thing." Hayley drew in and released a long, frustrated breath. "And so now it's up to me and my friend to do what *they* should have done in the first place."

"I never touched those girls."

"And which girls might you be referring to?"

He said nothing.

"More than one examiner determined that both of the Vicente girls were raped."

"I'm not saying they weren't, but it was their father who raped them, not me."

"I wonder how it was that *your* DNA was found on the girls?"

"We were neighbors. He planted my sperm. Took used condoms right out of the garbage. It wasn't me."

"And what about the daughter of your latest girlfriend? Who raped her?"

"That woman is crazy. I met her *once*."

"Well, I guess those pictures all over the news of you and the little girl at the park and the zoo were just the mother's imagination."

"Let me go right now," he warned. "You're starting to piss me off."

Hayley looked at Kitally, who put down the sharpened knife, picked up the duct tape, ripped off one more piece, and taped his mouth shut.

"You're not the only one who's pissed off," Hayley said. With every word out of his mouth, she'd felt the rage building within. She was so tired of assholes like him taking advantage of innocent young girls. Owen Dunham should have been left in prison where he belonged.

Muffled noises sounded beneath the tape as they both put on latex gloves. Hayley looked at Kitally. "Should we cut off his balls, or do you want to perform surgery to try to sterilize him instead?"

"Hell, yes, I'll give it a try," Kitally said, retrieving the knife. "Although I think castration might be the way to go."

The muffled cries rose in pitch.

Kitally went to the side of the bed. "Maybe we should carve *rapist* across his forehead." Kitally put the tip of the knife against his forehead. "Don't move or you might end up losing an eye."

The man growled.

Kitally pulled the knife away.

"What is it?" Hayley asked.

"I changed my mind. I'm going to perform a vasectomy instead. More of a challenge, less mess, and we'd still be making sure he won't reproduce." She climbed up on the bed. It took her a moment, but she made the first tiny incision. The man moaned and quivered all over. "Easy, easy there now," she said. "I don't know. Even if he holds still, I'm not sure this will work. It's a delicate procedure."

"Yeah, I'm not sure it's worth the bother," Hayley said. "Give me the knife."

Kitally climbed off the bed, and Hayley took over.

"Just count yourself lucky that I'm only going to cut off your balls," Hayley told him as she moved to the side of the bed. He was huffing wetly now against the tape. "I could remove just one, but I think your crimes justify the removal of both. I'm leaving your penis for now."

His face was red from exertion, his wrists and ankles raw from trying to free himself.

"You'll be sterile," she said matter-of-factly. "The procedure should reduce the production of testosterone and hopefully your desire to rape." She lifted her shoulders in a shrug and then leaned over, grabbed a handful, and cut his testes off in one clean swipe.

He thrashed and bellowed obscenities beneath the tape.

As far as Hayley was concerned, Owen Dunham fell into a particular grouping of rapists: the worst of the worst. He deserved to die for what he'd done to those girls. She could guarantee there were more victims out there. How many lives had Owen Dunham ruined?

Hayley's heart was racing. She felt a tremendous urge to pick up the knife and plunge it into his heart. The last time she didn't finish a job like this, her mom had ended up a casualty of that mistake. But Kitally was standing nearby, and killing the man was not part of tonight's plan. Maybe he would bleed to death or infection would set in. She could only hope.

"If this doesn't work," Hayley said, close to his ear as she slid his bloodied parts into a plastic bag, "if you rape again, I guarantee you I'll be back for the rest."

When she straightened, she held up the bag.

Her work was done here.

His testicles would be buried in some open field or maybe thrown into the river. She would make it impossible for a surgeon to sew them back on. Been there, done that.

CHAPTER TWO

He carried pen and paper to the table out on his balcony where he could see the magnificent view of the American River. Peaceful. Tranquil. The morning sun hit the water just so, making it sparkle. He then filled his glass with his favorite energy drink, opened his leather-bound journal to its opening pages, which he'd left blank all this time until he felt inspired to supply this introduction, and began to write.

I am a natural born killer. Although some people might beg to differ, I would say I am normal, as far as normal goes. Throughout elementary school, the teachers always liked me. I suffered no psychological abuse while growing up.

Never wet my bed. Not once.

Neither have I abused alcohol or drugs.

I make friends easily, but I prefer to be alone.

You might be surprised to know that I feel things . . . really feel things: emotions, sentiments, and desires. I have them all. I never pretend to be happy or sad. The emotions are right there to be viewed, like the angry scars etched across so many people's wrists. Unlike most of the people I have encountered throughout life, I am rarely angry or stressed. Drama is something I steer clear of at all costs.

Let's see. What else?

I have amazing and supportive parents. After forty years, Mom and Dad are still together. And still alive, which was no small feat on my part, thank you very much. There were many times when I wanted to take the butcher knife from the kitchen and carve their hearts out.

Yes. You heard me right. I wanted to kill my parents, butcher them. I wanted to kill them so many times, in fact, it forever boggles the mind to see them alive and thriving. My dad has one of those buzz cuts, along with a big nose and a craggy face. Mom is prematurely gray, though petite, perky, and cute. Not only do they make me smile, seeing their faces also makes me shake my head. They have no idea how lucky they are: two people in their fifties, buzzing around town, always bragging about their only son, the same son who killed their only daughter . . . my sister.

For me, killing is a lot like having an intense craving.

Have you ever been on a diet and you're watching TV and a commercial comes on? Some big-breasted broad is biting into a big, juicy, perfectly cooked hamburger? Makes my mouth water every time.

Well, that's how it is for me when it comes time to kill someone. Same exact thing. Same sensation, multiplied by one hundred. When the urge hits, my mouth waters, my heart pounds. Sometimes I manage to hold off for a day or two, maybe even a week, but in the end there's no stopping me. Somebody out there is going to die. Mostly I already know who it's going to be.

These victims of mine did nothing to me. My urges have nothing to do with anger or resentment. They were simply in the wrong place at the wrong time. So I killed them.

And the reason is this: I like death.

No, let me rephrase that. I love death.

The idea of the soul rising up, perhaps to make its way to earth again in one form or another, intrigues me. The grim reaper is pure genius. *Predation is orgasmic. Death by malnutrition and disease, not so much. Suicide fascinates me. Accidents aren't half-bad—if there's a car crash, I'm definitely the one craning my neck, causing traffic jams as I try to get a good look at some random victim of circumstance.*

But nothing beats killing a human being with my own two hands.

My favorite part is watching closely, intently, as the eyes lose their luster, until the only thing left is a dull, blank stare.

Like most serial killers, I did start with animals. It makes sense, doesn't it? Most critters are easy to control. Clueless, really. I used to enjoy watching the animals fight for their last breath. But killing people is so much more of a thrill. I wish I could explain it well enough for you to understand.

It's a compulsion.

Yes. I have a compulsion to kill. I was born with the yearning to kill. When I was eight years old, I killed my first human being—my four-year-old sister. My palms are sweaty just thinking about it. My heart is drumming against my chest. I take a deep breath.

Thirty years have passed since that day.

There are times when I am confronted with remorse. I even hate myself for a moment or two. But more often than not, I feel gladness that she was able to pass so effortlessly once she began to sink. Her eyes were wide open as she descended to the bottom. Her arms and legs hardly moved at all. To this day, I think she knew what was happening and she accepted it. I remember it all so clearly. You see, I have what researchers call highly superior autobiographical memory. This allows me to remember episodes from the past in detail. But even though I have the ability to recall these events in full HD color, I still put every detail in this leatherbound journal.

Why?

Because as much as I love reliving the details stored in my brain, I adore rereading my own vividly descriptive passages filled with sensory details that whisk me back to a time and place where I can see the fear, smell the tangy blood, and taste the panic in the air.

I have other ways of remembering these incidents, too, but we'll get to that later.

Back to my first kill.

The moment I saw the red rubber ball roll over the edge of the pool and hit the water, I became tense and very alert. My heart rate accelerated.

With her uneven ponytails and big green eyes, she pointed at the ball floating there and asked me to get it for her.

I looked around, but I already knew my parents were out front talking to the new neighbors who had just moved into the house next door. I knew she couldn't swim, but I told her to go ahead and get the ball herself.

She didn't hesitate. She headed that way, reached for the ball, straining every tiny muscle in her arms. But the ball bobbed farther away, just as I knew it would. She reached for it one more time, and that's when she fell in. Water splashed as my little sister fought for her life. She struggled valiantly that day, instinctively paddling both arms, swinging madly until one of her hands got a good solid grip on the pool's edge. Not only was I stunned by her fight for survival, I was panicked by the thought of her tattling on me. I had no choice but to kneel down and pry her little fingers off the edge, one at a time until she had nowhere to go but down.

I could go on and on about that day: the look on Dad's face right before he jumped into the water. My mom falling apart, all snot and drool. The neighbors, complete strangers, trying to console everyone.

I remember feeling afraid.

Once I realized my sister was truly dead, I missed her. I still do. But I would do it all over again if given the chance.

I have killed many times since then.

I have never shot anyone, never used a gun. Much too loud, for one thing. What good would it do to call attention to myself? Like many killers, and so-called normal people, for that matter, I like control.

Who doesn't?

When I overpower someone, I prefer to strangle them. I rarely drug my victims because most medications take all the fire out of their eyes.

I don't know why I'm so passionate about killing.

There are days when I wish I could stop.

No, not days, but moments. There are moments, long moments, when I wish I could stop killing. But I'm thirty-eight now, and if there is one thing in life that I'm certain of, it's that I will never stop.

If it makes you feel any better, I rarely rape or torture my victims. If that gave me a thrill, I might, but I'm not your typical serial killer. I'm not trying to play cat and mouse with the authorities. There was one particular FBI agent who intrigued me for a while there, but he's dead now. I have no desire for notoriety. My ego is plenty healthy enough as it is.

I simply want to keep doing what I do best.

I want to kill people. And then write in my journal. And paint. I will always paint.

I am almost finished with my latest work of art, which involves my last kill. It's the eyes I'm having problems with. I can't get the right look because it was dark outside. She was walking in a half-decent part of town, but it was an unusually dark night devoid of stars, and she was alone. The moment I spotted her, I opened my window, slowed my vehicle to a leisurely pace, and proceeded to warn her about the perils of being out alone at night. She looked worried, assured me she was almost home.

That's what they all say.

I drove ahead, parked around a bend, and waited for her. She didn't see it coming. Everything considered, it was all very anticlimactic.

Ahh, I hear the newspaper hit my front door. Wonderful. Will there be any news of the woman's death? The anticipation is delicious. Today, or someday soon, I'll have my answers: Who was she? What was her age? Her story? Everyone has a story.

I must go. The suspense is killing me.

But first, there is one more thing you should know about me. Above all else, I am an incessant liar. White lies, black lies, green lies. It doesn't matter. I love death and deceit. In fact, the truth is, my parents are now dead. I killed them both five years ago. They left me no choice.

Until next time,

ZT

CHAPTER THREE

Lizzy pulled her car into a parking space and shut off the engine.

The corporate SRT building in Folsom was a giant block of steel and concrete dotted with windows. Stacey Whitmore, anchor with Channel 10 News, sat beside her in the passenger seat. All the way here, she'd been clicking one of her perfectly manicured fingernails on the console. "I don't like this one bit," she said, not for the first time.

Lizzy felt a muscle tighten beneath her cheekbone. Up until now she'd just let her whine, but the time had come for Stacey Whitmore to grow a spine. "If you can't do this, then I'll take you back to your house right now." She reinserted the key in the ignition. "I'm sure Derek Murphy will be more than willing to help me out."

"Put your keys away," Stacey said. "The last thing I want is for you to call Derek Murphy every time you have a new story." Stacey looked squarely at Lizzy. "If anyone finds out about this, though, I could lose my job."

For the past few weeks, Lizzy's focus had been on Wayne Bennett. He was rich and powerful, and he used that power to take advantage of young women. He was the worst kind of predator. People, young and old, thought they could trust him. He was a self-made millionaire. But like many highly successful leaders, he was seduced by money and power, and somewhere along the way he had lost his moral bearings.

"Wayne Bennett is scum," Lizzy said. "You read the testimony from those three young women. And you know he won't call your boss to complain or to find out what's going on—the last thing he wants is the media coming around and asking him more questions."

"The judge dropped the case against Bennett. Why would he do that if there was enough evidence to bring Bennett to court and let a jury decide?"

"I talked to Grady Orwell, the prosecutor on the case, and he said the judge dropped the case on a simple technicality during preconference. You know as well as I do that power and money buy a lot of privileges, including time."

"You think the judge took a bribe?"

"I think that's obvious." There was a long pause before Lizzy added, "Somebody needs to get this guy off the street, and I have a feeling it's going to have to be me."

"There are hundreds, if not thousands, of rapists in Sacramento. Why him?"

"Because he has easy access to too many young people. The young women he purports to be helping put their trust in him because everything about him appears to be on the up-and-up. He's a wolf in sheep's clothing. By the time he strikes, these young women don't know what hit them. The worst part is that he thinks he can get away with it."

"He might be right."

"Not if I can help it." Lizzy anchored strands of hair behind her ear. "Listen. Think about all the young women you'll be saving from his abuse if I can get the proof I need and get this guy behind bars where he belongs. Karma will pay you back in triplicate."

"What sort of proof do you really think we'll get out of him today?"

"I want you to ask him about Miriam Walters. Ask him what he knows about her disappearance."

Silence.

"So, what's it going to be?" Lizzy asked. "Are you in?"

"I'm in. But you owe me."

Lizzy took a look outside. It was mid-April. The air coming through the vents was cool. White clouds billowed against a backdrop of gray sky.

"There he is," Stacey said, pointing. "That's his car pulling into the lot."

"Where? Which one?"

"The cream-colored Mercedes."

"Let's go."

Before Stacey could answer, Lizzy got out of the car, opened the trunk, and began to gather the video equipment she'd asked Stacey to bring. The Channel 10 News logo would make it all look official.

Stacey climbed out of the car and came around to the back. She took the microphone Lizzy handed her. She looked professional in her matching two-piece suit. Her hair and makeup were flawless.

"Ready?" Lizzy asked her.

"Three questions and then we go."

"That's right." Lizzy slid on a pair of black-rimmed eyeglasses that were nothing more than clear glass. Usually her hair was tied back in a ponytail, but today she'd taken the time to curl it. The last thing she wanted was for Wayne Bennett to recognize her as a private investigator from one of the many cases she'd worked on. If everything went as planned, he would think she was a camerawoman, and he wouldn't pay her any mind.

Lizzy was halfway across the parking lot when she spotted him as he neared the entrance to the building. "Hurry up," she told Stacey. "We're going to lose him."

Wayne Bennett was six feet tall, probably 170 pounds. His dark hair was thick and speckled with silver. His suit was well tailored. His shoes newly shined. Every step, every movement was sharp, rhythmic. He never looked their way.

"Mr. Bennett," Stacey called out, her heels clacking against the pavement. "Congratulations on your CEO of the Year Award."

He stopped. Turned. Smiled into Lizzy's camera.

Stacey was brilliant. She knew exactly what would get his attention.

"Hi. Stacey Whitmore with Channel 10 News."

He nodded. "What can I do for you?"

"You have gotten a lot of bad press lately despite all the great work you do with the underprivileged kids. I thought it was only fair that someone point out the good you've done for our community."

He straightened his tie, stood a little taller.

"The Sacramento area is home to a vast array of top-notch companies, and it's the CEOs who get the job done," she went on. "How does it feel to be included on the roster of those to be rewarded?"

"I am honored to have been selected and to be in such good company."

"Could you tell us about your organization outside of SRT, and about some of the work you do to help so many young men and women in Sacramento?"

He fairly beamed. "I'd be happy to. Five years ago, I started Opportunity Knocks, a nonprofit company that receives sponsorships and donations from many of the area's businesses. SRT is the biggest contributor. My team works closely with underprivileged kids who are right out of high school. We give them a crash course in technology and then teach them necessary social skills. Basically, we build a bridge between those less fortunate and the companies that end up employing them because they have been through our program. We have a very high employment rate."

"I understand you work especially closely with young disadvantaged women who might not otherwise have the chance to intern with large companies like SRT."

"That's right," he said. "Well, young men and young women. Every young person in our program has gone through a rigorous selection process that ensures that every participant is well motivated and eager to learn. Their only disadvantage is the environment they were born into. In six months' time, they are ready to go out into the world and interview for jobs they would have otherwise had no business seeking. Over fifty percent of these gifted men and women are given internships and then go on to accept well-paying jobs."

"One particular young woman has been extremely outspoken about the work you do. Her name is Tammy Walters. Her sister, Miriam Walters, has been missing for five days now."

Bennett stiffened. Through the camera lens, Lizzy saw the muscles at the hinges of his jaws pulse. Stacey was holding her own, refusing to flinch. At the bottom of the frame, Lizzy saw his left hand roll into a fist. At first Lizzy worried he might take a punch at Stacey, threaten her at the very least, but his voice was calm when he said, "I think I read something about this in the newspaper, but I don't know either of the women, so I really can't add anything to the discussion." He glanced at his watch. "Time has gotten away from me. I do need to run."

He was not going to get away that easily. Leaving Stacey behind, Lizzy followed Bennett to the entrance. "Are you saying you've never met Miriam Walters?"

"That's exactly what I'm saying." He stopped short and turned, as if he'd just realized it wasn't Stacey asking the question. He looked Lizzy over, his eyes hardening. "Do I know you?"

The double doors slid open, and Mr. Bennett slipped away without waiting for an answer.

"No," Lizzy said, "but you will."

CHAPTER FOUR

Kitally came through the front door with a newspaper in hand and a smile on her face. "We did it." She laid the newspaper on the coffee table in front of the couch where Hayley was sitting. "It worked. Wallace is going to jail."

Lizzy had just entered from the main hallway. She crossed the room to see for herself. "For how long?"

"Ten years."

"Better than nothing," Hayley said, clearly not overwhelmed with excitement.

"Are you kidding me? Ten years is a long time. Wallace will be sixty-two by the time he gets out."

"This is a good start," Lizzy said. "Our number five man is off the street. Cross him off the list."

To make it happen, they'd targeted a well-known thief in the area, filched some already stolen merchandise, and then planted the goods in the rapist's garage. It had been Kitally's idea. Stealing from one criminal to put away another. Not a bad deal.

"We really did it," Kitally said again, self-satisfaction scrawled across her face. "We put away a rapist without using violence."

"You did good," Lizzy agreed.

"What about Bennett?" Kitally asked Lizzy. "Any luck with that today?"

"Bennett isn't going down easy. The man owns half the town—judges, cops, elected officials, you name it. Deep pocketbooks buy loyalty."

"What did he have to say about Miriam Walters?"

"Said he didn't know her, but the good news is that now we have it on tape."

"What good will that do?" Hayley wanted to know.

"Bennett killed Miriam Walters. I'm sure of it. By the time they find her body, I plan to have enough proof to bring him in for questioning. If I can get my hands on a picture of the two of them, anything that will prove that Bennett knew Miriam Walters, I will have the video showing he lied. Why would the man lie about knowing the girl if he was innocent and had nothing to do with her disappearance?"

"I suppose," Hayley said, then shook her head. "I don't understand how the judge could let him off. Three different women were willing to appear and swear to his guilt. It makes no sense. Now that he knows who was willing to talk, he might use intimidation to shut them up."

Lizzy said nothing. Bennett's lawyers had ripped all three of the women's reputations to shreds, convincing first the public, then the judge, that all three of them were after Bennett's money. The lawyers harped on the fact that the women had waited a year to make any accusations. Why so long? Because they wanted his money.

Lizzy had talked to one of the women involved. Instinct told her she was telling the truth. But now they were all scared, she'd told Lizzy. One of their friends—Miriam Walters, a very pretty eighteen-year-old—was missing. And all three women had a good idea who was responsible.

• • •

It was midnight when Hayley drove slowly through West Sacramento. Her window was rolled down. The only noise was the rattle of her engine, and Kitally, who couldn't stay quiet for more than a few minutes at a time.

"So who are we going after tonight?" Kitally asked.

"It's the only woman on the list. They call her the Ghost, but the problem is we don't have a name."

"What's the deal with her anyhow?"

"I used to spend a lot of time on these streets. A while ago, a shop owner in the area pulled me aside and told me that his people, as he likes to call the homeless in the area, were being harassed by a crazy woman. The police, if they're even looking, haven't been able to catch her, so I figured she needed to be put on our list."

Kitally watched the road ahead. "She steals from these people who have nothing?"

"It's worse than that. She attacks the homeless . . . usually while they sleep. Both women and men, young and old, it doesn't seem to matter—beats the shit out of them. One elderly man almost died from head trauma. Apparently, she attacks for no reason at all. I talked to two different people who got a pretty good look at her, but we're going to need to track her down somehow, see what else we can find out. She's been described as slender-bodied. She has a thin face with high, pointy cheekbones and light-colored eyes. Someone else called her a sinewy white girl with spiky blonde hair, bushy eyebrows, and pale skin."

"Sounds like she would be easy to spot, even in the dark."

"I thought so, too, but I've been making the rounds for a while now and I have yet to get a glimpse of her. Apparently, many people in the area have heard of her. They've even rounded up a posse to look for her, but she's elusive. She's cocky, too. Comes back to the same exact places, time after time."

"That's a little freaky. She must have eyes in the back of her head if everyone is watching and waiting for her and yet she manages to show up at the precise moment when nobody's paying attention."

Hayley made a left at the stop sign, and then pulled to the curb, parked, and turned off the engine.

"What are we doing?"

"Just taking a stroll through the park, since one of the people I talked to spotted her here once. Long shot, but we have to start somewhere."

They climbed out. Kitally hitched her bag around her shoulder and followed close behind.

Hayley had been to this same park many times before. It always felt like home. Tonight was a quiet night. If she didn't know better, she would guess all the criminals and rapists in Sacramento had taken the night off. The thought made her smile. Not because she thought it was remotely possible, but because it was so damned absurd.

She lit up a cigarette and took a drag. "Is it true that you once had a brother?"

"Who told you about Liam?"

Hayley had been meaning to talk to Kitally about her brother for a while now, but there never seemed to be a good time. "Maybe Tommy mentioned it," Hayley said as they walked along. "I don't recall. What happened to him?"

"Long story short . . . my family was visiting a foreign country and he was taken."

Although Kitally talked a lot, she rarely spoke about herself. Hayley felt compelled for some reason to draw her out. "Your parents must have offered a hefty ransom to get him back."

"They did. They go back to Buenaventura, the main port of Colombia, every year. Usually when children are taken, it's for money. The authorities have no idea what happened. They suspect he was sold to the highest bidder."

"How old was he when he was kidnapped?"

"Liam was six and I was eight. One minute he was walking next to me, and the next he was running across the street. It all happened so fast. He'd be sixteen now. If I had just run after him instead of trying to find my parents first, he never would have been taken."

"You would have both been kidnapped."

"Maybe so, but Liam wouldn't be alone."

"That's not true. I doubt those types keep siblings together."

Kitally was quiet.

"You better not be blaming yourself for something you couldn't do anything about."

"My dad blames me enough for both of us."

"I bet he's angry at himself, not you."

"Why?"

"Are you kidding me? Because he didn't have the good sense to keep his six- and eight-year-old kids within sight in a foreign country." After a long pause, Hayley added, "You're a good person, but you're obviously a little off, if you know what I mean."

That got a laugh from Kitally. "Maybe someone needs to look in the mirror."

"We all know I'm fucked up. I am beyond repair. But you," Hayley said, "you have a chance, if you can get your shit together and get past it. I bet your dad started screwing around after your brother was taken. Your family still has a chance to turn itself around, but someone, probably you, needs to push to make it happen."

"Why do I get the feeling I'm in therapy?"

"Because I don't think you understand how lucky you are to have a mom and a dad who love you."

"I promise to think about everything you said," Kitally told her. "Are you done?"

Hayley didn't answer; she just let the conversation drift away. They both did. There wasn't anything more she could say or do to lessen Kitally's pain. Life wasn't fair. That wasn't ever going to change.

It was a while before they reached the center of the park.

Hayley heard a noise, stopped, and looked around. Kitally was checking something out farther back, standing still and peering into the night. She must have heard the same thing.

A scuffling noise sounded to Hayley's left. There was movement behind a patch of dense shrubbery. Bending over, she put out her cigarette, then unsnapped the sheath around her ankle and pulled out a three-inch blade. She took a careful step toward the brush. Better to be on the offense rather than be caught off guard.

"Who's there?" Hayley called out.

The noises stopped. No rustling of leaves or crackling of twigs.

"Step out of there or I'm calling the police."

"Leave me alone."

It was a female voice. Young. Whoever it was sounded exhausted, as if she'd just run twenty miles. Hayley marched forward and spread open the thick brush, surprised to see a girl lying on her side in a makeshift bed of dirt and leaves.

Kitally joined them. "What are you doing out here all alone?"

Hayley guessed the girl's age to be about sixteen, maybe older.

The girl struggled to get to her feet. "I could ask you the same thing."

"Except we're not alone," Kitally pointed out.

She was olive-skinned. Her long dark hair was a tangled mess. Her eyes were dark, too. Kitally looked at her sideways. "Are you pregnant?"

"Maybe."

Hayley snorted. It was obvious she was pretty far along. Probably in her last month or so.

"Maybe we should take her to the hospital."

"Leave me alone." The girl shooed them away. "I can take care of myself. And I don't need to go to a hospital. I'm pregnant—I'm not bleeding to death."

"Why are you out here?" Kitally asked.

"None of your business."

"How old are you?"

"Same answer." She picked up a flimsy bag, heaved it over her shoulder, and started to walk away.

Kitally stayed on the girl's heels. "I don't know what kind of trouble you're in, but we're not leaving without you. We can take you to a friend's house. Or maybe you have a relative living nearby. If neither of those options sound appealing, my friend will be forced to call the police."

The girl twirled about. "Why?"

"Because there's no way we're leaving you here in the dead of night all by yourself," Hayley said.

"It's dangerous out here," Kitally added.

"You two are unbelievable. Sure," she said, struggling not to drop her things. "You can take me to my sister's place a few blocks from here."

"Can you at least tell us your name?" Kitally asked.

The girl kept walking. "Why do you need to know? You haven't told me your names."

"I'm Kitally, and this is Hayley."

"OK. Fine. My name is Salma. There, are you happy?"

Kitally gave Hayley a look.

The girl bitched and complained all the way to the car.

They drove in silence for more than a few miles toward the address she tossed off, but Hayley suspected the girl had no place to go. If she really had a sister living nearby, why was she sleeping in the park?

"So what's your sister's address again?" Hayley asked.

"Drop me off right here. This is close enough."

Hayley ignored her, made a left on Sixteenth and then turned right and merged onto Interstate 80.

"Where are we going?"

"Since you obviously don't have any place to go, I'm taking you home with us."

"I believe that would be considered kidnapping in most states."

"We live with one other woman, Lizzy Gardner," Hayley went on, ignoring Salma's sarcasm. "There's an extra room. At least you'll be safe."

"I don't want your handouts."

"You look like you could pop at any moment. Do you really want that happening behind a bush in the park?" Kitally asked.

That seemed to do the trick. Salma sank back into the seat and kept her thoughts to herself for the rest of the drive.

CHAPTER FIVE

Wearing a brown cotton robe and white socks that came up to his knees, he made his way across the hardwood floors. He caught his reflection in the refrigerator and laughed. His hair was all over the place. With the Sunday paper tucked under his arm, he sipped his morning energy drink as he made his way to the kitchen table. Drinking too many of these energy drinks was said to cause restlessness, palpitations, and shaking, just to name a few of the top ten side effects, but he wasn't worried. Like anything else, it was all about moderation.

It was the weekend. He'd slept late. After taking a seat, he slid the rubber band off the newspaper and unfolded it. He took another gulp as he read today's headline in the *Sacramento Bee*: "Sacramento Strangler Strikes Again! Businessman and Philanthropist Mark Kiel's Daughter Found Dead in Capitol Park."

Within a heartbeat, his surprise turned to amusement. Who would have thought the billionaire's daughter would be running alone late at night? The nights were chilly and dark this time of year. She had been asking for trouble.

He shook his head.

Damn. Mark Kiel's daughter. This would change everything. The public outcry. He could hear it now.

The mayor and every other official who received "contributions" from Kiel would have most of the city's law enforcement on the case sniffing every bloody trail, perhaps digging up cold cases, dead bodies here and there, victims who had been denied justice, random killings whose faces he could still see in his mind's eye. There were so many and yet here he was, enjoying the view from his balcony.

If Special Agent Shayne were still alive, things might be different. That man had been hot on his trail and yet now he would never know how Shayne had managed to get so close. He had attended Shayne's funeral, watched as people closest to him grieved. Agent Shayne's fiancée had stood stoically to the side while an elderly woman he assumed was the agent's mother fell to her knees, her arms draped over her son's coffin, and wept.

Lizzy Gardner. The thought of her sparked an idea. Perhaps he would check up on the gal and see how she was holding up. After keeping track of Jared Shayne for so long, he felt as if he knew her, rather quite like the dead sister he once had.

It hit him then—felt as if he'd been clunked on the head with a stick.

A moment of clarity was all he'd needed.

Everything happened for a reason, and everything was playing out exactly how it was meant to be.

He'd been on a downhill spiral of late, hadn't understood what he was feeling, didn't know what was wrong with him. He absolutely did not appreciate the heavy waves of overwhelming melancholy that hit without notice. Definitely a new experience for him.

When it came to killing, he'd done his homework. He liked to think he was extraordinarily careful, but the truth was he'd left clues on or around every single one of his victims. What made him do that? Was he looking to get caught? Did he want recognition, after all?

Perhaps now was the time to change things up.

He folded the paper neatly in front of him. He would strike quickly and randomly over the next few weeks, over and over, often enough to make the investigators' heads spin.

A dead body here, another one there.

They wouldn't know which way was forward and backward, let alone up and down.

Maybe he would find someone to bring home for a while.

Excitement burst open inside him as a plan began to form.

If he were to do that—bring a potential victim home, that is—he would need a place to keep her. He lifted a brow. He would need a dark room . . . windowless . . . a place where—

His thoughts were interrupted by the sound of the doorbell.

He walked to the front entry and looked out the peephole. Saw the neighbor kid, Landon, and opened the door.

"Good morning, sir. My mom was wondering if she could borrow a cube of butter. She's making oatmeal cookies, and I'm supposed to tell you we'll pay you back after she goes to the store. I'll bring you some cookies, too. If you pick out the raisins, they're pretty OK."

This wasn't the first time the neighbor kid had come for a visit. He had to admit the kid was sort of cute. He especially liked that the boy showed respect by calling him "sir." He leaned his head out the door, looked both ways. Neither of the child's parents was hanging around. Interesting. Other than waving hello every once in a while to the adults, he'd only ever had a conversation with Landon. Opening the door wide, he said, "Come on in."

Without a care in the world, the kid stepped inside. He craned his neck as he looked at all the artwork covering the walls in the entryway. "Wow," Landon said. "Did you paint all these pictures?"

He shut the door. "I did." He guessed the boy to be about ten or eleven years of age. An all-American kid with a mop of tangled brown hair and freckles that looked like blood splatter across his nose and cheeks.

"Why does everyone in your paintings look dead?"

He looked the kid in the eyes. "Maybe because they are."

Landon's big brown eyes doubled in size. "Really?"

He felt a tightening in his chest. *Really.* Then he smiled and said, "Nah, just pulling your leg, Landon. Come on, let's get Mom some butter."

Detective Chase was on the phone, but he waved Lizzy into his office and into a seat in front of his desk.

After being shot in the left shoulder, the detective had ended up in the hospital for nearly a month. He'd lost a lot of blood and for a while there the doctors weren't always sure he was going to make it. She'd known better than that. Although she had to admit he looked like crap. He had a sling around his left arm, dark circles under his eyes, and he looked as if he'd lost at least fifteen pounds since she'd seen him last.

As soon as he hung up the phone, she said, "You wanted to see me?"

His sigh came out sounding like a dying engine. "Nice to see you, too."

"I'm glad to see you pulled through," she told him. "I had no doubt you would make it."

"Because of my stubborn and determined will to live?"

"Something like that."

With his good arm, Chase pushed a manila file across the desk.

Lizzy opened it up and looked through a half dozen eight-by-ten color photographs. The date stamped on the back told her the pictures were taken three months ago. A man with a bag over his head. Dead. Suffocated. A close-up revealing duct tape over his mouth. Red markings around his wrist.

Confused, Lizzy looked across the desk at Chase. "What's this about?"

"I was hoping you could tell me."

"Listen. I know you don't think what I do is important, but I take my clients and my job very seriously, and I have a hell of a lot of work to do. I don't have time to play games with you. I've never seen this man before. So, for that reason, I ask again . . . what is all this about?"

"It's about Hayley Hansen."

"What about her?"

"We have reason to believe she might be involved."

She grabbed one of the pictures and held it up. "With this? Involved how?"

He shrugged.

"Hayley would never hurt anyone, if that's what you're implying."

"Do I need to remind you that she sliced a man's penis off?"

Lizzy poked his mahogany desk with her finger for emphasis. "Brian Rosie deserved what he got, and you know it. She did her time for that. Everything that girl does is for the good of others. She has been handed a shit-for-nothing life, and yet she does all she can to make other peoples' lives better."

"Well, the guy in the pictures here might argue with you about that. I have a witness who can put her in the area within an hour of that scene you're looking at."

"Judging by these pictures, I would say this is a suicide."

He sighed. Rubbed his chin. Sighed again. "Listen to me," he said at last. "I'm going to be as blunt with you as I can. I've been hearing stories about you and your girls trying to take the law into your own hands. I don't like it, and I won't allow it to go on. You and your whole merry band need to stand down."

And that's when Lizzy saw a telltale sign in the detective's eyes. This wasn't about the man in the photo or Hayley. This was about something else altogether. It was about Wayne Bennett. The detective was trying to pull a fast one on her. He wanted Lizzy to think he had the goods on Hayley, something to throw in her face and get her to behave. "He talked to you, didn't he?"

"Who?"

"Oh, don't give me that innocent look," Lizzy said. "You know who—Wayne Bennett."

He fidgeted just enough so that Lizzy knew she was right. "And what did you tell him, Detective? That you would give me a good talking-to, let me know that Mr. Wayne Bennett is off-limits? I have pictures of him talking to Miriam Walters, the girl who was in his program and who is now missing. And yet he told me he'd never met her in his life." Although Lizzy had yet to see any actual pictures of Wayne and Miriam together, she'd heard they existed. They better, because she was banking on it.

Detective Chase scratched the side of his head. "Bennett works with hundreds, maybe thousands, of young people in Sacramento. You think he would remember every single young woman he ever met? Be reasonable."

"Miriam Walters isn't the type of girl you would forget. She's tall and statuesque—a young Beyoncé. A guy like Bennett wouldn't forget a girl like that."

Detective Chase leaned forward and then squinted in pain and quickly readjusted his posture. "You're right," he said, apparently giving up on his other tactic. "I'm telling you to lay off. Miriam Walters is a troubled young lady. Everything we've learned about her points to her being a runaway."

"That is such bullshit. What happened to you anyhow? What's that Top Cop award all about? Why are you here in Sacramento? What did you do? Shoot your partner? Take a bribe?"

He stiffened. "I'm not going to let you get to me, Gardner. You're having a difficult time dealing with the loss of your fiancé. I get that. The world is a dark, unfriendly place filled with people who feel they are owed something. Everyone else is just plain sad. They have given up on the world, maybe life. But you fall into another category. Something between the evildoers and the people who have lost all hope. You need to pull yourself together, Gardner. It's time for you to sit down and take a long hard look at what you're doing and where you go from here."

Before Lizzy could respond, he added, "This thing with Bennett is complicated, and I really don't need you sticking your nose in other people's business."

Lizzy kept her gaze on his. "Thanks for the sermon. Are we done here?"

"Not until you promise me you'll stay away from him."

"Not in a million years. Go ahead and arrest me for disobeying your orders because I'm going after that man with a vengeance. He's been molesting and abusing women for too long. It's going to stop. And you," Lizzy said as she came to her feet, "should be ashamed of yourself. I wonder if you'd be telling me to back off if you had a daughter or a sister who had been assaulted by that pervert."

Lizzy walked to the door, and then turned to face him one more time. "If you change your mind and decide to do the decent thing, let me know. I don't plan to stop gathering evidence against this man until I have enough proof to put him away for a long, long time, but I sure could use a little help. If your conscience ever speaks to you, you know where to find me."

After shutting the door behind her, Lizzy wove around desks and people until she was walking through the main door. She marched across the pavement until she reached her car and climbed in behind the wheel.

Her hands were shaking. She'd never felt so angry, so confused, and yet so determined to see one man put away. Her outrage and resentment bubbled inside her, so close to the surface. Her fingers curled around the steering wheel. Everywhere she looked—narrow-minded, prejudiced, biased people.

Evil.

The world had never felt so stifling and restricted, so small.

And Hayley.

Would Hayley ever step that far over the line?

Maybe.

Yes, there were times when she appeared to be a walking time bomb, but she was also, without a doubt, one of the most caring people Lizzy had ever met. Unless it was in self-defense, Hayley would never take a life. And yet something niggled deep down inside Lizzy . . . something coarse and foul, something that smelled a lot like doubt.

CHAPTER SIX

Lizzy had been sitting at her desk inside her office on J Street in Sacramento, doing nothing but listening to the sound of her breath, when the door opened. A wisp of cool air and the smell of coffee and doughnuts followed her sister, Cathy, inside the office. Her morning was quickly going from bad to worse.

Cathy set a cup of coffee and a white paper bag on the corner of her desk and then pulled the strap of her purse up higher around her shoulder. "Are you here alone?"

Lizzy managed a nod, wishing her sister would go away and not come back some other day.

"You haven't returned my calls."

Lizzy said nothing.

Her sister took a seat in the chair facing Lizzy's desk. "I'm sorry. About everything . . . about Richard and all the ugly things he said to you . . . but mostly I'm sorry I haven't been there for you." Cathy reached out and put a hand on top of Lizzy's. "Talk to me. Please."

Lizzy didn't like seeing her sister in pain, and yet she felt helpless to help her feel any better, afraid to say the wrong thing, afraid that in the end, no matter how hard they both tried to say and do the right thing, they would both be eaten alive by past events and crippling guilt.

"I'm the one who should be apologizing," Lizzy finally said.

"Why? What do you mean?"

"I've done nothing but cause trouble since the day I was born. I've left a clear path of destruction: Mom and Dad, you, Brittany, Hayley, Jessica, Kitally, and Jared. If it weren't for me, Jared would still be alive. Do you have any idea what that man did for me?"

Cathy watched her closely as she waited for her to continue.

"Jared lifted me from the depths of hell. That man asked for nothing in return. He would have been happy to live a nice, quiet, simple life . . . just the two of us. He talked about having kids someday, taking them camping, watching them play sports, a normal everyday life. But when it came to settling down, I fought him—why? What was so important about my work that I couldn't fathom a simple life?" She looked around the office, held her arms out wide. "Look around you. What do you see? I'm not exactly changing the world, am I? I gave up a beautiful life for this." She forced air through her nose. "I let Jared die for *this*."

"Lizzy, it wasn't your fault. You were both in a dangerous business. You both knew the chances you were taking. And I'm sorry, but this is no time to feel sorry for yourself. If Jared were here now, he would want you to pick yourself up and carry on. You know he would."

"I think you should go."

"No. I'm not finished. I know you're hurting, and I know you don't want to hear about what Jared would do or not do, but it's the truth."

Lizzy fiddled around with the papers in front of her.

"I kicked Richard out of the house," Cathy blurted.

And there it is, Lizzy thought. *One tiny step for mankind. One itsy-bitsy teeny-weeny drop of hope amid a lifetime of despair.* She looked up at her sister, away from all the mounds of paperwork and meaningless notes. "I'm glad."

"I was hoping you might consider moving back into the house with me."

Lizzy shook her head. "No. You and Brittany need time to yourselves."

"Brittany will hardly look at me," Cathy told her.

"All the more reason for you two to spend time alone, without Richard or me to complicate matters. Talk to your daughter," Lizzy said. "Be honest. Tell her the truth. Brittany deserves to know everything."

"She keeps asking about you, Lizzy. She wants to see you. Brittany needs to know that you'll be all right."

"Not now," Lizzy said. "Not yet."

Cathy released a weighty breath. "Brittany was accepted into Sac State. You know how creative she is, and, well, it turns out she's interested in studying art. She won't start until the fall, of course, but she's been invited by the famous artist Ian Berg to take an art class. There will be other artists helping out, but Ian Berg will be overseeing it all."

"I've heard of him. That's really great. Tell her congratulations."

Cathy sat there for a moment longer, waiting for something more. Finally, she came to her feet and headed for the door.

"I will call her," Lizzy said. "I promise."

"Eat a bagel, Lizzy. You look as if you're trying to starve yourself to death."

And that was it. She was gone, leaving Lizzy alone to punish herself with her self-hatred and dark thoughts of the past and future.

For the rest of the day, Lizzy did her best to lose herself in busy-work. At three o'clock, an elderly man came through the door with a file tucked under one arm. His walk was slow, his back hunched, his cane trembling as it fought to keep him upright.

Lizzy stood, ready to help.

"Sit down," he said. "I'll get there."

Lizzy did as he said. She folded her hands on top of her desk and then watched him closely, ready to jump up and help him after he fell. But against all odds the old man made it all the way to the chair in front of her desk without any mishap. He took a seat and then tucked his cane between his knees.

"What can I do for you?"

"Thought you'd never ask."

Lizzy gave him a smirk.

"I have a job for you and your girls. Are they around?"

"Nope. It's just you and me. Why don't you tell me what the problem is?"

"Somebody killed my wife."

Lizzy released a steadying breath. She hadn't thought the old man could surprise her, but she'd been wrong. She had no words.

"Aren't you going to ask me who did it?"

"Who did it?"

"I'm not sure yet, but I intend to find out, and I'm hoping you will help me."

Lizzy scratched a nonexistent itch on her neck. "Mr. . . ."

"Call me Gus."

"Gus. How old are you?"

"Why? Do you have some sort of age limitation?"

"No. Never mind. I don't think I'm the person you should be talking to."

"The police have swept away my concerns as senility and paranoia. Is that what you're doing?" He handed Lizzy a thin manila folder that looked as if it had survived two wars. "Don't just stare at it," he told her. "Open it up."

Despite his crotchety tone, she did as he said. A medical report sat on top of the pile of papers. She skimmed through it. "It says here that your wife, Helsie, died of chronic heart failure."

"Lies."

Lizzy continued to flip through the pages. "I don't see anything that even remotely suggests homicide."

"She told me more than once that friends of hers, perfectly healthy people when they arrived at the nursing home, were dying. In the end, I believe Helsie knew too much about whatever was going on in that place. She said they were asking her a lot of questions, and she was sure they would come after her, too."

"Who was asking her questions?"

"Staff members at Shady Oaks Nursing Home."

"According to this report," Lizzy said, "your wife had dementia."

"More lies. Told by the doctors hired by Shady Oaks."

"How long was she there?"

"Two years."

"If she didn't have the disease and she was healthy, why would you agree to put her into a nursing home?"

He laid a shaky fist on top of Lizzy's desk. "Yes, it's true. Helsie was diagnosed with vascular dementia four years ago."

Lizzy sighed.

"It's not what you think. She went for regular checkups, and her doctor was always surprised by how sharp she was. She knew exactly what was happening to her, physically and mentally. Sure, she had difficulty walking down stairs and she tended to burn the chicken every once in a while, but I swear her memory, more often than not, was better than mine. And then, two years ago, out of the blue, Helsie announced that she wanted to go to a nursing home where complete strangers could look after her." The old man looked down and away. When his gaze met Lizzy's again, his voice was rough. "I was angry at first. It felt like she was abandoning me, but there was no talking her out of it. Later I came to realize she didn't want to be a burden to me. She even admitted that sometimes she woke up in our bed and didn't know who the man was lying next to her."

"I'm sorry."

Lizzy could almost see the memories swirling about inside his head, all the memories of the life he once knew. "Helsie died two months ago. Heart failure." He shook his head. "Makes no sense. She was in great shape. I went to visit her every day."

"So how did she seem in that last week before she passed away?"

He shook his head, slowly, regretfully. "That's the kicker in all of this. My son thought I needed a break. It took some doing, but he finally convinced me to come visit him in Montana. We set up camp in the mountains where nobody could bother us. The weather was surprisingly good for that time of the year so we even stayed an extra few days. By the time I returned home, Helsie was dead."

Lizzy's heart went out to the man.

"I had a dozen missed calls by the time I returned. The nursing home's chief medical officer told me she died of heart failure caused by clogged arteries. It didn't make sense, but I was in shock and why would I doubt what the doctors told me?"

"I don't know," Lizzy said. "Why are you doubting them now?"

"Because of an anonymous note I found in my mailbox." He gestured with his chin toward the folder. "It's in the very back."

Lizzy flipped through the file and picked up the handwritten note. It had been written on a simple stationery with a squiggly design in the bottom right-hand corner. The message was short and sweet.

EVERYTHING IS NOT WHAT IT SEEMS. NEED AUTOPSY.

Lizzy looked at Gus. "Did you have the body exhumed?"

"I tried. My application was denied. I guess that only happens in the movies. I should have requested an official autopsy when I first learned of her death. But like I said before, I wasn't thinking clearly at the time."

"I understand."

"I thought you would."

"How is that?"

"I've read about you. I'm sorry for your loss."

"Thanks."

"Do you think you'll be able to help me?"

She stared into Gus's rheumy gray eyes. "I can try, but you should know that I'm having a difficult time just getting through the day."

"I call it teetering on the edge of insanity," Gus said.

She looked at him for a long moment. There was something about the old man that calmed her. She couldn't put her finger on it exactly, but it was simply there, like the air that she breathed.

"I don't have much money," he went on, "but I can help you out if you ever need any work done."

Lizzy tapped her pencil against her chin. She didn't want or expect anything from Gus, but she didn't want to offend him, either. "What kind of work?"

"You name it . . . plumbing, electrical. Whatever you need done."

Lizzy offered him a hand. "Well, Gus, it looks like you've got yourself an investigator."

They shook hands. For an old guy, his grip was surprisingly strong.

CHAPTER SEVEN

Hayley walked outside, where Kitally was waiting by the car. Instead of her usual avant-garde getup, she wore jeans, T-shirt, dark sunglasses, and a white baseball cap. Hayley might not have recognized Kitally at all if it weren't for the rainbow-colored dread hanging over one shoulder.

The jeans and T-shirt complete with silly logo weren't the only things throwing Hayley off. There was an eleven-by-fourteen magnetic sign on Kitally's Toyota. It read: H & K House Cleaning Services. In the backseat of the car were buckets and mops and all sorts of cleaning supplies.

"Looks like you thought of everything."

"Pretty much," Kitally said, holding up a T-shirt with the H & K logo. "This one's for you."

"I'll pass."

Kitally shrugged. "Your loss. Do you have the flash drive?"

Hayley patted her pocket and then held up a large envelope filled with porn.

Kitally looked inside the envelope. "Gross. Where did you get these?"

"I've been collecting all sorts of goods that could be used as evidence we might need to put these guys away. This is just one of my gold mines."

"Maybe you should have left those pictures wherever you found them so we could report that particular weirdo."

"No way," Hayley said. "The loser I took these from likes to look, but he doesn't touch. Those guys are a dime a dozen. We can get him anytime. Right now, we need to focus on the pervs who are doing the most damage. And Holmes needs to be put away. Besides, he's number three on the list."

"I didn't see anything on the news or in the paper about Owen Dunham, did you?"

"Never heard of him."

Kitally lowered her voice. "The guy without balls . . . does that ring a bell?"

Hayley stepped closer and said in a low voice, "Listen. Unless we're talking to Lizzy about any of the people on our list, it's best if you don't ever mention his name again. Let it go. That's how it has to be, OK?"

"Got it," Kitally said before they both climbed into the car.

On the drive from Carmichael to West Sacramento, Kitally said, "Do you think this will work?"

"It has to." Donald Holmes was a guard in the state women's prison. After a yearlong investigation, he was convicted of raping two teenagers and yet all he'd gotten for it was community time and probation.

"Did the investigators ever talk to any of the women in the prison who filed complaints?"

"No," Hayley said. "They're merely prisoners, so they don't count."

"What little time I did in detention was enough to make me realize I don't ever want to end up in prison," Kitally said. "I have to say, I am beginning to feel the weight of everything we've been doing lately."

"What do you mean?" Hayley had never spoken a word to Kitally, Tommy, or anyone else about the man whose life she'd taken months before. Sometimes she woke up in a cold sweat at the thought of what she'd done. She couldn't say she regretted it—the man had destroyed too many lives to count—but still, the act itself had left a bad taste in her mouth. Nobody else knew, and she was determined to keep it that way. "I thought you were excited about Wallace getting ten years," Hayley said. "What happened to the enthusiasm?"

"I guess I'm having second thoughts. Me, you, and Lizzy are all risking doing more time than this rapist. And for what?"

"You're not making sense," Hayley said. "This is all coming out of left field."

"I just read about a case where a hacker was able to expose a rapist, but the hacker ended up doing more time than the rapist. Not cool."

Now they were getting somewhere, to the root of Kitally's change of heart. "Calm down," Hayley told her. "I don't know the details of the case you're talking about, but we're not going to get caught. I'm going to plant the child porn on Holmes's PC and place the drugs and the pictures inside his house, somewhere where the cops won't be able to miss it. Then we're going to use this nifty throwaway phone that criminals love so much and call 911 to report a rape currently taking place inside his house. Done deal."

"We're taking a lot of chances to put away one rapist out of a thousand. And like you said the other day, how long will they keep him behind bars after he's caught?"

"You're looking at this all wrong," Hayley explained. "It may be only one guy, but we're helping dozens of future victims by getting this guy off the streets. You have to keep your eye on the prize. This is less about putting the rapist away and more about helping innocent women and young girls who don't stand a chance against monsters like Holmes."

The rest of the drive was quiet.

Thanks to satellite maps, they already knew exactly where to park when they arrived at Holmes's house. Holmes didn't get off work until eight o'clock at night. It was the middle of the afternoon. They had plenty of time. No wife, kids, or girlfriends to worry about. Kitally was the lookout. If anyone parked in Holmes's driveway or at the curb in front of the house, if anyone walked anywhere near his place, Kitally would send Hayley a warning text.

"This shouldn't take long," Hayley said before climbing out of the car. "Fifteen minutes tops, unless I have trouble getting into his computer." The guy was pretty active on social media for a sociopath. Tommy had befriended Holmes under the guise of having similar interests in video war games. It didn't take Tommy long to figure out what sort of equipment Holmes was using.

Hayley climbed out of the car and headed across the street for Holmes's front door, leaving the cleaning supplies behind.

Kitally watched Hayley go. It was true. She'd been having second thoughts about this whole vigilante thing, mostly because she had seen the look in Hayley's eyes when they were dealing with Owen Dunham. If she hadn't been there, Hayley might have taken things too far. And that made Kitally nervous.

Nothing had been the same since Jared's funeral.

Sometimes life didn't just go on, after all. Sometimes the world really did stop turning on its axis because that's how it felt.

Lizzy was angry at the world, and Hayley seemed to walk a fine line between compassion and coldheartedness.

She watched Hayley disappear inside Holmes's house. Hayley was good. She made breaking and entering seem like child's play.

Kitally focused her attention on the street in front of her. The houses on both sides were small and nondescript. At the end of the block, there was an empty lot littered with trash. A white sedan drove by. It was a woman driver. The lady kept her gaze straight ahead, didn't appear to notice Kitally sitting behind the wheel of the car, waiting as the minutes slowly ticked by.

Her cell phone vibrated. She picked it up and looked at the caller ID. *Mom.* She'd have to call her back later.

Two kids on bikes were headed her way. She didn't know whether to hunker down in her seat or sit up a little straighter. She opted for leaning over and looking through the glove box. If they slowed down even a little bit, she would text Hayley.

The kids cruised past without a glance her way.

She looked at the time. Only seven minutes had passed.

She sucked in a breath and then slowly released it. Every time a breeze blew by, the branches of the trees creaked and swayed. She looked at her phone. No texts from Hayley. No need to worry.

Her phone vibrated.

It was Mom. Again. *Jesus.* She hit Talk. "Mom, I really can't talk right now, but since you've called twice in five minutes, I figured it must be urgent."

"I just wanted to make sure you would be able to come by the house next week and water the inside plants."

Now she remembered. Her parents were going on another trip. The Greek islands. "I'll water the plants. I promise."

"Is everything all right?"

"I'm fine. You and Dad have fun, and I'll come visit when you get back."

Unfortunately, it was never that easy to get off the phone with her mom. Every call required a comprehensive update on the family, which included second and third cousins Kitally had never met. By the time Kitally finally pulled herself free, another fifteen minutes had passed. Hayley had been inside Holmes's house for twenty-two minutes.

Kitally looked around. Nobody in the neighborhood was out and about. Nobody checking their mail or mowing their lawn. She took a good look at Holmes's house with its faded pink paint job. The walkway was uneven and cracked. The lawn was decorated with a few sporadic weeds. Blankets hanging over the windows made it impossible to see inside. Curling her fingers around the door handle, she was about to get out when she saw a car approaching. She decided to sit still, wait until the car passed before she made her exit.

But the car didn't pass by at all. The Honda Civic pulled into the driveway.

It was him. Donald Holmes. He was home early.

Shit.

She grabbed her cell phone and quickly texted Hayley. *Holmes is home. Get out of the house!*

Holmes walked to the door. He was short and stocky. His clothes were wrinkled and baggy. Hopefully Hayley would hear him using his keys to get in the front door.

He stepped inside and shut the door behind him.

Seconds turned into minutes.

She kept waiting to see Hayley running around the side of the house, but nothing happened. Her nerves were shot. She couldn't take it any longer. She climbed out of the car, went to the front, and opened the hood. Then she headed for the house and knocked on the door.

The door opened. Up close, she could see that his gut hung over his pants and a light sheen of sweat covered his brow. He held the doorknob with one hand and a can of beer with the other. His brown wiry hair curled around two monstrous ears.

Kitally shivered.

"What are you selling, little girl?"

"Nothing." She tried to peek over his shoulder. "I'm having car troubles." Without looking behind her, she gestured across the street toward her car. "Would it be possible to use your phone?"

He glanced at the car, then gave her a once-over before taking another look across the street. "That's a nice car. Where's your cell phone?"

"I forgot to charge it last night," she lied. She couldn't understand why Hayley wasn't making a run for it, but maybe by calling him to the door she'd given her a chance to climb out a window or run out the back door. "Maybe I'll just try the engine one more time. Sorry to have bothered you."

Before she could leave, he grabbed hold of her shoulder, his hand clamped so tight she could feel the rough edges of his fingernails through her shirt. "You can use my phone," he said.

She stepped inside. The door shut behind her. A lock clicked into place. She headed left toward the kitchen, but he stopped her again and pointed to the right. "The phone is this way."

She followed him down a narrow hallway. The place smelled like body odor. The guy obviously didn't own a bar of soap.

There were two bedrooms. Both doors were open. Holmes walked ahead while she stopped to look inside the first bedroom. There was a futon covered with dirty clothes. A desk with a computer sat in front of the bedroom window. *Where is Hayley hiding?* "Don't you have a phone in your—"

A hand clamped over her mouth.

She hadn't seen or heard him step up from behind her. He dragged her backward into the next room. Not only was he overweight, he was strong, and he had her flat on the ground with her hands wrenched back behind her, nearly three hundred pounds keeping her down. She wriggled, tried to get air to her lungs. It was no use.

Moving an inch or two at a time, Hayley wriggled her way out from under the bed. *What was Kitally thinking, coming into the house?* She had single-handedly compromised their plans.

On her feet, Hayley looked around the room. All that came to hand was an old stapler on the desk. It was a real warhorse, at least. The thing felt as if it were made of wrought iron.

It shouldn't have surprised her to see Kitally beneath the big man in the next bedroom, but it did. She swung the stapler with all her might at his head, but merely clipped him when he turned at the last instant. The effort she put into the swing caused her to lose her footing and stagger backward into a dresser.

He was fast for a big man. He jumped to his feet and reached out for Hayley before she could catch her balance. Yanking her arm behind her, he twisted until she had no choice but to give in. He had her in a headlock.

Kitally was on all fours, her chest heaving as she caught her breath. Hayley watched her use the wood frame of the bed to slowly pull herself upward. Her legs wobbled like a newborn deer's.

They were fucked.

But apparently it was all show. When Kitally whirled around, Hayley wrenched her head to one side, giving Kitally room to jam the heel of her hand into Holmes's nose.

Bone crunched.

Hayley yanked herself free, but Holmes reeled around, blood gushing from his nose as he blindly planted his knuckles into Hayley's left cheekbone.

Growling, Kitally struck him in the throat, then used her body weight to throw a sharp elbow dead center into his torso, finishing with a right knee to the groin.

Holmes grunted and fell to the ground.

Hayley and Kitally took off at the same time, down the hall and out the door. Hayley slammed the hood of the car down just as Kitally jumped in behind the wheel. Hayley leaped into the passenger seat right before Kitally hit the gas.

When Hayley looked back, she saw Holmes charge out the door holding his face, stopping in the middle of the street. He was still standing there when Kitally took a sharp left and disappeared out of sight.

Hayley opened the mirror on the visor. There was already some discoloration, and her eye was swollen and half-shut. "What the hell were you thinking?"

"Excuse me?"

"You heard me. Why did you come after me? That was never part of the plan."

"All you had to do was text me," Kitally said, "and let me know you were having problems getting shit done in there. I thought you had fallen into a black hole. When Holmes drove up and I didn't see you drop out of a window or come running around the side of the house, I knew I had to do something."

"Stupid move," Hayley said. "I had it under control. And the reason I didn't text you back was because I had crawled under the bed and I couldn't reach my phone. I could hear Holmes in the kitchen, rifling through the refrigerator. Once he settled down, I was going to sneak out the back door."

"You were on the wrong side of the house. The back door, if there was one, was on the other side."

"Then I would have crawled through the fucking window."

"You said you would be fifteen minutes."

"No, I told you to give me thirty."

Kitally shook her head as she kept her eyes on the road in front of her. "That's not what you said."

Hayley opened the glove box and pulled out the throwaway phone. Then she called 911 and reported a rape taking place inside the house on 1273 Florence Drive in Sacramento. She told them to hurry, and then she hung up the phone before they could ask for a name.

CHAPTER EIGHT

Lizzy had worked late last night and didn't get home until well past midnight, when the only noise outside was the chirping of crickets. By the time she awoke, the sun was up and the day had started without her.

She staggered into the bathroom. A dizzy head prompted her to hang on to the counter for support. She felt hungover; with dark circles under her eyes, she looked hungover, too, and yet she hadn't had a drink since Hayley found her in the office drowning her sorrows in a bottle of scotch three months ago.

It took her fifteen minutes to get through her morning routine. Downstairs, she found Kitally at the kitchen table, eating scrambled eggs.

"Morning," Lizzy mumbled. "How did everything go with the prison guard? Any problems getting in and out?"

A girl stepped out of the main part of the kitchen and into view. Her black hair was pulled back into a bun. She was olive-skinned, ridiculously young, and pregnant.

Lizzy cocked her head and said, "Who are you?"

"I'm Salma. Who are you?"

Lizzy looked at Kitally. "What's going on?"

53

"Hayley and I were driving around looking for the Ghost when we happened upon Salma sleeping in the park."

"So you brought her here?"

"There's plenty of room," Hayley said from the main living area.

Lizzy lifted both palms in question. "Are we opening up some sort of home for misfits?"

Kitally's eyes widened in surprise. "I don't know. Is that what we are—misfits?"

"I can cook," Salma said, "and I—"

Ignoring the girl, Lizzy turned around and walked into the other room, where Hayley was sitting on the couch, tapping away on the keyboard, absorbed in whatever she was working on. "We can't talk openly if she's going to be staying here," Lizzy said.

Hayley looked up.

"What happened to your face?" Lizzy asked. "Who did that to you?"

"It's not as bad as it looks."

"Did Holmes see you?"

"Yep. He saw us both."

Lizzy stood stock-still. Heat rose from her toes to her neck.

"It was my fault," Kitally said as she entered the room behind Lizzy. "I should have let Hayley handle things, but I got worried and screwed everything up."

"Yeah, well, it doesn't really matter why or how," Lizzy said. "We're shutting this so-called operation down."

"Not yet," Kitally said. "There's still a good chance they caught Holmes with the porn that we planted inside his house and he'll be locked up. In fact, he could be behind bars right now as far as we know."

"Don't either of you get it?"

Kitally and Hayley waited for Lizzy to tell them.

"You weren't ready," Lizzy said to Kitally, angrily stabbing the air for emphasis. "I knew you weren't ready, but I let you talk me into moving forward. And look what happened. He saw both of your faces. It's over."

"You're overreacting," Hayley said. "Holmes can't prove we were ever in his house. He has no idea who we are, and I bet you he doesn't have a clue as to why we were there to begin with."

"Tell that to Detective Chase. He's got his eyes on you," she said to Hayley. "He's got a file this thick." She used her fingers to show her exactly how big the file was. "He's got pictures and witnesses who say they saw *you* in the area where a dead man was found in his apartment—a man who supposedly put a bag over his head and committed suicide."

Hayley sighed and went back to whatever she was doing before.

Kitally shot Lizzy a confused look. "What does that have to do with Hayley?"

"That girl," Lizzy said, ignoring Kitally and pointing in the direction she'd last seen Salma. "She's gotta go."

"What happened to helping others whenever possible?" Kitally wanted to know.

"Do you see those words carved on my fucking forehead?"

"Wow," Kitally said. "I get that you've got some major issues to deal with, but you don't have to be such a bitch."

Lizzy took a breath, tried to calm herself. "I'm going to my room to grab a few things and then I'll be out for most of the day."

"What about Shady Oaks Nursing Home?" Kitally asked.

"What about it?"

"You told me over the phone yesterday that you needed to talk to me about checking the place out."

"Yeah, well, figure it out. The file is on the desk in the office," she said as she walked off.

"I've never seen her so pissed off," Kitally said after Lizzy walked away.

Hayley shrugged. "She'll get over it."

"Should I leave?" Salma asked.

"*No*," Kitally and Hayley both said at once.

Tammy Walters and her four-year-old son lived in a one-bedroom apartment off Forty-Second Street. Long, unkempt dry grass and broken-down fencing surrounded the outside of the building, but the inside of the apartment was clean and neat, if sparsely furnished.

Tammy sat on a sofa, and Lizzy sat in an overstuffed chair facing her. "What can you tell me about your sister Miriam?"

"Do you mean what kind of person is she? Her hobbies, her goals?"

"Sure," Lizzy said. "Anything that might tell me what she's like."

Tammy thought about it for a moment. "Miriam is my best friend. Although we have the same birth parents, you wouldn't know it once you looked at the two of us together. Miriam is tall and slender but with curves—you know what I mean?"

Lizzy nodded.

"But me—well, take a look at me—I've got a lot of meat on these bones and being five feet, three inches, nobody ever accused me of being tall."

She laughed, but Lizzy could see that her heart wasn't in it. Although she talked as if her sister was still alive, the probability of that being the case was growing slimmer every day.

"Not only is Miriam beautiful," Tammy said, "she was always the brightest student in school." She sighed. "I'd be lying if I said I was never jealous of Miriam, because I was. And if her own sister is sometimes jealous, think how many girls in high school were. I used to joke and call my sister 'poor beautiful Miriam.'"

Tammy's son brought over a toy, and, without missing a beat, she connected a plastic robot arm and leg and then handed it back to him. "There you go," she said. "Momma loves you." The kid ran back to his pile of toys in the middle of the apartment.

"Do you know how Miriam met Wayne Bennett?" Lizzy asked.

"Yeah. I do." She pointed to her chest. "It was *me*." She fiddled with her tight black curls. "After I heard that a girl I knew was handpicked by Wayne Bennett to be in his program, I called his office. I was outraged that my sister wasn't chosen, and that's when I found out that Miriam had never even applied." She shook her head. "Why didn't I just leave well enough alone?"

"We would all make different decisions and choices if we could see into the future."

"Yeah, well, how many people make choices that put a loved one's life in danger?"

Lizzy lifted a shoulder and left it at that.

"Anyhow, I talked Miriam into applying, and, of course, she got into the program. If she wasn't so damned beautiful, Wayne Bennett probably never would have paid her any mind. But as it was, he took an immediate interest in my sister and that was that."

"Did she complain about him?" Lizzy asked.

"No. It was way worse than that. Poor beautiful Miriam fell in love with Wayne Bennett."

"Really?"

"Yep. It took Miriam about twenty-four hours to fall for the guy. As if she knows what love is, right? She's eighteen. He's way too old for her. I just figured it was a harmless infatuation. Think about it," Tammy said, leaning forward, her voice lowering. "Tall, handsome, distinguished, smart, and compassionate. A well-respected man looked up to in the community, a man who wasn't satisfied with making millions of dollars but who claimed to have a burning need to help others." Tammy moaned in disgust. "If my sister had made a list describing her perfect mate, Wayne Bennett would have fallen at the top of the list."

They both watched Tammy's son run around the apartment making airplane noises, his wooden airplane rising to the floor and then back to the sky, around and around. The kid stopped in front of Lizzy, his airplane held frozen in holding mode. "Are you gonna find Aunt Miriam?"

"I don't know," Lizzy said. "I sure hope so."

The little boy took off again. When he was out of earshot, Lizzy said, "In your opinion, is it possible Miriam and Mr. Bennett formed an intimate relationship?"

"Not only is it possible—it happened. Our father is an asshole, so Miriam moved in with me. She's been living here with my boy and me for a while now. After she met Mr. Bennett, I would get daily updates. If he so much as looked at her, I heard about it. The first time he took her to dinner, I thought her head would explode from excitement alone."

"Did she know he was married?"

"She's a smart girl, remember? Of course she did."

"So she must have known it wouldn't last forever."

"She was book smart, I guess, not exactly relationship smart. Like a lot of mistresses out there, Miriam thought she was special."

"So what do you think happened? Do you think he told her it was over and she left town?"

"Nope. Not even close. I've heard rumors that Miriam had met someone else, a younger guy, so, in my opinion, I think one of two things happened. Miriam either threatened to tell the world about their relationship if he didn't leave his wife, or she told him about this other guy and Bennett didn't like it."

Tammy sighed and then wiped away a tear. "She can't be dead. She just can't be. He must be keeping her against her will somewhere, like maybe in his mountain cabin. I heard he had a vacation home in Lake Tahoe. All rich people have one of those—don't they?"

"You told me over the phone that you had a picture of them together. Can I see it?"

Tammy laughed. "Bennett would not allow Miriam to take pictures of them together." The look on Tammy's face was a sly one. "He wouldn't allow her to use her phone when they were together, either."

Lizzy frowned. "We need proof."

"Calm down, girlfriend. You see, Mr. Bennett had no idea who he was dealing with. Just because Miriam couldn't pull out a cell phone or take pictures of them together, that didn't mean her friends and family couldn't."

Tammy picked up an envelope and dumped its contents onto the coffee table between them. Pictures of all sizes slid out, some falling to the floor.

Lizzy scooped up the ones from the floor. "Did your sister know about this?"

"You bet. It was her idea."

Lizzy examined one particular photo: a clear shot of Miriam and Wayne Bennett enjoying a candlelit dinner for two. "Do you know where this was taken?"

"I sure do."

"How about date and time?"

"Yep. I got it all."

Lizzy's adrenaline kicked in. "I'll need a list of friends and family, anyone who might have seen Miriam with Bennett. I will also need her last place of employment and anything else you can give me."

"I'll make you a list right now."

CHAPTER NINE

Up until three weeks ago, when she discovered she was pregnant, Lorry Jo Raciti considered herself to be lucky in life. Not a perfect life, but a good one.

She and her second husband had been married for ten years. They had three children who meant the world to her. The problems all started when she returned to the workforce. She was an assistant for a slew of engineers at a software company in Folsom. Going to work, interacting with other adults, getting respect—not to mention a paycheck—was a high she hadn't experienced in a very long time.

But she'd blown it. She'd let one of the engineers get the best of her: tall, handsome, great-smelling cologne—a drink after work and then instead of driving her back to work where her car had been left in the parking lot, he'd gotten halfway to their destination and pulled over to the side of the road.

She had more than a hunch he wanted to kiss her.

She wanted to kiss him, too.

Under the pretense of getting some air, needing a moment to think about whether or not she would allow him one quick kiss, solely to get it out of her system, she got out of the car. He climbed out, too, and the next thing she knew, he took her hard and fast on the hood of his Camaro.

It was exhilarating, intoxicating: the best sex she'd ever had.

And that was it.

Ten minutes of hot and heavy, mind-blowing sex ended up being ten minutes she would never forget for as long as she lived.

Not because the man or the sex was unforgettable, but because she was pregnant.

This morning, like any other morning, she woke up, kissed her husband, got dressed, and then made sure the kids arrived at school on time. Instead of going to work, though, she came here, to the American River. She had grown up in Sacramento, and this trail—with its views of the meandering river, leafy trees, and so much wildlife, a picture that would stay with her for days—was where she always went when she needed to unwind or to think things through.

If she were going to keep this baby, she would need to tell her husband the truth. After the birth of their third child, he'd had a vasectomy. Her only other option, as far as she was concerned, was to have an abortion and never tell a soul.

The sun's rays hit the water in a way that made the river look as if crushed diamonds had been sprinkled over the top. Nature at its best—alive and welcoming.

Although her earbuds were in place, it was only for show. When she wanted to think, didn't want to say hello to people she passed, she wore the buds in hopes of being left alone. Since they weren't connected to anything, she could still hear the water as it lapped gently against the shoreline. She could hear the birds chirping and the rustling of leaves and tiny feet against bark as the squirrels chased one another, circling a tree.

Her thoughts progressed to the matter at hand, and she tried to imagine what her unborn child would look like. Boy or girl? Blonde or brunette? All of her kids were so different, in both looks and personality. Would this child have her blue eyes? She imagined her other children playing with the new baby, arguing over whose turn it was to hold him or her next. She had two girls and a boy. Her son would love to have a brother. Did her husband love her enough to make this work?

She lifted her gaze to the sky and smiled as the tremendous weight of indecision lifted from her shoulders.

Everything changed in that moment.

She knew she had made a mistake. There was no getting around that fact. But she would do everything in her power to make her marriage work. Her mind was made up. Chills swept over her. She would keep this baby.

The distinct sounds of someone approaching startled her. Lost in her thoughts, she'd momentarily become unaware of her surroundings. Before she could turn around, an arm circled her neck and a rag was stuffed into her mouth.

She struggled for breath.

And then she fought for her life and the life of her unborn baby. She couldn't die! She kicked her attacker in the shin. Not now. Certainly not today.

She clawed at his face, determined to leave a mark.

It was such a beautiful day.

Even now as she was dragged over the slope of a hill, the sharp edges of twigs and rocks digging into her back, she could see the morning rays of the sun peeking through the trees.

Someone would help her.

There were always so many people on this path. But this wasn't Saturday or Sunday. Today was a workday.

Help me, please.

Her children needed her. She found the physical power to fight on. She kicked him again, kicked him hard, but she could already feel her strength leaving her.

She thought of her husband. Would he ever know how sorry she was?

She prayed he would never learn of her condition. But if he did, she prayed he would find it in his heart to forgive her.

Well hidden beneath the leafy canopy of a giant oak, he had watched and waited. Every so often a biker would whiz by, a group of runners, or the occasional couple taking a morning walk. The pathway veered along the American River, a watercourse that ran from the Sierra Nevada mountain range, converged with the Sacramento River, and eventually emptied into the San Francisco Bay and then the Pacific Ocean.

He loved to watch the kayakers and paddleboarders skim across the river from his balcony at home, but his newest plan had forced him out of his rut to try something new.

He was in no hurry this morning, yet it wasn't long before he saw a lone walker on the horizon. Yes, she was walking this way. He could see wires dangling on both sides of her face. She had buds in her ears. Not a smart move. No cell phone on hand, at least that he could see. She walked at a good clipped pace, would be upon him any minute now. As long as no other walkers, runners, or bikers showed up, she would be the chosen one—his next victim.

From his spot on the hill, he could see just far enough both ways, far enough to see that the timing couldn't be better. The moment the woman passed him, he headed out from under the tree and onto the trail, making quick work of catching up to her. His hand came around her face, and she opened her mouth to scream just as he knew she would. He shoved a rag into her mouth to muffle her cries as he dragged her into the cover, past the place where he'd been watching the trail, deep into the thickest part of rocks and trees.

Damn.

She was a fighter.

She kicked and she hit.

Even after he had her on the ground face up, his legs straddling her, the weight of him holding her down, his hands around her throat, she managed to rake sharp fingernails across his face. "You bitch."

He clamped his hands around her neck and squeezed until he thought the pads of his thumbs might go through her flesh and come out the other side.

Her eyes widened, wild with fear. He felt her heart rate race, watched her cheeks redden. He grew hard watching her expression shift from anger to terror.

Even as he stared at her, unblinking, he felt her arms go limp at her sides.

Now she had stopped fighting altogether. Her legs had gone slack beneath him.

His gaze became one with hers. He couldn't look away even if he wanted to. She might not realize it as she took her last breaths, but she was special. He would remember her for the rest of his life. She was magnificent. Her eyes, as blue as the clear waters of Tahoe, had turned a stormy cerulean right before they lost their luster. On canvas, she would come alive.

Overcome with joy, filled with orgasmic satisfaction, he finally released his hold on the woman. He inhaled deeply and closed his eyes as he filled his lungs with the smell of fear, death, and ultimate control.

He pulled out a two-inch blade and cut away her clothes, then sliced through flesh from left to right, then a clean diagonal cut from her collarbone to her hip bone, and then straight across. He finished his signature with one last horizontal cut.

This time he'd made sure to leave a mark big enough so every crime scene technician who came within ten feet of the girl would see it.

Taking a step back, he took a good long look at his bloody artwork. He stared at her, unsure of the mix of emotions he was feeling. He wasn't ready to leave, but he had no choice. He tilted her head just so, fixed her hair as best he could, and then spared her one last glance before he walked away.

Heading back toward the trail, he stopped to bury an item he'd brought with him—a mirror. He scooped out the rich soil, placed the mirror inside, covered it up, and gently patted the soil until it was hardly noticeable. Back on his feet, he inwardly scolded himself for leaving the object. But he hadn't been able to help himself. It was a small but essential part of the composition—the mirror was the artist's reminder to reflect and speculate, to look inside oneself to gain self-knowledge. With a heavy sigh, he peeled the gloves from his hands, rolled them into a ball, and slid them into his pants pocket. Hidden behind brush and trees, he heard talking: two women discussing their marital woes. He took a quiet breath, held perfectly still, and waited until they were far enough up the trail that they wouldn't notice him.

He crossed the path, admiring the vast array of trees, all different shades of green, some with silver-tipped leaves. Making his way toward the river, his latest victim all but forgotten for now, he found himself wondering why he didn't do this more often. The great outdoors: blue skies and the fresh smell of fish, plant, and earth all mingled into one.

Crisp air brushed his face and still he considered it to be fairly warm for the month of April. Halfway down the trail, he saw the very tip of his yellow kayak peeking out from under the brush.

Upon reaching it, he leaned over and picked up his life vest. He slipped it on—you could never be too safe when it came to large bodies of water—and, when he was certain the river, at least as far as he could see in either direction, was devoid of people, he slid his kayak into the smooth water, carefully took his place inside, and began to paddle for home.

CHAPTER TEN

Lizzy's longtime therapist, Linda Gates, placed a cup of hot green tea on the side table next to the couch where Lizzy was sitting. Then she picked up her notebook and sat down in her leather chair. "I have an unusual request."

"What is it?"

"There's a woman I've been seeing for a while now. She lost her husband and their three small children to a drunk driver."

Lizzy had no idea where Linda might be going with this. Not once in all their years together had she uttered one word about another client. But Lizzy sat quietly and waited to see what she had to say.

"You might have read about it in the paper. Her husband wanted to give her a break, so he decided to take the kids to his parents' house fifteen minutes away. They never made it."

More waiting.

"She read about what happened to Jared, and she thought you might benefit from having someone to talk to. Someone who has dealt with a tragic loss of a loved one."

"Isn't that what I pay you for?"

"I agree with her. I think it might be helpful for you to talk to someone who has dealt with a traumatic and unexpected loss."

"I think it's a stupid idea."

"Why?"

"People all over the world are dealing with shit worse than mine or hers. She'll never be the same, and neither will I. We all just have to keep on moving, get through another day and then another until it's all one big blur again." Lizzy lifted a shoulder. "We all heal in our own way and in our own time. You know that."

"I'll tell her you're not ready to talk to anyone."

"Tell her whatever you want, Linda. Tell her I'm sorry for her loss. While you're at it, you might think about telling her the truth."

"And that is?"

"That it might not get any better. That the days get longer and the nights get darker. Her best days could well be over."

"We don't know if that's true."

"I guess we'll have to agree to disagree."

"I'm worried about you, Lizzy."

Lizzy uncrossed her legs, then crossed them again. She picked nonexistent lint off the couch.

"You seem angry."

"No. Really?"

"Who are you angry with?"

"Everyone."

"You're angry with me?" Linda asked without reproach.

"Yes, even you. I've known you for what, eighteen years, and I don't know anything about you, but you know everything about me. That's fucked up. And, let's see, I'm angry with my mother. She didn't come to my wedding, which was probably a good move, since she could have been shot and killed had she made the effort. But she didn't come. She's alive and well. So, would it kill her to call me every once in a while? And then there's my sister." Lizzy waved a hand through the air. "I'm not even going to bother going there—the list is too long. But you know who I'm really pissed off at?"

"Who?"

"Myself. I hate *me*. I hate every choice I've ever made. I hate being around people. I hate seeing my reflection staring back at me, always judging. I hate the way food feels on my tongue and the way I never taste anything. I hate the ugly gray skies every time I look up. The six o'clock news makes me sick to my stomach. I hate the drizzly rain out there today. I mean, if you're going to rain, you might as well pour. Give us some real water, not this half-ass shit. I hate my life. Most of all, I hate being so fucking angry." Lizzy clamped her mouth shut. She was finished.

A long, drawn-out moment passed before Linda said, "You have every reason to be angry."

"Well, thanks," Lizzy said as she started to stand up. "Are we done?"

"Not quite." Linda straightened. "I've been married and divorced twice, and I never had children." Linda put her notebook aside. "Not because I didn't want them, but because I was born with a fixed number of eggs and the health of those eggs declined as I got older. I'm fifty-eight now. It's too late for me."

Lizzy slid an arm into her jacket.

"Both husbands refused to use donor eggs and both went on to remarry and have children of their own. One of them married my best friend, with whom I no longer speak. When I get lonely, I play the violin. I love going to operas. I spend most of my life sitting here in this chair listening to others without passing judgment. I listen to their stories and I see their sadness, feel their grief, and I know, above all, I cannot cry. It would be unprofessional to do so."

Lizzy slid her other arm into her jacket and shouldered her purse, her gaze never leaving Linda's. And then she sat back down and listened.

"Through my clients, I have learned forgiveness. So many hours I spend sitting in this chair, wanting to tell someone what to do, but I sit quietly and listen because I know that if I can draw in my own thoughts and listen really well, I'll be more helpful to them. I have learned over the years that we are all children at heart and that we all need to be heard and understood. I have carried hundreds of stories deep within and when my clients hurt, I also hurt. When they mourn, I mourn with them. And through it all, my heart has grown bigger and stronger and for that I am eternally grateful."

"Thank you," Lizzy said as she came to her feet once again.

"You're welcome."

Lizzy stopped at the door and said, "I'll see you next week."

"I'll be here."

CHAPTER ELEVEN

The only nursing home Kitally had visited in her lifetime was the one back east where she'd last seen her grandfather. It had been a happy place. There was always laughter and entertainment, piano music or singing. On one of her visits to see her grandfather, the staff had set up a little petting zoo outside, complete with miniature goats, rabbits, and sheep. They held classes—yoga and dancing. Even the people in wheelchairs used to dance.

But Shady Oaks Nursing Home in Orangevale was nothing like that.

One lady sat lopsided within her wheelchair, abandoned in the hallway, facing the wall. Kitally looked around. Would anyone notice if she walked over to the woman and turned her chair around so she could look at something other than a wall?

"Can I help you?"

The woman behind the front desk was looking her way. Her frizzy brown hair was clipped back. Her face was pinched.

"I called a few hours ago about getting a tour of Shady Oaks," Kitally said. "My mom and I need to find a place for my grandmother."

Exasperated, the woman picked up the receiver and said over the loudspeaker, "Janice Unger. Please come to the front desk."

After she hung up, she said, "Janice will be here momentarily. Please take a seat."

Kitally grabbed a magazine and settled into one of the plastic chairs lined up against the wall. Her gaze promptly returned to the woman in the wheelchair. She had yet to see the woman move a muscle. *Is she asleep? Dead? Does anyone care?*

Figuring she could ask Janice about it when she arrived, Kitally skimmed through the magazine.

"*CAW! CAW!*"

Kitally jerked to attention.

The frazzled woman behind the desk merely groaned. "There she goes again."

Kitally followed her gaze to the woman in the wheelchair. She wasn't dead, after all. She came to her feet and did it again. "*CAW! CAW!*"

The call of the wild. Within seconds all sorts of animal noises erupted from different sections of the building. The distinct moo of a cow was followed by the neigh of a horse. Then came a meow and a dozen barking dogs.

What the hell is going on around here?

If the frizzy-haired woman didn't look so thoroughly agitated, Kitally might have laughed out loud. By the time the animal noises began to die off, a very round woman with short stubby arms and legs waddled toward the front desk.

Frizzy-haired lady pointed at Kitally.

The woman waddled her way. "I'm Janice Unger. Nice to meet you. Let's go."

Kitally returned the magazine to the pile on the table, then hurried to catch up to the woman. She followed Janice to the left, away from where the woman sat in the wheelchair. "What was that all about?" Kitally asked.

"What?"

"The animal noises."

"Oh, that was just Ms. Trumble having some fun. She loves animals, and I think it makes her happy to hear all the animal sounds."

"So," Janice said as they walked. "You're looking for a place for your grandmother?"

"Yes."

"How old is she?"

"Um, seventy-six."

"She's young. You realize we're a full nursing-care facility, not just assisted living. She needs twenty-four-hour medical care to be admitted."

"Yes, I know. Mom is taking care of her now, and it's becoming too much of a burden for her."

"Does she need long-term care or short-term?"

Kitally was at a loss. The truth was her grandmother had died when Kitally was very young. "I'm not sure at this point. If I could just have a quick look around, then report back to my mom, that would be best."

Kitally followed Janice into a large room. "As you can see, this is the recreation room."

Kitally couldn't see that at all. There was no music. No life. Three women played cards, but that was the extent of the entertainment.

Next, she was shown the cafeteria, the kitchen, the outside area that consisted of two plastic chairs and a weathered bench. There wasn't anywhere nice to sit and enjoy the day. The sound of the freeway was deafening. No birdsong. No greenery. She hadn't thought about it before, but Kitally realized she didn't like the idea of growing old. She thought of Helsie, the reason she was here. Dementia was an awful disease. If the woman had been abused, had she known what was happening to her? Were there moments of clarity where she knew exactly where she was and what was going on? Stuck in this place with no one to protect her. Not cool.

"What do you think about Shady Oaks?" Kitally asked.

Janice used her fingernail to dislodge something from her tooth. "It's a great place. I'd bring my mother here if I could afford it."

Kitally didn't believe it for a moment. "Could I see the rooms where residents sleep and spend most of their day?"

"We're all filled up at the moment. I'm not allowed to disturb our residents. I'm sorry." She picked at a scab on her arm. It took every bit of restraint Kitally could muster to not make a face.

"Janice Unger," a voice called over the loudspeaker. "Please come to the front desk."

The woman glanced at her watch. "Oh, would you look at that. It's time for my next tour."

"I just need a little more time," Kitally said, sniffling. "I just can't imagine bringing my grandma to a nursing home and leaving her." She wiped at nonexistent tears.

The woman shifted uncomfortably on her feet.

"Go on," Kitally said. "I just need a few minutes to collect myself. I know the way out."

"OK. If you're sure."

Kitally turned her back to the woman and sniffled again as she headed for the weathered bench. The moment she heard the door swing shut, Kitally stood up and followed her into the building. She headed back the same way Janice had brought her. In fact, she saw Janice talking to the new visitors. The frizzy-haired woman was no longer standing behind the desk, giving Kitally a chance to head the other way. The lady in the wheelchair was gone.

In the first bedroom she came upon, Kitally saw an elderly woman being spoon-fed her lunch by a middle-aged woman wearing a green Shady Oaks smock. Nobody noticed her standing a few feet from the door. Everything in the room looked neat and orderly.

The next room was empty, which was odd considering she'd just been told the place was full. She walked inside. It was a small room, twelve-by-twelve at the most. No windows. Claustrophobic. She stepped back into the hallway and continued on, peeking inside each room. Every other room was unoccupied. She had no idea what she was looking for or expecting to see. She just kept walking.

"Hey, you."

She backed up a few steps until she saw an old man sitting in bed.

"Yeah, you," he said.

Kitally stepped inside his room. The place smelled like unwashed skin and disinfectant. She tried not to wrinkle her nose. "Do you need something?"

"Are you new around here?"

"I don't work here, but I could try to find someone."

"I just need you to get me an extra blanket." He pointed across the room at the high dresser with the TV on it.

She opened one drawer after another: socks and underwear, adult diapers, T-shirts. No blankets.

"Nothing in there?" he asked.

"No."

"Go back into the hallway and in the next room you'll find an old broad named Betty Ackley. Tell her I need one of her blankets."

"Maybe I should just ask one of the staff members for a blanket."

"No," he said firmly. "Next room on the right. Ask Betty."

Kitally sighed. "Sure. OK. I'll be right back." Unlike the other rooms she'd seen so far, Betty's room was larger. She even had a window, although the view of the parking lot was nothing to get excited about. Still, it was better than nothing. The TV was on, the volume turned up. A soap opera.

"What do you want?" the woman asked, loud enough to be heard over the TV.

"Um . . . the man in the next room needs a blanket. He said to ask you for one."

"Are you his daughter?"

Kitally shook her head.

"Niece?"

"No."

"Well, who the hell are you?"

"I'm just here for a tour. My mom and I are looking for a place for my grandmother."

"Don't bring her here. No matter what you do, don't bring Grandma here."

"Why?"

"Look around, honey. Open your eyes."

"It really is that bad?"

"Worse than bad. I should have had children. Maybe then someone would break me out of this joint."

Before the woman could say anything else, another woman wearing a green smock entered the room. "Got yourself a visitor, Betty?"

"I sure do. Dixie, I'd like you to meet my grandson's girlfriend. Isn't she pretty?"

"She's gorgeous," the nurse said without glancing her way.

As the woman in the green smock set up a tray of food next to her bed, Betty winked at Kitally and said, "Why don't you go ahead and grab a blanket for Cecil?" She pointed to the dresser. "Bottom drawer."

Kitally did as she said. On top of the dresser there was a calendar and an assortment of pens and stationery. Stationery with a squiggly design on the bottom right corner. The exact same stationery she had seen inside Lizzy's file.

Could Betty Ackley be the one who wrote the note and had it delivered to Gus? Could Kitally have really stumbled upon the person she was looking for that quickly? No way. Nothing in life was ever that easy!

Kitally bent down, opened the bottom drawer, and pulled out a blanket.

After the orderly finished setting up Betty Ackley's meal, she finally took a moment to look at Kitally. And that's when the woman's eyes narrowed. "Where's your badge?"

"Badge?"

"All visitors must wear a badge."

"Oh. It must have fallen off."

"You can't be in here without a badge."

"My name is Kitally," she said, more for Betty's benefit than the nurse's.

"Don't care if your name is President Obama. You can't be in here without a badge."

"It's OK, darling," Betty said to Kitally. "Take Cecil his blanket and next time you come, make sure you wear your badge and bring me some chocolates, too."

"I'll see you in a few days," Kitally said before making her exit.

Betty nodded. "I'll be here."

CHAPTER TWELVE

Standing outside the door to her office downtown, fishing around inside her bag for the keys, Lizzy heard someone call her name and glanced over her shoulder. It was Jessica Pleiss, her very first employee, now ex-employee and rookie FBI agent, running toward her.

"What are you doing here?"

"I just flew in an hour ago," Jessica said, catching her breath. "I rented a car and came straight here. I have a meeting in an hour, so I thought I'd see if you were here. After I didn't see your car, I decided to get a coffee, but then I saw you and here I am."

They embraced, and then Jessica pointed to the coffee shop up the street. "I'll go get us both a coffee. I'll be right back."

"Nothing for me," Lizzy said. "My stomach has been acting up."

"Have you had a checkup recently?"

Lizzy gave her a don't-mother-me look. "Go get your coffee," she said, shooing her away. "I'll put away my things and heat the place up so we can talk and you can tell me why you're here in Sacramento before you run off."

"Sounds good."

Lizzy used to stop to admire the etched sign on the door: LIZZY GARDNER INVESTIGATIONS. But not any longer. The sign, the business, everything about the place left a bad taste in her mouth. She would sell the business today if she didn't need it as a cover for their extracurricular activities.

Hurrying inside, she dropped her purse in the bottom desk drawer, then put away any files or notes that might raise a red flag. Jessica had no idea what she, Kitally, and Hayley were up to, and Lizzy planned to keep it that way. Jessica was a law-abiding citizen, a straight shooter who happened to work for the FBI.

Jessica returned five minutes later, coffee in hand. "Did you know that the Bernsteins sold the coffee shop?"

Lizzy shook her head.

"According to the new owner, they were robbed. Twice. They couldn't take it any longer and they moved away. Clear across the country."

"I can't blame them."

"What? Don't tell me you're thinking of moving."

"I'm just taking it one day at a time."

Jessica sank into the seat in front of Lizzy's desk. "How are you doing, Lizzy? How are you holding up?"

"I don't want to talk about me. Tell me why you're here."

Jessica's gaze roamed over Lizzy's face as if she was searching for answers. Finally, she exhaled and said, "I'm sure you've heard about Mark Kiel's daughter. Killed while taking a run through the park."

Lizzy nodded.

"I can't say too much, but there are at least two other homicides that occurred in the past few months that are being reexamined for connections."

"And they wanted you on the case because . . . ?"

"Because the FBI is getting involved and Jimmy Martin asked me to help him out. It will be good for me to get some early exposure to these sorts of crimes."

"What about Quantico?"

"I still have a few weeks of training left. I'll be flying back and forth."

Lizzy nodded. "Good for you."

"There's more. Another body was found during my flight over here this morning."

"Where?"

"Right off of the American River trail. Not too far from Kitally's house in Carmichael."

Lizzy stiffened.

"With Brittany getting into Sac State and with you taking your morning and/or evening runs, I thought you should know."

"I appreciate it." Lizzy rubbed her chin. "How did you know about Brittany getting into Sac State?"

"She called me."

Silence.

"Your niece is worried about you. You should call her."

"I will. Do you have a place to stay?"

"I thought you'd never ask."

When Lizzy arrived home at six o'clock, she found Salma sitting at the dining room table, playing solitaire. "There's some vegetarian biryani in the refrigerator if you're hungry."

"What is it?"

"A classic Indian dish with basmati rice, potatoes, carrots, peas, and lots of spices."

Lizzy plopped her purse on the table. "Thanks. I'll give it a try. Where's everyone else?"

"Kitally is in her bedroom, and I haven't seen Hayley all day."

Lizzy wrinkled her nose as she walked toward the family room. "What's that smell? It's not your yani dish, is it?"

"It most certainly is not. And it's called biryani, not yani." Salma sniffed the air. "It does smell in here, though. Kind of smells like seafood, doesn't it?"

Lizzy walked around the main room, trying to find the source of the smell. "Yes, that's it. Smells like rotted fish. Makes me want to gag."

"I mentioned it to Kitally, but she couldn't smell it. I thought maybe I was going crazy."

Lizzy gave up on finding the source of the smell. As she walked back toward the kitchen, she said, "I'm sorry about the other day. I haven't been myself lately."

"Don't worry about it. It wouldn't feel like home if everyone walked around with smiles on their faces."

Lizzy forced a smile, and then opened the refrigerator and pulled out the container holding the dish Salma had made. She popped the lid and gave it a precautionary sniff. Nope, that wasn't the smell. If the rotting-fish stench didn't go away soon, she was going to start opening windows. She put the container in the microwave and pushed a few buttons to heat it up. "I have a friend coming here to stay for a few nights. She should arrive any time now."

"Oh. I can move out of the bedroom and give her some privacy."

"She can sleep on the couch. She'll be fine."

The quiet settled between them while Lizzy waited for dinner to heat up and Salma played her card game.

"If you need any help with anything, let me know," Salma said.

"I will. So, what's the deal with you anyhow? Do you have family in the area?"

The girl nodded. "I do. Not that you'd know it. Since they found out I'm pregnant they're not talking to me."

"What about the father of the baby?"

"He's around."

When Salma grew quiet, Lizzy went to the table and took a seat across from her. "How old are you?"

"Eighteen."

Lizzy didn't believe her. "You look much younger."

"That's what everyone says."

"Are you a runaway?"

She rubbed her swollen belly. "No."

"Do your parents know where you are?"

She shrugged.

"If you tell me where you live or give me a number, I could call and talk to them."

"Listen, this isn't something you can just jump in and fix. My father is not happy with my choices—that's a nice way to put it. The cultural differences between my boyfriend and me make it impossible for my family to accept him. My brother can be a hot-head. If they find out where I am, who knows what could happen? So no, no phone calls. If you don't want me to stay, I'll leave. I didn't ask to come here. Your friends dragged me here against my will."

Lizzy didn't like the ultimatum. She also didn't like the idea of the young girl roaming the streets. She needed to think things through and figure out what to do with the girl. With a baby on the way, she couldn't stay here indefinitely.

CHAPTER THIRTEEN

Annie Shepard staggered out of the doctor's office. Her cell phone was inside her purse, and she could feel it vibrating against her thigh. It was probably her husband, calling from work to find out the results of the latest test.

A tear ran down her cheek.

Standing in the hallway, her only thought was, *Oh, my God. Oh, my God.*

She wasn't ready to talk to her husband. Not yet. She just needed a moment to herself to take it all in. She'd never felt so damned happy in her life.

Deliriously happy.

After all these months of staying strong, refusing to cry or show emotions, she was a wreck. Her heart pounded inside her chest. Her hands felt clammy; her legs wobbled beneath her bony frame. It boggled her mind to discover she'd never really seen this coming. It was a miracle. And she knew it.

As she followed the carpeted hallway, making a left and then a right, she recalled taking this same walk through these same hallways two years ago, almost to the day.

She'd been given an upsetting diagnosis that day—told she

had ovarian cancer. One year to live was the most they could promise her. Tops.

She'd spent the last twenty-four months of her life doing everything she could to reverse the cancer that had dared to invade her body and turn her life upside down. After getting a second and third opinion, each diagnosis grimmer than the last, she'd had surgery, and then chemotherapy followed by radiation. Not to mention a radical change in her diet. Despite the weakness in her arms and legs, she began to exercise, which consisted mostly of stretching and taking long walks. Every day. When she wasn't exercising, she was reading self-help books. All very inspiring and positive books: *No Fear for the Fearless. You Can Beat the Odds. Don't Look Back, Moving Forward.*

Not once had she allowed herself a pity party. In fact, the minute she had walked out of this same building two years ago, she had refused to accept the verdict. She would not go out without a fight.

And today, she'd learned she had won.

Her cancer was in full-blown remission.

She would live long enough to see her children grow, marry, have children of their own.

She stopped right there in the middle of the hallway and let out a "*Yippee!*" She blushed when an elderly couple passed by, gawking at her. After they disappeared inside the elevator at the end of the hallway, she let out another whoop, and then she laughed out loud.

She couldn't remember the last time she'd laughed—a real honest-to-goodness laugh that made her insides thrum like this.

Things were going to change, she decided as she continued toward the stairwell at the end of the hallway. She needed to try new things. Live a little.

She spared a quick glance at the elevator as she walked by.

By nature, she'd always been a scaredy-cat. There were quite a few things, in fact, that scared the bejesus out of her, and the top two on her list were bridges and elevators.

After turning away from the door to the stairwell, she turned back toward the elevator. As she bit down on her bottom lip, she looked at the shiny metallic doors in a new light. She'd lost track of the number of times someone or another told her that the elevator was the most used transportation on earth. Elevators required regular inspections and maintenance, they would tell her. Elevators were perfectly safe. Accidents only happened in the movies or on TV. If there was an emergency, there were call buttons for just that reason.

She reached out and hit the red Down button.

Then she waited.

Since he still had plenty of time before his meeting, he'd taken the first empty parking space he could find on the side of the road and decided to head for Capitol Mall to do some people watching. Once his meeting was over, he planned to visit the Crocker Art Museum, one of his favorite places in Sacramento. The new wing was nice, light and spacious, but he treasured the original Crocker with its elaborately carved wood, dark colors, and stained glass. He always felt at home when he visited.

As he'd walked along the sidewalk, he watched various people pass him by without a second glance. With his neatly trimmed hair and casual suit, he was one of them. Everyone was rushing to work or perhaps to lunch.

After he'd noticed an elderly couple exit an underground parking garage, something possessed him to head that way. It was almost as if he were being pulled by some magnetic force.

There were very few cars parked within the garage, and despite it being daytime, the area was dark. Bits of trash were scattered about. No security whatsoever. A black hole in the middle of a bustling city.

The elevator doors to his left opened, startling him. Before the doors could shut again, he rushed over and used his right foot to hold the doors open while he stepped inside. He had no idea where he was going or what sort of building this was, but it was such an odd little hole in the wall, he couldn't resist.

There appeared to be three floors. A short ride, no matter which button he pressed. He pushed the button with the number 3, hoping to feel a jolt before takeoff.

No jolt. No fun. Not until the doors parted and he found a tiny bird of a woman waiting to get on the elevator. Her eyes were twinkling until she saw him frowning.

"I'm afraid I'm lost," he told her, bedazzling her with one of his wide grins.

"Are you here to see Dr. Roth?"

"Yes, Dr. Roth. Am I on the right track?"

Her frown bloomed into a smile that made her eyes sparkle again. She pointed to her left. "It's a bit of a maze, but his office is that way," she said.

He stepped off the elevator, holding the door for the woman to get on.

"Thank you," she said after she'd stepped inside.

"Anything for such a lovely woman."

He let go of the door, saw her blush as the doors slowly moved toward each other. Before the doors met, though, he grabbed hold of the edge of a door and squeezed his way back inside the elevator. "I forgot something," he said.

Five seconds passed before the doors began to close again.

"It's a lovely day, isn't it?" he asked her.

How fitting, Annie had thought, that the elevator doors would open and such a handsome and distinguished-looking man would be standing before her. Her day kept getting better and better.

After she'd pointed him in the direction of Dr. Roth's office, she'd stepped into the elevator and felt a ripple of anticipation rush through her body. Instead of being afraid, she'd felt a thrill she couldn't explain if she tried.

When the man turned and stopped the elevator doors from shutting so he could step back inside, a moment of trepidation had fallen over her, but any worry was short-lived. He had simply forgotten something.

"It's a lovely day, isn't it?"

He had a rich and pleasing voice. He asked the question in such a way that made her feel as if he knew she'd just been handed a second chance to live life. His eyes were so blue, his smile so bright, she had a difficult time looking away. "Today is the best day of my life," she said cheerily.

He smiled again and said, "You have no idea how happy that makes me."

Their space was limited, but he stepped closer, all the while looking at her with a fiery intensity.

Her pulse raced.

He lifted his hands, and for a moment she actually thought he was going in for a kiss.

"I'm a married woman," she said as his fingers brushed over her throat, her eyes never leaving his.

"Even better," he said. And then his hands clamped hard around her neck and he began to squeeze. It was then she noticed not only his crooked nose but four faint lines across her cheek. Scratch marks he'd tried to cover up.

This wasn't his first time. He'd killed before. And he would kill again.

Today was not the first day of the rest of her life, after all.

It was her last.

If only I'd taken the stairs, she thought as the elevator lurched to a stop and her legs crumpled beneath her.

CHAPTER FOURTEEN

Lizzy had been sitting behind the wheel of her car in the parking lot at a shopping center in West Sacramento for over an hour. Kobi Millard worked at the bank. She was one of many women who had been sexually assaulted by Wayne Bennett. Kobi was also one of the women whose reputation had been damaged before the judge ruled there was not enough evidence to hold a trial.

Lizzy needed to talk to her, and she figured Kobi Millard had to take a lunch sooner or later.

Her stomach cramped, and she winced in pain.

Damn.

She white-knuckled the steering wheel, reminded that she needed to make a call to the doctor. Something was definitely not right. It was time for a checkup, and she'd already missed one appointment. About to turn on the engine and ask her voice-activated phone to call her doctor, she stopped when she saw Kobi walk out the front door of the bank and head for her car.

It was about time.

The woman's sleek black hair was rolled up high on her head, her bangs sweeping across one eye. She wore a two-piece gray suit and black heels. Kobi climbed into a silver Toyota Corolla with a dented bumper.

After Lizzy followed her car for less than two miles, Kobi made a right and parked in front of a grocery store. Lizzy parked nearby, jumped out of the car, and caught up to her before Kobi could enter the store. "Hi, Kobi, my name is Lizzy Gardner, and I need to talk to you."

Kobi stopped and looked Lizzy over, her eyes scanning from head to toe. "You've got balls, lady, coming around, following me. I already told you on the phone I didn't have anything to say in the matter of Wayne Bennett." She pivoted, ready to walk off, but Lizzy grabbed her shoulder. "Get your hands off me."

Lizzy let go. "I don't have a recorder on me, Kobi, I swear. Not even a phone. I just need to know the truth. I can't get the monster or even go after him if nobody will straight up tell me the damn truth. Is he raping young women enrolled in his program?"

A heavy sigh escaped Kobi as she looked around the parking lot. Finally, her gaze met Lizzy's again. She nodded and said, "Yes."

"Did he rape you?"

A very subtle nod was her response.

"But he paid you off, and that's why you refuse to talk," Lizzy stated instead of questioned.

Kobi's somber expression turned to fury. Her anger tightened all the features on her face. The woman smoothed out the bangs covering her forehead and straightened her shoulders, lending power to her stance and fire to her eyes. "You're a bitch, Lizzy Gardner." She then jabbed her finger into Lizzy's chest.

"Ouch."

She did it again.

"Knock it off!" Lizzy looked down to see if she was bleeding.

"He didn't pay me one cent. He threatened my life and the life of my daughter. Valerie is my everything. If he finds out I talked to you and messes with my family, I will come after you myself. I swear I will."

"I'm sorry," Lizzy said.

"No, you're not. You wouldn't still be standing here if you were."

"He's ruining so many lives," Lizzy told her, "and he's getting away with it. It's only going to get worse. Miriam Walters is still missing, and yet I can't find anyone who will talk to me."

Kobi's head fell. Her chin nearly hit her chest.

"We both know she's probably dead," Lizzy said. "And we both know who killed her. My girls and I have been following him for weeks. With or without your help, I will catch him in the act and I'll make sure he's put behind bars for a very long time."

"Tomorrow night, after work," Kobi blurted. "Six o'clock. He's asked one of the women in the program if she would like to be interviewed for the chance to work for a very lucrative company. He's told her the pay starts at sixty thousand."

"You're no longer in the program. How do you know this?"

"I have my ways. Just like you. The girl was warned, though. But sometimes we don't listen because we all like to think we're special, don't we?"

"So there won't be an interview. He'll take her somewhere else instead?"

Her eyes narrowed. "You didn't hear any of this from me. Me and you," she said, "we never talked. And don't you ever come anywhere near me again—you hear me?" And then Kobi Millard turned around, spine stiff and head held high as she made her way toward the store's entrance.

Lizzy watched the house, her gaze on the electric gate in front of a long driveway lined with palm trees. Even from here she could see the fountain with trickling water in front of the grand entrance to Wayne Bennett's mansion.

What is he doing at this very moment? His wife probably shoved dinner in front of him and then watched the clock, waiting for him to leave. She probably didn't give a rat's ass what her husband did after he left the house. Women like Mrs. Bennett weren't stupid. He'd already been arrested once, long ago, for molesting an underage female. And Lizzy could guarantee he'd be arrested again. In fact, she was going to make sure of it. Mrs. Bennett was probably counting the minutes, waiting for a nice quiet respite from the evil man who shared her bed.

But did Mrs. Bennett ever stop to think of her husband's victims?

Were diamonds and pearls worth living with a disgusting, manipulative excuse of a man?

Lizzy counted to ten and reined in her anger. She'd never met the woman. She shouldn't judge. She wanted to throw up. Every thought of late, every bit of focus, was on taking Bennett down. She couldn't stop if she wanted to.

Lizzy sipped water from her reusable bottle, and then rubbed her stomach. She felt bloated and uncomfortable. She unfastened the top button of her jeans and was rewarded with instantaneous relief. It was six o'clock already, and she began to wonder if Kobi had the date and time wrong. Maybe tonight wasn't the night, after all. And that's when the iron gates to the monster's lair slid open.

It was him. Time to take care of business.

The video camera hooked to her dashboard was ready to go. She turned it on, waited until he was far enough ahead, and then followed him down the street. She'd been doing surveillance long enough to know she needed to stay a safe distance away.

Tammy Walters had confirmed that Bennett preferred to do his evil business under the cloak of darkness. He'd rarely taken her sister Miriam out during the day. The problem for Lizzy was that ever since he'd been under public scrutiny, he'd been more careful. He was a patient man. But although he had deep pockets, he'd already called in a lot of favors. She could only hope he was running out of people to bribe.

As she followed him, making sure not to miss a traffic light before merging onto the highway, it angered her anew that he used his position in life to take advantage of these young women. He was rich and handsome. A reputable man like Wayne Bennett made it easy for the women being mentored to throw caution to the wind. He was their savior—the man who could change their lives for the better. He took dreams into the palm of his hand and crushed them.

Fifteen minutes later, she followed him off the highway and through a maze of smaller side streets, bringing them to La Riviera. Many of the houses on this particular road had weeds for lawns and broken windows. Most of the mailboxes had been dented in or were missing altogether. Kids vented, got their frustrations out by damaging other people's property. And then they went on to become gang members, druggies, rapists, whatever. Nobody gave a shit.

Two blocks away, parked at the curb, Lizzy watched a young girl leave her apartment, turn back, and wave at whoever stood at the door before she climbed into the black sedan awaiting her arrival.

It boggled the mind to see the man at work. Not a care in the world. Right there out in the open for everyone to see. He wasn't afraid of anyone. He was king of the world, powerful and in control. The hatred she felt for the man continued to grow in intensity. He used his success to manipulate people and make them do things to satisfy his revolting desires. Wayne Bennett's father had been a well-respected businessman in Sacramento, all the way up to his death. Wayne Bennett attended the best schools. He married well and went on to have two kids. He made his family proud. After his business flourished, he decided to give back to the community. But apparently that wasn't enough.

She followed the black sedan. The red light on the video assured her it was still recording. Her phone rang, lighting up the screen on her dashboard. It was Hayley.

No need to turn video off since it would not record sound. "Answer call."

"Lizzy. It's Hayley. Are you there?"

"I'm here. What do you need?"

"I thought we were going to have a meeting tonight?"

"We'll have to move it to tomorrow night."

"You're not following Wayne Bennett on your own, are you?"

"Why do you want to know?"

"The man is dangerous."

"He's no different than the others on our list."

"Since the disappearance of Miriam Walters, we agreed that Wayne Bennett should be a two-man surveillance at all times."

"Gotta go."

She disconnected the call. It was growing dark now, but the traffic was light, making for an easy tail. A mile and a half later, he took a right onto a lonely-looking street. As Lizzy drove on past, she saw his brake lights flash halfway down the block. After pulling a quick U-turn, she eased to the curb at the intersection in time to see a garage door finish opening and Bennett pull the car inside. Lizzy watched the door clamp shut.

What the hell was going on? She'd been expecting Bennett to pull into an abandoned warehouse or a parking lot, but a house?

After walking up the block for the street number, she returned to her car and called the police. She reported suspicious activity at the address, then dialed Kitally's number. She didn't want to knock on the door and give herself up too early. What if Bennett was there to pick up another girl? But why would he have pulled his car inside the garage?

"What's up?" Kitally asked.

"I need you to use the Realtor database and look up an address for me. I need to know who a certain house belongs to at 552 Indian Drive in West Sac."

After Lizzy was put on hold, she rolled down her window to get a better look at the neighborhood. A dog barked in the distance. The row of houses on both sides of the street across from her looked the same, mostly one-story homes with small yards. Despite the zip-up hoodie she wore, shivers coursed up her arms. Thoughts of Jared drifted over her just as Kitally came back on the line, saving her from feeling the wave of darkness that came over her every time memories surfaced.

"You're not going to believe this," Kitally said. "Most of the houses in that area belong to the JR Millennial Company, owed by Wayne Bennett himself."

"Interesting," Lizzy said. "If you could find out how many homes he owns in the Sacramento area, that would be appreciated. Just give me the information when I see you next, OK?"

"Not a problem. Be careful."

Lizzy disconnected the call. She focused her attention back on the house into which she'd seen Wayne Bennett disappear.

The lights were on. No cries for help. Nothing unusual. The police were notoriously slow. Nothing new there, either. More than anything, she wanted to knock down the door and catch him in the act. She considered doing a search around the perimeter of the house. In the end, if she really wanted to get this guy, she needed to be patient. She needed to do things by the book.

At least for now.

At last she was relieved to see the lights of a police cruiser headed her way. The cruiser turned down the street and pulled into the driveway of the address she'd given the dispatcher. Two cops exited the vehicle, went to the door, and knocked.

It was a long while before the door opened.

One of the officers tried to peek inside, but his partner put a hand in front of his chest to stop him. They were talking to whoever had answered the door. Even smiling.

What were they doing? "Go inside," she muttered under her breath.

From the looks of it, they weren't going to do anything at all.

She'd had enough. She turned off the video.

Fuck doing things the right way—staying low and keeping out of sight—all bullshit. She got out of her car, slammed the door shut, and marched down the middle of the street toward the house.

She joined the officers at the door.

Bennett looked disheveled. No jacket or tie. The top buttons of his shirt were undone, low enough to see a smattering of chest hair.

"Ma'am," one of the officers said, "I'm going to have to ask you to back off."

"Not until you enter the house and talk to the young woman inside. She's underage, and I believe she was brought here under false pretenses." Lizzy made a show of reading both men's badges, setting name and numbers to memory.

The officer on her right looked uncomfortable. His partner, not so much.

"Officer Tagaleri," she said. "If you leave here without questioning the woman inside, I will make it my business to report both of you to the chief of police."

"Go back to your car, ma'am, and let us do our jobs."

Before she could protest, he put a hand on his holster.

She looked from the officer to Wayne Bennett.

The man glared at her. His usually handsome face was pale and splotchy, his body stiff with ire. Recognition flickered in his eyes.

It was time to walk away.

Regaining control of her emotions, she turned around and headed back for her car, feeling three pairs of eyes on her back. Her mind was made up. If those officers left the premises without checking the house first, she would go in and take care of business herself.

She slowed her pace, took her time walking down the street and toward her car. She'd hoped Bennett wouldn't recognize her as Stacey Whitmore's camerawoman, but the undeniable glimmer she'd seen in his eyes before she'd walked away told her he knew exactly who she was.

When she reached her car, she opened the door and climbed in behind the wheel and turned the video on. Within minutes, a crying young woman, ushered by one of the officers, was helped into the backseat of the police car.

Lizzy took a breath and waited for the officers to drive away.

The girl was safe for now.

But Bennett knew what she was up to, which meant things were about to get ugly.

CHAPTER FIFTEEN

The first thing Claire Kerley saw when she walked into her bedroom was the crayon marks scrawled across her bedroom walls. Walls she had spent an entire weekend painting herself. She dropped her backpack on the floor.

She could hear her little brother and sister fighting in the other room, arguing over who got the front seat on the way to the grocery store with Mom.

Before she could close her door, her older brother, Cameron, walked in and took a seat on the corner of her bed.

He was eighteen going on thirty. Their mother had remarried and had two more kids, another boy and girl. Judging by the way they argued, they would grow up to be just like her and Cameron.

"What do you want?" she asked.

"What's the matter with you?"

"Are you kidding me? Look around. Those little monsters take my things and write on my walls. And that man Mom married took away my phone and car for a week. That's just plain cruel."

"They found a bag of weed in your room, and it didn't help that you called Mom a bitch. The punishment was justified."

"Did you come in here just to remind me of what a horrible person I am?"

"No, I came in here to tell you about something I saw at school today. You're not going to like it, but I didn't want you to hear from anyone else."

"What is it? Are you and Megan breaking up?"

"No, we're fine. This is about you," he said, "not me."

Downstairs, Mom yelled goodbye, and the house fell silent. Claire waited for her brother to say whatever it was he had on his mind, but he seemed hesitant. "You're driving me crazy, Cameron. Out with it."

"It's about Luke. After practice, I saw him making out with Jasmine Perkins behind the gym."

"That's a lie."

He shook his head. "They were going at it pretty hot and heavy."

"Luke despises that girl. God, this is a new low. You've never liked Luke. You're just jealous because he's the quarterback and you're a lineman."

He sighed. "I wasn't going to show you this, but if my character is going to be called into question, I guess I don't have a choice." He fiddled with his smartphone and then positioned it so they could watch the video together.

Her stomach roiled. It was true. Luke and Jasmine were all over each other.

Claire dug around in her backpack until she remembered she no longer had a phone. She hated her stepdad, Dave . . . hated her whole damn family. She had to get out of here before she suffocated.

Cameron followed her down the carpeted stairs. "Where are you going?"

"Out. I just need some time alone, OK?"

"I guess, but you better get back before Dave gets home."

"I'm tired of Dave telling me what to do. He's not our dad."

"Dad didn't just leave Mom, you know," Cameron said to her back. "He left all of us, Claire, and never looked back. You need to get over it. You need to stop being angry at the world because of Dad. Stop acting like a spoiled brat and grow up."

Claire walked out of the house and slammed the door behind her. More than anything, she wished she could move far away and never talk to any of them ever again. By the time she got to the end of her street, she was shivering from the cold. What an idiot she was . . . leaving the house without a jacket. *Stupid.*

She looked over her shoulder. She wasn't about to go home while Cameron was there. He would just laugh, rub it in her face that she couldn't stay away for more than five minutes. So she kept on walking. She rubbed her arms as she went, thinking about how unfair life could be.

As he drove along, he found himself thinking about the David Ligare exhibit that would soon be showing at the Crocker Art Museum. One of a handful invited to attend a private preview of nearly eighty works, he'd been so caught up in throwing the police off his trail, he'd forgotten about the impending event until this very moment. Ligare's works were poetic. He created order in a chaotic world.

Right now, though, he needed to take care of business, finish what he'd started. The media was finally getting fired up. In today's paper, one journalist warned the people of Sacramento to be alert. After finding a body near the American River and then the woman in the elevator, reporters took it upon themselves to give credit to the Sacramento Strangler.

Hmm. Maybe they were finally catching on. He would love to be a fly on the wall at the Federal Bureau of Investigation.

Sometimes the media could be downright clever. For instance, dubbing Albert Fish the "Werewolf of Wysteria" because of the rumors that he lusted for blood under a full moon sounded as if a little thought actually went into naming the killer. But the Sacramento Strangler? If memory served, he wasn't the first person in the area to strangle a few people to death.

The Sacramento Strangler, he repeated in his mind. *Bah. Boring. Bland.* For now, he had to let the nickname go. He had more important things to worry about.

He was on a mission.

Today he had something special planned. This would be his first kidnapping.

Disguised with a beard, hat, and sunglasses, he drove on the back streets, making his way toward Watt Avenue, where he planned to find, at the very least, a prostitute or a homeless person. He had a room readied back home. The last owners had gone to a lot of trouble to build a wine cellar. Narrow stairs led deep underground into a dark, windowless room. The perfect setup for what he had planned.

His victim, a female—age didn't really matter—would be bound and tied. Perhaps he could make videotaped messages to send to the media.

No. Too dicey.

He wasn't sure how long he would keep her. Maybe just a day or two. He'd figure it all out as he went along.

He knew it was risky, bringing one of his victims to his house, but that was the whole point. He'd forgotten how thrilling it could be to pursue something new and exciting. He would get to know his victim before he took her life. He'd never known any of his victims before killing them. Just thinking about it gave him a thrill, a sensory delight.

He inhaled. Life had become too predictable. Taking a chance, going in pursuit of such an experience, was downright intoxicating. He'd all but forgotten his need for high-level stimulation. Some people needed gambling, sex, or drugs to achieve such a mental rush. He just needed this.

With his gaze focused on the road ahead of him, he could hardly believe what he was seeing. *Would you look at that?* A young girl. A hitchhiker, of all things. "Fate is a fickle fellow," he said with a laugh as he passed the girl before slowing and pulling off the road.

In his rearview mirror, he watched her run to catch up to him. She reminded him of sunshine and innocence. The girl didn't bother leaning forward and looking through the passenger window to see who was driving. She just climbed right in and said, "Thanks," in a breathless voice. "I was beginning to wonder if anyone would ever pick me up."

"Not a problem," he said as he made quick work of merging back onto the road. "Where are you off to?"

She flipped her shiny blonde hair to one side, then looked at him with bright-green eyes. "I just need to get away."

"Anywhere?" he asked.

She flung a hand through the air, as though literally throwing caution to the wind. "I'll go wherever you're going."

"Are you sure about that?"

"Absolutely." She looked him over. "You look pretty harmless to me."

That particular comment elicited a grin.

Her laughter sounded like tiny twinkling bells.

"It'll be dark out soon," he told her. "Perhaps you should let me drive you home." He would do no such thing, of course, but he figured it would put her at ease if she thought he was a straitlaced, worried old man.

"No way!" was her immediate response. "My family is nuts. I can't take it any longer."

"I only had a sister, so I wouldn't know."

"Did she die?"

He nodded. "She drowned at a very young age."

"I'm sorry."

"It was a long time ago."

"My mom remarried," she told him. "My stepdad is a dick. I have a younger brother and sister who scribble on my walls and make a mess of my things. My older brother can't seem to mind his own business. He thinks he's my father. Like I really need another one of those. And that's not the worst of it," she said with a sigh. "My boyfriend, Luke, is a two-timing asshole."

Cry me a river.

"Do you have any weed? I'm dying to get high." She adjusted herself in the passenger seat, sat up taller. He could feel her looking at him. "How old are you?"

"None of your business," he said. "Open the middle console. You'll find a plastic bag inside."

She did as he said. Picking up a clear baggie filled with yellow pills, she smiled and said, "Well, well, what do we have here?"

"They're called *magic*," he said, his voice lined with an air of grandiosity, although really, the yellow tablets were nothing more than sleeping pills. "They're new, a party drug. And they're spectacular."

"Like ecstasy?"

"Even better. A bit of magic will take you on a trip you won't want to come back from."

"You don't look like the druggie type."

He shrugged.

She examined one of the pills. "How many should I take?"

"Two or three should do the trick. If you reach around to the back, you'll find a water bottle."

She did as he said and then unscrewed the top of the water bottle and took a sip. "After I take these, do you think you could drive me to my boyfriend's house?"

"The two-timing asshole?" he asked.

"Yeah," she said with that twinkling laugh of hers, "that's the one." She popped the pills into her mouth and chased them down with water. Then she put the bag back where she'd found it. "There. I took three. Luke lives at 8815 La Casa, not too far from here."

"We're about ten minutes from La Casa," he said. "That's a nice area."

"Yeah. His parents are loaded."

She was doing it again—staring at him. He didn't like it.

He spared her a glance, surprised by the way her smile lit up his insides. She wasn't quite so annoying, after all. Her skin was flawless. If he could capture even a small fraction of her innocence on canvas, he would be a happy man.

"You're a pretty cool dude," she said.

"Thanks."

"I want to be flying like a kite when I talk to Luke. I'm going to march right up to him and tell him exactly what I think of him."

Keeping his eyes on the road, he made sure to go the speed limit. He didn't need unwanted attention from other motorists.

There was something so refreshing about the girl. She was fearless. He felt sort of bad she wouldn't ever get the chance to tell her dickish boyfriend what she thought of him. It would have been an interesting scene to witness.

"After I talk to Luke, do you think you could take me home?"

"Change of heart?"

"No," she said with an exaggerated shiver. "I really do hate them all, but I don't want my mom to worry. She freaks out easily—you know what I mean?"

Yes. He knew exactly what she meant. The thought of her mother freaking out sent a shudder through his body—the good kind. "Don't worry," he told her. "After you talk to Luke, I'll take you anywhere you want to go."

She turned away from him, her eyes back on the road in front of them as she rested her head against the leather seat.

He drove well past the exit to La Casa. Twenty minutes later, when he pulled into his two-car garage and shut off the engine, she'd long been fast asleep.

CHAPTER SIXTEEN

It was after five when Hayley heard Lizzy return from a run around the neighborhood. She found Hayley and Kitally waiting for her in the living room.

"We're ready to have a quick meeting when you are," Kitally said.

"OK, let me grab a few things and we'll do this." In another minute, Lizzy returned holding a file, and she took a seat in an upholstered wingback chair facing the couch. She looked at the clock. "Jessica won't be returning for another hour, at least. Let's talk about what's on the agenda for the next few weeks."

"I think we should talk about Wayne Bennett," Hayley said.

There was noise in the kitchen—the shuffling of drawers and the opening and closing of the microwave door. They all sat quietly and waited for Salma to finish what she was doing. It was at least five minutes before the girl walked into the living room, holding two bowls of popcorn. "Here," she said, setting the bowl on the coffee table between them. She made eye contact with Hayley and then Lizzy. "OK, I can take a hint. I'm outta here."

The girl's stomach looked like a watermelon. It was hard for Hayley to believe she could walk without falling over.

As soon as Salma disappeared, Lizzy said, "This is never going to work. Maybe we should update one another at a later date."

"We just have to make do," Hayley said.

"You two need to find out what the deal is with Salma . . . if she has family who's worried about her."

"I'll see what I can find out," Kitally said.

"About Wayne Bennett," Hayley went on. "Have you found anyone who will testify against him?"

"Not so far. It's going to be tough. Bennett's threatening his victims and their families with their lives."

"What about the young woman he had with him last night? The girl who left with the police?"

"They took her to the station to fill out reports, but she refused to press charges against him."

"I have an idea," Kitally announced.

"Let's hear it."

"As I mentioned to you on the phone, Bennett owns at least a dozen rental homes, including the one you visited last night. Why don't we set up cameras in every house that isn't occupied? If and when he takes someone to one of the houses, we'll have a video recording of what he's doing."

"Tommy has agreed to install the cameras if we can get access," Hayley added.

"Not a bad idea," Lizzy said. "Although illegally obtained evidence won't be admissible in court."

"Unless we say that the videos were sent to us by an anonymous person."

"Well, even then, probably. Still, it's worth a shot. Let's set up surveillance on the homes to see which ones are empty and go from there." Lizzy opened her file and looked through her notes. "Owen Dunham. I've been meaning to ask you two about him."

Hayley shrugged it off. "We dealt with that problem."

Lizzy lifted a brow. "So what happened? The plan was to place stolen items in the trunk of his car."

Lizzy turned to Kitally. "Hayley seems to have lost her voice, so why don't you fill me in."

Kitally crinkled her nose but didn't say a word.

"One of you better tell me what's going on or the meeting is over."

Hayley grunted. "I cut off his balls and tossed them in the river."

Lizzy looked perplexed. "You're kidding, right?"

Hayley shook her head.

Kitally refused to make eye contact.

Lizzy looked over her shoulder as if she thought someone might have overheard. Then she turned back to face Hayley and said in a low voice, "What would possess you to do such a thing? You don't think you're going to be the first person investigators think of? Three years ago, you cut off a man's penis and now someone's testicles, and you don't think anyone is going to put two and two together?"

Silence.

"What is your ridiculous fetish with male body parts any-how?"

Hayley refused to answer such a ridiculous question. Lizzy wasn't herself and hadn't been for a while now. If it were up to Hayley, every convicted rapist would have his testicles removed. "Owen Dunham and I do not share any connection whatsoever," Hayley told Lizzy matter-of-factly. "Our paths never once crossed before that night. I never even heard his name until he showed up on our list." Hayley lifted her hands in frustration. "You might feel better about this if you look at the file and read over his long list of criminal activity."

"I guess I should be happy you didn't kill the man," Lizzy said as she looked deep into Hayley's eyes. "Because you're not a killer. Don't you ever forget that."

"Hayley threatened to come back and remove whatever was left if he went to the police," Kitally added. "I think Dunham got the message loud and clear."

Hayley stared back at Lizzy, unblinking, refusing to look away as she waited for her to move on to the next guy on the list. Because, clearly, Lizzy would not be able to handle the truth. The harsh reality was that Hayley had gone back that very night and taken care of Dunham for good. Kitally and Lizzy would never know what happened. It only mattered that Dunham would never have a chance to hurt anyone else again.

Lizzy's shoulders visibly relaxed before she said, "So all evidence was removed?"

"Trust me," Hayley said. "It's all been taken care of."

"I'd like you both to stay away from Dunham and Holmes for now." Lizzy looked over their list. "What's going on with the Ghost?"

"Nothing so far. There hasn't been a sighting in days."

"Well, good. Maybe she's lost interest."

"What about Scott Shaffer—number four on the list?" she asked next.

"As far I can tell, he's been lying low and staying out of trouble," Hayley said. "I'll keep an eye on him and let you both know when he's on the prowl again."

"Sounds good. Other than doing surveillance on Wayne Bennett's properties," Lizzy said, "I need you both to go to Miriam Walters's place of work."

"The missing girl?"

Lizzy nodded.

"Where does—or did—she work?"

"At the mall. It's all in the file, along with a short list of people who might have seen Miriam with Bennett."

"What exactly do we want to know?" Kitally asked.

"We need to talk to anyone who might have been in close contact with Miriam before she disappeared. Did she mention going away for a while? Do any of her coworkers know what she used to do after she left work? Did she ever talk to anyone about Wayne Bennett? Did she ever meet him for lunch? If so, where did they go?"

They heard the rattle of keys before the front door opened. It was Jessica, home early. She left her belongings on the table and joined them in the living room. "Hey, what's going on?"

"Nothing," Hayley said.

"You all look pretty serious for it to be nothing."

Lizzy shrugged. "Just getting up-to-date on a few things."

"That's right," Kitally said, her voice a little too cheerful. "We were talking about Lizzy's newest client, Gus. He lost his wife, and he thinks someone at the Shady Oaks Nursing Home is responsible. In fact," she said, turning to Lizzy, "I've been meaning to talk to you about the note that was written on the stationery in your file. I'm pretty sure I found a match."

Jessica stepped closer and picked up the list of names. "What is this?"

Lizzy snatched the paper out of her hand and tucked it inside the file on her lap.

"What's going on?" Jessica demanded.

A phone rang.

It was Lizzy's cell. She picked up the call as she came to her feet and walked away from the group as she listened. When she returned, she had her coat and keys. "I have to go. I've got a live one."

"Does it have to do with Wayne Bennett?" Hayley asked.

Lizzy nodded.

"President of SRT? *That* Wayne Bennett?" Jessica asked.

"One and the same," Lizzy said. "He's using his nonprofit organization to take advantage of young vulnerable women."

"And he's getting away with it," Kitally added.

Jessica followed Lizzy to the door. "So who was that on the phone?"

"A girl named Olimpia Padula who says Bennett raped her. She's willing to talk, even if it means sitting in front of a jury and telling her story."

"Mind if I come along?"

Lizzy shrugged and then turned back to Hayley. "You two get busy working on the things we discussed. We'll talk later."

"What about Gus and the nursing home?" Kitally asked.

"Take care of it," Lizzy said before she left the room. "You can fill me in later."

Moments after Lizzy and Jessica left the house, Kitally saw Salma peer into the living room. "Is it safe?"

Kitally smiled. "Yeah, they're gone. You can come out of hiding."

Salma came in and eased herself into a chair with an enormous sigh. Kitally knew it wasn't possible, but it seemed as if the girl's belly had expanded since the last time she'd seen her.

"Your boss can be scary at times," Salma said.

"She's really not so bad," Hayley said. "She's just angry at the world right now."

"I don't know if *angry* is the right word," Kitally said. "When I look into her eyes, I don't see the same Lizzy Gardner. This new Lizzy seems possessed."

Hayley sighed. "She'll be fine. She just needs time."

"Well, I didn't want to tell you this in front of Lizzy," Salma said, "but I've been meaning to talk to you about the Ghost."

That got Hayley's attention. "Yeah, what about her?"

"I think I know who you're looking for."

"Do you know her name?" Kitally asked.

"No, but before I slept in the park, I was living with a friend who was dating a guy who lived on Fedora Street. He had a roommate who looks just like the person you two were discussing the other day: skinny, pale-skinned, and she had white hair that she gelled to make it look like she had a porcupine on top of her head. You can't miss her. She definitely stands out in a crowd. And she's funny about her sneakers."

"How so?"

"She has a dozen pairs of white sneakers, and if she gets a scuff mark, she throws a tantrum."

"That's gotta be her." Hayley looked at the time. "I'll pull up a satellite map on the Internet, and you can show me where she lives."

"Why don't we go for a drive," Salma said, "and I'll show you exactly where the house is."

Kitally got up, ready to go, but Hayley hesitated, probably conflicted about having a pregnant teen as a ride-along.

"I need to get out of here," Salma said. "I haven't been outside since you two brought me here."

"My car?" Kitally asked.

"I just filled my tank," Hayley said. "We'll take the Chevy."

Hayley and her beloved hunk of junk, Kitally thought, but she gave her a one-handed salute. "Whatever you say, boss."

They took the ramp to US 50 West and continued on to Business 80 toward West Sacramento. Kitally was sitting in the passenger seat, and she turned to the side to look at Salma. "How are you feeling?"

She rubbed her belly. "Fine."

"You look like you're ready to explode. How does it feel to have a person growing inside you?"

Hayley shook her head at Kitally's question but said nothing.

"It's a strange sensation," Salma said. "Especially when the baby kicks like it wants out."

"Bizarre," Kitally agreed.

"Yeah, it used to do somersaults, I swear, but now that there's less room in there, it sort of hurts when it pushes its feet into my ribs."

"Ouch."

It was quiet for a moment before Salma said, "So when's Lizzy's baby due?"

"What do you mean?" Kitally asked.

"She's pregnant, isn't she?"

Hayley frowned. "What makes you say that?"

"I don't know. Seems obvious. Every little smell makes her sick to her stomach, she hardly eats, and she has a definite baby bump."

Kitally looked at Hayley. "Do you think she could be?"

"No. I think Salma has baby on the brain." Hayley looked into the rearview mirror. "No offense."

Salma smiled. "No offense taken. Besides, I know I'm right. Everything I said, plus her mood swings and the stuff she eats."

"She did turn down a Rice Krispies Treat the other day," Kitally said. "And come to think of it, she doesn't drink coffee anymore. I thought that was odd."

"Take the next exit," Salma told Hayley.

In another few minutes they were on the 1600 block of Madrone Avenue. Unfamiliar turf for Kitally. All three of them were quiet as Salma pointed and told Hayley to take a left.

"Never mind," Salma said. "That might be her up ahead."

Sure enough, a skinny girl dressed in black jeans and a dark sweatshirt with white spiky hair was heading for the gas station on the corner.

Hayley pulled into the gas station just ahead of the girl and told Kitally to roll down her window. "Hey, you," Hayley called.

Unconcerned, the girl turned toward them and strolled over to the window. "What's going on?"

"You wouldn't happen to know where we could find some weed, would you?"

"I might." She leaned lower so that she could see all the way to the backseat. She pointed a finger toward Salma. "Don't I know you?"

Salma's eyes widened. "I don't think so."

The girl snapped her fingers. "You're Jane's friend, Salma. Why don't you girls wait right here while I head inside and buy some smokes?" She smiled and then touched the collar of Kitally's blouse. "I like your shirt."

"Thanks."

"There's a decent party happening a few blocks away," the girl said, walking backward toward the mini-mart. "Maybe you can give me a ride."

"Sure thing," Kitally said. After she watched the girl disappear inside the mini-mart, she said, "We'll give her a ride straight to the police station on Jefferson Boulevard."

Hayley looked over her shoulder at Salma. "So that's the same girl, right?"

"That's her. She hasn't changed a bit," Salma said. "If we're giving her a ride, we need to be careful. That girl has a mean temper, and there's no telling what she might do."

Kitally looked at Hayley. "We found the Ghost. Should I go inside and keep an eye on her?"

"I think that's a good idea."

Before Kitally could get out of the car, Hayley grabbed her arm. "Never mind." She gestured toward the parking lot behind the building. The girl was sprinting across it. "Looks like she's making a run for it. Buckle up."

Hayley gunned it, squeezed her way between the guy pumping gas and the mini-market. A man filling his tank held his arm high in the air and shook his fist at her.

The Ghost was fast, running toward a chain-link fence and then vaulting over it into a backyard and disappearing without losing a step.

"Whoa, can she fly or what?" Kitally said.

The Chevy's tires squealed as Hayley made a sharp right out of the gas station, bouncing over the curb and tossing them around inside the car, lifting a grunt from Salma in the back.

Hayley shot down the block and made a right onto a quiet neighborhood street, hoping to cut the girl off on the other side. The Ghost couldn't have made it through all the yards in the block, but Kitally saw no sign of her.

As Hayley swept around the next corner, circling the block, the underbelly of the car began to shake and the wheels rattled. "This thing doesn't sound good," Kitally said. "There's smoke coming out from under the hood. You need to pull over!"

Hayley ignored her.

"Oh no!" Salma cried out. "Not now!"

Glancing over her shoulder, Kitally found Salma wincing in pain. Her clothes, along with the backseat, were weirdly dark. No, not just dark. Wet.

"She just jumped another fence at the end of the block," Hayley said. But when she floored it, the car shook and the engine hissed in protest.

"Shit, shit, shit!" Hayley said as the car slowed. She pummeled the gas pedal with her foot, but it didn't do any good. The engine died. Holding tightly to the wheel, she coasted slowly to the curb.

Leaving the keys in the engine, Hayley jumped out of the car and headed after the Ghost.

"Get back here!" Kitally shouted. "We have a problem!"

It was no use. Hayley was gone.

Kitally looked back at Salma. "Don't you dare have that baby right now. This is not a good time."

Salma panted, her face red and pinched. A sheen of sweat covered her forehead. She did not look well.

Kitally grabbed her cell phone, exited the car, and ran to the corner to read the street signs. She called 911 and told them what was going on and where they could be found. Then she hung up and ran back to the car.

When she opened the back door and looked inside, she didn't like what she saw. She knew how to make a bomb. Hell, she could sew a designer dress by hand without using a pattern and speak Mandarin and Italian fluently, but she knew nothing about bringing a baby into the world. The notion that she'd ever find herself in this predicament had never once come to mind. If the girl had been choking, she could do the Heimlich, but helping someone birth a baby was nowhere near her forte.

Whatever. Get a grip, she told herself.

Just then, Salma cried out in pain. The high-pitched shriek hit every nerve ending in Kitally's body.

Salma was in a fetal position; her eyes were squeezed shut, her teeth clenched.

"Help is on its way," Kitally told her between Salma's squeals of pain. "Logic tells me you probably shouldn't push yet."

"Get out!"

"OK. Jeez. Just trying to help." Kitally looked across the street, relieved to see Hayley heading back their way. She ran to the front of the car and waved her hands. "Salma has gone into labor. An ambulance is on its way."

Hayley jogged across the street. "She's having a baby *in my car*?"

"Hello? She's having a *baby*. And by the way, your car is a dump. A little amniotic fluid isn't going to hurt anything."

Hayley opened the hood and plunked her hands on her hips. "I need to call a tow truck."

"A tow truck? There's a baby being born in the backseat of your stupid car, you selfish bitch. What don't you get?"

Hayley gave her a quizzical look before she walked over and took a look inside. Her gaze connected with Salma's. "That baby of yours isn't going to wait for the paramedics, is it?"

Salma grunted. "I need help."

"You got it," Hayley said as she climbed in.

CHAPTER SEVENTEEN

"Thanks for letting me come along for the ride," Jessica said as soon as they drove off. "I really need to talk to you."

Lizzy stiffened. "She's not a killer."

"Who's not a killer?"

Shit. Lizzy figured Detective Chase or Jimmy had talked to Jessica about Hayley. Wrong again. She needed to calm down and get her act together. Hayley was not a killer, and therefore Lizzy needed to stop freaking out about it. "Nothing. Never mind," she said. "What do you want to talk about?"

She could feel Jessica's eyes on her.

"Are you OK?" Jessica asked.

"I'm fine. Just spit it out. What do you want to talk about?"

"The Sacramento Strangler."

"What about him?"

"The killer works quickly. He strikes without leaving any evidence or witnesses. He appears to be getting more brazen, killing in broad daylight and in public places where lots of people are around."

"So why are you telling me this?"

"Because it's becoming clear the killer had a connection to Jared."

119

"How so?"

"The night before what was to be your wedding day, Jared talked to the deputy assistant director and told him he was close to having a name. They were set to meet the following week to talk about it."

"Are you saying the Sacramento Strangler could have something to do with Jared's death?"

"No, I don't think so. My point is Jared was killed before he had a chance to reveal what he knew about the Sacramento Strangler."

"I see. Is Jimmy handling the case?"

"No. He's involved, but Kenneth Mitchell is the man in charge."

Lizzy said nothing. The name Kenneth Mitchell didn't ring a bell, and she'd been too wrapped up in her own problems to worry about the Sacramento Strangler.

"They want to talk to you," Jessica told her.

"Who? Jimmy?"

"And Mitchell."

"It would be a waste of all our time," Lizzy said. "Jared rarely talked about the cases he was working on. Mostly because I think he preferred to leave work behind when he stepped through the front door, since we both dealt with the darker side of reality all day long."

"We need to find this guy, Lizzy. He's now been linked to more than a dozen victims."

"What have you found?"

"It turns out he's been leaving a mark. His signature. He's probably gotten a good laugh that nobody has figured it out."

"What does his signature look like?"

"A symbol, a *Z* or an *N* with an extra line through it. It's this mark that has allowed us to connect the older victims with the newer ones."

"Sounds pretty obvious. What took them so long to connect the dots?"

"The killer's mark isn't always so apparent. Sometimes it's so small, it's hard to see. For instance, on one body, he left a tiny mark behind the victim's ear. Recently, though, they have requested bodies be exhumed, and in many of the cases they are finding the mark on the scalp under the hairline, between toes, inside the mouth."

"Interesting."

"It's exciting," Jessica said. "A real game changer for this case. It turns out he didn't just strangle his victims; sometimes he drowned them or cut their throats. Victims are mostly female. Recently, though, he's picked up the pace, killing much more frequently and more randomly. And that tells me he's either gotten bored or he's decided to have fun with investigators."

"Any witnesses at all?"

"Not so far. Nobody credible anyhow. And no forensic evidence, either. Mitchell believes there is more than one person involved."

"And you?"

"So far, I'm betting on one man, aged thirty-four to forty, considering how long he's been killing. He probably started at a very young age, maybe as young as twelve years old. I believe we'll be digging up bodies for years to come."

"What's your reasoning for believing he started at such a young age?"

"The typical serial killer is male, between the ages of twenty-five to thirty-five. Our guy's been at it for eighteen years, at least. Because of the changes in his MO and the lack of lust involved in the earlier killings, I believe he was very young when he first started killing."

"Twelve years old," Lizzy said, shaking her head.

"It's not unheard of. Look up Mary Flora Bell and Norma Bell, no relation. They were caught before Mary could be considered a true serial killer by definition, but still, ten years old."

"I don't know why any of this would surprise me," Lizzy said, "but it always does. In any event, it sounds like the guy's getting reckless. At some point, they always do."

Jessica kept her gaze on the road. "I think you're right. The girl he found on the American River trail was probably his first attempt at getting messy."

"He's *trying* to get messy? Why do you say that?"

"Everything was still too precise."

Lizzy said nothing as she waited for Jessica to elaborate.

"I've been examining pictures from the crime scene for days. It seems obvious the killer is trying hard to do things differently, but the mark isn't the only thing he leaves behind. In fact, if he didn't have the one thing most serial killers have, he might have thrown us completely off track."

"What's that?"

"A larger-than-life ego."

"So what is it? What's he leaving behind?"

"It's peculiar, and I can't possibly remember them all, but to give you an idea, he's left a clock, a book, a candleholder, even a fasces."

"Fasces?"

"A bundle of rods, usually around the handle of an axe. A symbol of power."

"That is strange," Lizzy agreed. "What did he leave with the latest victim?"

"At first they came up empty-handed, but I figured if it were the same killer, there had to be something in the vicinity. You see, he doesn't always leave the object on the body. Sometimes he buries it nearby or hangs the item from a tree. Mitchell wasn't happy with me, but hell, I didn't ask for this, so Jimmy finally talked Mitchell into sending crime scene technicians back to the scene. Sure enough, they found a vintage mirror buried deep under the soil a few feet away from where they found the woman's body."

"A mirror? Do you know what that means?"

"Not a clue."

There was a moment's pause before Jessica said, "So, will you consider coming with me to talk to Jimmy?"

"I'll think about it," Lizzy said as they turned in to the parking area of an apartment complex.

They climbed out of the car. It was getting dark, and a cold breeze swept across Lizzy's face. She pulled out her cell and read the note she'd made earlier: *Olimpia Padula. Apartment 6D.*

They headed up more than one flight of stairs before they found her apartment. Lizzy knocked on the door and waited.

"Who is it?"

"Lizzy Gardner. We talked on the phone thirty minutes ago."

"Who is that with you?"

If she told the woman Jessica was with the FBI, she'd never talk to her. "This is Jessica Pleiss, my assistant."

The door opened a crack. Olimpia Padula took a long look at both of them before she removed the chain and gestured for them to come inside.

Once they were seated, Olimpia said, "I heard through the grapevine that you were on some sort of personal vendetta to see Wayne Bennett pay for what he's done to me and others."

"Vendetta?" Jessica asked, though she was looking at Lizzy when she said it.

Lizzy raised her hand, letting Jessica know that now was not the time to butt in. "Call it whatever you want," Lizzy told the woman. "I want to see the man behind bars where he won't be able to hurt anyone else."

"Amen to that," Olimpia said. "Where should I start?"

"Anywhere you'd like."

Olimpia took a breath. "I thought I was the luckiest woman on earth," she began. "Not only had I made it into Wayne Bennett's prestigious program, I was selected for an interview with Tom Lungren, the president of a million-dollar consulting firm right here in Sacramento. Mr. Bennett called me the day of the interview and told me specifically to take a shower, do my hair, and dress up nice." She made a face. "The idea of the man calling me to remind me to take a shower was off-putting, to say the least, but I was too excited about the interview to worry about it much. I did exactly what he asked me to do. Do you have any idea how much a new dress and shoes cost?"

Before anyone could respond, she added, "It cost me my entire paycheck. I can hardly afford food, let alone rent, but I spent my paycheck on a dress and shoes."

Lizzy made notes as the woman spoke. There weren't too many people willing to talk about Wayne Bennett. She didn't want to miss a thing.

"Mr. Bennett picked me up in his nice shiny black sedan," Olimpia continued. "He was wearing a dark suit and tie. The man even got out of the car to open the door for me." She took in a breath. "I can't deny it. He looked good. He was wearing some sort of spicy aftershave, and he smelled good, too." She locked gazes with Lizzy. "I thought I was on my way . . . know what I mean?"

Lizzy nodded, anything to keep her talking.

"Have you ever heard Wayne Bennett give one of his speeches about poor girls like me being the future?"

"No," Lizzy said, "I haven't. But I've seen and heard him enough times to know he can charm the lollipop right out of a little girl's clutches."

Olimpia fidgeted. "I thought it was strange when he brought me to some old dilapidated house with shingles falling from the roof. Who does interviews in a run-down, low-rent shack with a rusty mailbox?" She shook her head. "Nobody does. But did I listen to my instincts and run off? Did I tell him I'd changed my mind and wanted to leave? Nope," she said, her voice trembling now. "I followed the man inside, and then I took the drink he offered me. After three sips, I began to feel woozy."

Olimpia buried her face in the palms of her hands and began to cry.

Jessica moved next to her on the couch and patted her hand. As Lizzy watched Jessica, she felt a sense of pride she didn't really understand. From the beginning, Jessica had been a lot like Jared. She believed there was more good in the world than bad. She was compassionate and caring, and when it came to her principles, she'd never wavered. Not once.

"I'm so sorry," Olimpia said as she sat up straighter. "I thought I could do this without crying. I guess I was wrong." Mascara trickled down her face as she said, "Wayne Bennett raped me. He did other things, too. Horrible, unspeakable things. At some point during the evening, I passed out. When I woke up, he was hovering over me. He told me to get dressed. We left the house and climbed into his nice car. On the way home, he explained what would happen if I ever told anyone about what went down."

"Did he threaten your family members?"

She smiled then. "He sure did. He threatened to do to my sisters what he had just done to me. He went into great detail about the fate of every family member if I talked to anyone at all. And then he pulled his car to the curb. But this time he didn't bother getting out. He just smiled at me as if we now shared a unique bond. And then he told me I was special and that he couldn't wait until next time."

"Did you go back into the program after that night?"

"Not a chance in hell. I called the rape crisis center and did everything they told me to do. I went straight to the hospital and filled out a police report. That same week, I heard you were spending a lot of time and energy trying to find someone to speak in court against Wayne Bennett. And I knew it would have to be me."

"I have to be clear about something," Lizzy told her. "Bennett is a very dangerous man, and I don't have the resources to provide round-the-clock protection for you."

"I'm not worried about him. I wasn't born yesterday."

"What about your family?" Jessica asked.

"That's the best part. He must have mixed me up with some other poor girl, because I don't have any family."

CHAPTER EIGHTEEN

"Where are you going?"

Nora Belle pulled her hoodie up around her head and face. "Out. I'll be back."

The fat slob, Michael, told her he'd like a kiss first, which she knew meant a blow job.

Fuck, she thought, as she headed back over to the couch, where she was always sure to find him if he wasn't working construction. It was the last thing in the world she wanted to do, but she liked having a place to come home to and food to eat, and it was the price she had to pay.

She didn't even bother looking at him as she unzipped his pants and got to work. Having his penis in her mouth was like sucking on a rubbery, slimy carrot. Maybe it was time to find someone else to keep a roof over her head. Guys like Michael were a dime a dozen.

"Hey, not so much with the teeth, OK?"

Fucking asshole. She thought about biting his dick right off. She might do it, too, just not this time. When she was done, she went to the kitchen sink and cleaned up, then walked out the door without another word.

The night was chilly. She rubbed her hands together as she made her way through the streets of Sacramento.

An hour had passed by the time she found the Naomi bitch. The woman was tucked away for the night in her red sleeping bag in the doorway of a long-shuttered discount store. Red bag, red hair. When Nora Belle first met her, the woman talked about how she used to be somebody, as if anyone fucking cared. How she went to college and used to have a job with the state.

Big fucking deal.

Nora Belle hated the woman like nobody else. Plopping down astraddle her now, she wrenched the sleeping bag down and started pummeling away. Every time her fist made contact with the woman's face, she felt a jolt of electricity race through her body.

Beneath her, Naomi struggled.

Someone shouted from under her. It was not Naomi's voice. She stopped what she was doing, climbed off, and pulled the sleeping bag all the way down so she could see who was in there.

"What the hell are you doing?" the guy asked, his nose bleeding all over the place.

She was on all fours, staring at the man. "Where's Naomi?"

"Who?"

"This is Naomi's sleeping bag. Where did you get it?"

"I found it on the side of the road." His hands were covering his nose. "I think you might have broken my nose."

She looked around, pushed herself up, and started searching through his shopping cart.

The loser staggered to his feet. "What are you doing?"

"What does it look like?" She grabbed a few of his things, including a picture that looked as if it might have sentimental value and ripped it into tiny pieces. "You're being inducted into the Ghost Hall of Fame."

The man had long red hair, just like Naomi. She was going to have to pay closer attention next time—not that it mattered. They were basically all the same.

He grabbed hold of her sweatshirt and yanked it down over her shoulder as he tried to stop her from going through his things.

She backhanded him, and he staggered back, leaving her to gape at the damage he'd done. "You broke my zipper! You just ruined my favorite sweatshirt."

She jumped on him then, bit his hand, and clawed at his face. All she could see through her blinding rage were the whites of his eyes as she ground her knee into his nuts, determined to show him what happened when someone like him dared to lay a hand on someone like her.

CHAPTER NINETEEN

Claire sat up and tried to figure out where she was. The room was dark. Her head was spinning. Her tongue kept sticking to the roof of her mouth. She needed water.

Where am I?

She felt around, using her hands to search in the dark. She was on a thin mattress covered with a sheet and a scratchy wool blanket. Her heart raced, pounded against her chest.

She crawled over the mattress until she could feel the ground. Smooth cement. Pushing herself to her feet, she kept her arms straight out in front of her, careful not to trip as she explored the room. The tips of her fingers brushed against a rough stone wall. She moved slowly, inch by inch, feeling around, hoping to find a window or a door. *Finally. A door.*

She tried the knob, but it was no use. The door was locked. Down on her knees, she tried to peek under the door. She couldn't see a thing. Back on her feet again, she crossed to the other side of the room and found a wall of empty wooden slots. She was in a wine cellar.

A clear image of the man's face came to her: he was wearing a hat and sunglasses. He had a crooked nose, an ugly, wiry beard, and a wide smile. The man who picked her up on the side of the road had brought her here.

How stupid could she be? Getting into the car with a stranger was bad enough, but then asking him for drugs and taking his magic pills? Hell, she didn't even know what kind of car he'd been driving. Four-door? Two-door? Blue? Green? She had no idea.

She sank down onto the mattress and tried to get a grip, tried to think.

Her mouth was dry. She couldn't remember ever being so thirsty. Once again she began to crawl around the room on all fours, hoping he'd at least left her some food or water. But there was nothing here. No windows. No table. No chairs. No food and no water.

"Are you awake?"

Her head snapped up at the sound of his voice. She scrambled to the door. "Please let me out. My family is probably worried sick about me. You have to let me call my mom."

"Oh, Claire. That would be foolish of me. You're a smart girl. I can't let you do that."

She banged on the door, didn't stop until her hands hurt from the effort. "Let me out of here, you sicko!"

She heard the squeak of metal. A sliver of light spilled through the top of the door. It looked like a mail slot. She stood on her tiptoes and found herself peering into gray-blue eyes.

She stepped back, put a hand to her chest, tried to catch her breath.

"Please," she said when she realized he might leave her there and never come back. "I'm begging you. I'll be good, but I don't like the dark. And I'm thirsty. My throat is dry. I swear, I can't breathe."

"My little drama queen," he said. "I'll get you a glass of water and something to eat. I'll be back."

The metal door shut with a clank.

She stood still. She needed to think. He said he would be back. As soon as he opened the door, she would attack him, claw at his eyes and then run.

Where was she, though?

If she escaped the wine cellar, would she find another locked door? And it didn't help that she was small and he was tall. Inside the car, the top of his head had looked as if it was only an inch from the roof. The weird hat he'd been wearing probably made him look even taller. The hat. The strange hat and sunglasses made sense. His beard hadn't looked right, either. It had to be a disguise. She never should have gotten into his car. What an idiot she was. And to think she had believed every word the man uttered. Right down to the ridiculous magic pills he happened to keep in his car. *Shit!*

She chewed on her thumbnail. She already knew she couldn't fight the man. Her little brother could practically pin her to the floor when they wrestled. When it came to fighting her way out of there, she didn't stand a chance.

Not without a weapon.

That thought set her in motion. She moved around in the dark until she could feel the wooden wine rack beneath her fingers again. She brushed her hands over every wooden slot, looking for a loose board. The squeak of metal—the slot in the door—stopped her dead. *Damn.* She'd have to wait. She dropped down on the mattress.

He had a flashlight this time, and the little beam of light hit her directly in the face.

"There you are." For a long moment, he merely stared at her, the beam of light roaming over her, his beady eyes unblinking. He was a creeper, all right.

"Stay right where you are, Claire. You need to understand how this works. You need to stay perfectly still. If you do anything that I don't tell you to do, bad things will happen. One wrong move and it's over. Now, Claire, I want you to nod your head if you understand. Can you do that?"

She nodded her head and prayed she would find a way out of there alive.

It wasn't long before she heard the door being unlocked.

The door opened. Using his foot, he pushed a doorstop in place to hold it open while he brought in a tray. There was a bowl of soup and a tall plastic cup filled with water. There was also a napkin and a spoon. The bowl and the cup were made of plastic. No help there.

He put the tray on the floor, then watched her closely as she reached for the water and gulped it down in thirsty swallows. She kept her eye on the spoon. It was metal.

"You are a thirsty girl," he said.

His voice grated on her nerves. The man disgusted her. She looked at him, tried to get a view of the room and the stairs behind him. Stone floors and narrow steps made of stone curved around the wall until they disappeared. It was like some sort of medieval castle down here.

"There's no way out," he said. "You can pound on these walls and scream at the top of your lungs all day long and nobody will hear you."

She started in on the soup. It was lukewarm and tasted like shit, but she was hungry. She needed to keep her strength up if she had any hope of escaping.

"What happened to all of that bravado I saw yesterday in the car?"

"That was before some creepy, disgusting old man brought me to his weird castle to keep me prisoner in his dungeon."

"There we go," he said. "Much better."

She kept her eye on the spoon as she lifted each spoonful of soup to her mouth. *Be patient*, she reminded herself, but the idea of sitting in this room for another hour, let alone another day, made it difficult to sit there and do nothing. She lifted her chin, looked him square in the eyes. "Why are you staring at me?"

"You're mesmerizing, Claire. I don't think you have an inkling as to what an absolute masterpiece you are."

"Let me go. I can't live here with you."

"Who said anything about living?" He picked up the tray and waited for her to put everything on it.

Dutifully, she placed her bowl on the tray. The spoon was clutched tightly within her fist. She wanted to jab it into his eye, thrust the hard metal into his throat, but she felt unusually weak. The bastard had put something in her soup. Her head began to spin. Her eyelids felt heavy.

"I bet you wish you were back home with that hateful family of yours—isn't that right, Claire?"

She wanted to spit in his eye, lunge at him, and rip that stupid beard from his face. But she was light-headed and tired. The spoon dropped from her hand. Her body sagged against the flimsy mattress. Instead of charging at him, she felt herself nodding in agreement right before she drifted off to sleep.

CHAPTER TWENTY

Lizzy pulled to the curb, screeching to a stop. She threw the car in park in front of the building where Stacey Whitmore worked. Stacey had made the mistake of leaving her keycard behind in Lizzy's car after their "interview" with Bennett. She'd left a message on Lizzy's phone to arrange its return, but Lizzy hadn't gotten around to dealing with it. Now would be the perfect time.

Stacey had been ignoring her calls for days now. Something was going on, and Lizzy aimed to find out what it was. She had been inside the station before. Had followed Stacey inside, knew what to do—assuming the keycard still worked. It was quite possible it had been deactivated when Stacey had been issued a replacement. Things would get more complicated then. Lizzy would have to feign frustration with the lock mechanism, then bluff herself inside when someone came to deal with her.

No plan B necessary: Lizzy slipped the card through the slot and opened the door into the building. The receptionist gave her a funny look, but Lizzy ignored her and kept on walking. She passed by a long row of cubicles.

Behind her, she heard someone calling out to her, but she ignored the voice and headed straight for Stacey's cubicle.

Stacey's head shot up when Lizzy entered her space. "Lizzy!"

"Hello, Stacey. Here's your keycard back." She tossed it on her desk. "Is there a reason you haven't been returning my calls?"

Stacey sorted through papers on her desk, tried to appear relaxed, but she was anything but. Her face had paled the moment she'd seen Lizzy.

"What's going on, Stacey?"

Stacey bolted to her feet then, grabbed hold of Lizzy's arm, and ushered her to an editing room. She shut the door. Then she crossed her arms and said, "Now you can talk."

"I have pictures of Miriam with Wayne Bennett," Lizzy told her. "Pictures of the two of them cuddling and eating dinner in a dimly lit restaurant. Dozens of them. I also have the video that you helped me tape. The one where Bennett looks directly into the camera and says he'd never heard of Miriam Walters."

Stacey let out a breath. "I need that video back."

Somebody tried to open the door. "Is everything OK in there?"

"We'll be out in a minute!" Lizzy shouted.

The door opened. It was a tall dark-haired woman with wild eyes. She pointed at Lizzy. "You're going to have to come with me, miss. You can't be back here without checking in first. I'll need your ID."

Lizzy walked toward the woman, shut the door in her face, and locked it. Then she turned back to Stacey.

"They'll call security," Stacey told her. "You don't want to end up in jail again, do you?"

"You're seriously pissing me off. Tell me what's going on right now, or I'm going to walk out there, find your boss, and tell him you've been working with me and that you borrowed station equipment to help me get a video of Wayne Bennett." Lizzy curled her fingers around the doorknob, ready to open it and follow through with her threat. The look she saw on Stacey's face said it all.

"Bennett got to you," Lizzy said.

"It's complicated."

"Bullshit. The asshole got to you, or maybe he had a little talk with your boss and he told you to back off." Lizzy shook her head. "You are now officially just like every other chickenshit reporter running around Sacramento with their tail between their legs." Lizzy scowled at her. "My God. I really never thought a scumbag piece of shit like Bennett would get the best of Stacey Whitmore. Remember how fired up you were when you started out, fighting to get stories with substance, stories that just might make a difference? What happened to that Stacey?"

Lots of frantic pounding on the door.

"I thought you were different from the rest of the talking heads."

"I thought so, too," Stacey said. "But things change, I guess. I thought I could make a difference and somehow save the world. What a crock of shit. Now I'm just hoping I can save myself. I really don't know what else I can say other than I can't be part of this reckless journey of yours."

"Then don't call me begging for any more stories," Lizzy said through clenched teeth.

Stacey shook her head in frustration. "You really don't get it, do you? Bennett is a dangerous man. We both agree on that. But I don't carry a gun, Lizzy. I'm not a fighter. You certainly aren't going to be able to protect me. I may not like it, but I can't do anything about it. I can't help you, Lizzy."

"Then I guess we're done here."

"I'm sorry."

Lizzy turned back to the door and opened it.

Two security guards with starched white shirts and shiny badges tried to grab hold of her arms. "Let go," Lizzy said, wrenching them free. "I'm leaving."

Shady Oaks Nursing Home looked slightly better than the last time Kitally visited. The smell of sanitizers was strong and the floors looked as if they had just been mopped. Even the dingy plastic chairs had been removed.

She walked up to the front counter and recognized the woman with the frizzy brown hair. She had the same annoyed expression scrawled across her face.

"Hi," Kitally said. "I'm here to see Betty Ackley. I'd like to check in."

"Weren't you here recently for a tour?"

"Yes, I was."

"I don't believe you mentioned you knew Betty Ackley."

"I don't believe I did," Kitally said. "Betty Ackley is the reason Mom and I are interested in checking the place out for my grandmother. Is there a problem?"

"She doesn't get too many visitors. It strikes me as odd, that's all."

Kitally glanced at the woman's nametag. Her name was Birgitta. "Can I please get a badge?"

The woman took her time, but she finally handed Kitally a clipboard with a list of names followed by blank spaces where she was to sign her own name.

With that done, Kitally made her way to the hallway with all the rooms where she'd first met Cecil and Betty. Unlike the front area, the hallway and rooms had clearly not been cleaned recently. The smell of urine and soiled bed linens became hard to ignore as she went along. Shady Oaks was definitely understaffed. The door to Cecil's room was closed, but she found Betty sitting in the chair next to her bed. Once again, the television was blasting.

Betty's eyes lit up when she saw her in the doorway. She picked up the remote and turned down the volume. "Did you bring me some chocolates?"

The woman might be old, but she was sharp. Kitally set her big leather bag on the edge of the bed, pulled out two boxes of assorted chocolates, and handed them to her. "I wasn't sure what you liked, so I bought you a little bit of everything."

"Thank you." Betty studied her for a moment. "I really didn't expect you to come back to see me. I was just trying to keep you out of trouble. The people around here can be frightening at times."

Kitally looked over her shoulder to make sure no one was within hearing distance before she said, "I came back for a reason."

The woman raised her eyebrows in question.

"Did you send a message to a man named Gus Valentine?"

Betty said, "Shhh," and then gestured toward the door.

Kitally went to it and peeked into the hallway. It was all clear. She shut the door and went back to where Betty was sitting.

"What do you know about Gus Valentine?" Betty asked.

Kitally kept her voice low. "I work for an investigative agency. Gus hired us to look into the death of his wife, Helsie. Are you the one who sent the note telling him to have an autopsy done?"

Betty put a trembling hand to her chest. "I am the one who wrote that note. Helsie was my friend. She knew something wasn't right about this place, but she died before we could figure out what was going on."

"Do you think her death was suspicious?"

"Yes. I think they killed her."

"Why?"

"Because she knew too much about what's happening around here."

The idea that someone might be killing off residents who were dependent on them made Kitally sick to her stomach. "You said the two of you were friends. Did Helsie tell you what she knew?"

"She was convinced they killed Marty."

"*They* being who exactly? An orderly? A doctor?"

"The whole kit and caboodle," Betty said. "All of them. This is a family-run operation. As far as I'm concerned, they're all under suspicion."

"Maybe we should alert authorities, fill out a report."

She shook her head. "It won't do any good. Helsie called the police, and look what happened to her. She died before they found time to come see her."

"You would think that might have raised a few red flags."

"You would think. But Birgitta convinced the police that Helsie had dementia and was upset because someone was stealing her Oreo cookies."

"How about you? How's your memory?"

"My brain is working like a newly oiled machine. Movie trivia is my specialty. Ask me anything."

Kitally thought Betty was kidding until the woman elbowed her and said, "Go on—ask me something."

"OK. Let's see. Who played Dorothy in the original *Wizard of Oz*?"

"Judy Garland. Too easy. Ask me another."

"What's the name of the movie starring John Wayne and Maureen O'Hara?"

"Ha! Trick question. They made . . . let me see . . . five films together. *Rio Grande, The Quiet Man, The Wings of Eagles, McLintock!,* and *Big Jake.*"

Kitally laughed. "The only one I knew was *The Quiet Man.*"

"Well, that was the best one." Betty narrowed her eyes. "How would you know anything about *The Quiet Man*?"

"Late-night movies," Kitally said. "Sometimes I have a difficult time getting to sleep."

"Huh," Betty said. "Well, enough playing around. Dixie will be making the rounds soon. We need to figure out how we're going to sneak into the main office and take a look around."

"What? We can't do that."

"Of course we can. I thought you were a detective."

Kitally shook her head. "No, I said nothing of the sort."

"You're here to ask questions about Helsie's death, aren't you?"

"Yes."

"And you do work for a private investigator, isn't that right?"

"True, but—"

"But nothing. You're a detective, and it looks like you've got yourself a sidekick. This is going to be fun."

"Wait a minute," Kitally said. "Let's pretend for a moment that we do somehow get into the main office. What exactly would we be looking for?"

"Anything and everything. Haven't you done your homework? Why do you think all the detectives on television bother sorting through people's garbage?"

"Good question."

"Those people are never looking for anything specific. They're looking for clues, and they don't know they're clues until they see them. And we're not going to see any if we're sitting in here eating chocolates, are we?"

"Good point," Kitally said. "So what's the plan?"

"This place is as good as dead after ten p.m. on most Friday nights. I need you to come back on Friday between ten and ten thirty."

Before Kitally could answer her one way or another, Betty added, "Just tap on the window, and I'll let you in."

Kitally walked over to the window and looked out at the parking lot. It wasn't a bad idea. There were thick shrubs that would help to keep her hidden. It might just work.

It only took a few minutes for Hayley to find a way into yet another run-down, three-bedroom house owned by Wayne Bennett.

Tommy was the camera expert, so he stood on the counter, feet firmly planted, while Hayley sat on the Formica counter and handed him tools whenever he asked for them. This was their third and last house for the night. They had installed motion-activated spy cameras inside closets, clocks, and now he was placing one inside a smoke detector. All the equipment had been purchased through the Internet. Serial numbers were removed, and they both wore gloves so there would be no fingerprints or evidence that would trace back to them.

"Could you hand me the clippers?" Tommy asked, his hand reaching downward in front of her face.

Hayley reached into the open bag, pulled out the wire cutters, and handed them to him.

"Thanks."

"Sure." When she failed to hear any snipping or moving around, she looked up and saw Tommy looking at her in a funny way. "What?"

"I was wondering if you would go on a date with me."

She laughed.

"Why is that funny?"

"'A date,'" she repeated. "It sounds so . . . I don't know . . . 1950-ish. It's like saying 'Let's go steady.'"

"Typical," he said, returning his attention to installing the camera.

"Typical in what way?"

"You are the biggest pain in the ass," he said without looking at her this time. "I've spent the past two hours getting myself all worked up to ask you out on a simple night out with me, and once again you're going to make me out to be a little boy who has no idea how to deal with a girl."

"Well, you sure as hell don't know how to deal with *this* girl."

He finished what he was doing and said, "You're wrong about that. I know exactly how to handle you, Hayley. I know what makes you tick. I see the way you look at me when you think I'm not looking."

She snorted.

"I know that at this very moment, you want nothing more than for me to lean over and kiss you. Not a simple little peck on the lips, either, but a real toe-curler."

"Toe-curler?"

"Yeah, an actual, honest-to-God kiss that'll curl your toes."

She didn't want him to know that his little speech had gotten to her, but damn it all, she was without words.

"Hand me that cover, will you?"

She did.

"And those two little screws," he said, without a *please* or *thanks*.

She scooped them up, pretended not to notice the way his fingers brushed over her palm as he took them from her.

Once he finished, he jumped down off the counter, put the tools in the bag, and then hopped up so that he was sitting beside her. "So, is that a yes or a no?"

She gave him one of her *are-you-fucking-kidding-me* stares. "I don't think it's a good idea."

"Why not?"

"Because I like things just the way they are between the two of us."

"You do not. You like me more than you're willing to let on. Everyone knows it, so just say yes. Go on a date with me, Hayley."

"Where would we go?"

"How about a concert in San Francisco? A lot of new bands play at the fairgrounds over there. It's cool. I think you'd enjoy it."

"I'll think about it."

"Fair enough."

"Guess what?" she said in hopes of getting his mind off her, them, the possibility of a date.

"What?"

"I think I'm ready to give up cigarettes."

His eyes lit up as if he'd just seen an elephant enter the room. "I can honestly say I never expected to hear you ever say that."

"Why not?"

"You've always said you only had one vice and you were never going to give it up. What made you change your mind?"

"Actually, I experienced my first bout of morning cough, and I didn't like it. I think it's time to give my lungs a break."

Tommy pulled his black knit ski cap over his head and then picked hers up and did the same for her, pulling the cap snugly over her ears. He looked into her eyes for a long moment and then released his hold on her.

Before he could step away, Hayley reached out and gently clasped her hands on to both sides of his face and pulled his lips to hers.

CHAPTER TWENTY-ONE

Lizzy followed Jessica into the building off Orange Grove. After they signed in, they were ushered through a long corridor by a petite woman wearing slacks, a white blouse, and a beige blazer. The click of her sturdy heels echoed through the hallway as they went.

With everything Lizzy and the girls had going on, the last thing she wanted to do was sit across the table from a couple of FBI special agents. In the end, she figured she didn't have much of a choice. There was no denying that Jimmy Martin was a good friend, but, more importantly, there was a killer on the loose. If she could be of any help, then she would do whatever she could.

The conference room they were brought to was spacious with four white walls. A picture of J. Edgar Hoover dominated one of the walls. In the center of the room was a long rectangular table where Jimmy Martin and Kenneth Mitchell awaited them.

Jimmy was a cancer survivor. He was in his midsixties. He looked good.

Kenneth Mitchell was at least twenty years younger, tall and slender, with light-colored eyes and thinning hair.

Jimmy stood and greeted Lizzy with a friendly embrace.

After introductions were made, Jessica and Lizzy took offered seats across the table from the two men. The woman in the beige blazer made sure everyone had water before she left, shutting the door behind her.

Jimmy got to it. "Kenneth here will be heading up the Sacramento Strangler case, and I'll be working alongside him at times. We wanted a chance to talk to you, Lizzy, and ask you a few questions."

Lizzy nodded.

"I'd like to begin by saying how sorry I am for your loss," Mitchell said. "Jared was well liked and respected for his single-mindedness when it came to solving a case. He was one of the brightest men I've ever worked with."

"Thank you."

"We realize this is an incredibly tough time for you," Jimmy added. "I think you know me well enough to know I wouldn't drag you here if it wasn't important."

"I understand."

"To start off," Mitchell said, "it's important that we ask you if Jared ever talked to you about any of the cases he was working on."

"He rarely spoke about work," Lizzy said. "Most evenings, I was the one who brought work home and then picked his brain for ideas."

He glanced at his notes. "Do you recall Jared ever keeping record of his daily activities, perhaps a journal where he might have kept tabs on people he interviewed or places he visited?"

"No. I would have known if he kept any sort of log."

He scribbled something on his notepad before continuing. "What about any phone calls? Do you recall Jared having any conversation at all that might have sounded strained in any way?

146

Perhaps you remember a change in his voice or demeanor, anything that might have stood out at the time as being out of the norm?"

She shook her head. "I can't think of a thing. The truth is, I was so busy I didn't have time to help Jared plan our wedding. You would have been better off talking to our neighbor, Heather, since she spent more time with him leading up to the wedding day than I did."

"Can we talk to her?"

"She's dead," Lizzy said bluntly.

"I see." Mitchell reached into his file and began laying out pictures of recent crime scenes in front of Lizzy. One photo was of a young woman among leaves and twigs, her body arranged just so. She had been sliced across the abdomen. There was also a picture of a handheld mirror with a gold finish. She figured that was the mirror Jessica had mentioned.

Among the other pictures was a magnified photograph of the mark the killer left on his victims. Jessica was right. The mark, in some cases, could easily be mistaken as a scratch or a cut. Some were big, some small. It looked like some sort of symbol. A capital Z with an extra line through it. There were also pictures of the other items found over the years: a clock, a sphere, a book, a bouquet of irises, a wreath of red roses placed around the top of a male victim's head. There were more pictures, but nothing made sense, so she stopped looking. "What do you think all of this means?"

"We've got a team of people working on it. A lot of ideas are being tossed into the hat, but so far we have nothing definitive and no correlation between any of the objects."

"It's there," Jessica said. "Right there in front of us. With every victim, he's giving us a clue, a piece of him. It's like putting together a puzzle."

Lizzy picked up another picture. It looked like a stone. "Is that coral?"

Mitchell nodded. "That was found in the front pocket of one of his youngest victims, a young girl strangled outside a rest-stop bathroom while she waited for her mother. She also had a watch clutched tightly in her hand."

"He wouldn't have had much time," Lizzy said.

"Which is why he didn't take the time to carve his mark into the girl. She's one of the few who does not have the symbol, but it's the timepiece that connects her to the rest. Her mother was adamant about having never seen the coral or the timepiece before." Mitchell pointed to a picture of the watch that was found.

"Four fifteen," Jessica said. "Could be another clue."

"Jessica mentioned that you thought Jared might have been close to identifying the killer. Why is that?"

"As you probably know, Agent Shayne worked this particular case for the last year after Gordon Presley retired. He's the one who first noticed the symbol or mark on two of the victims. We have reason to believe that sometime within a twenty-four-hour time frame before your wedding day, the killer or someone close to the killer made contact with him."

Lizzy paled. "Jared was at a hotel the night before our wedding. I talked to him for only a few minutes the next day." She drew in a steadying breath. "He didn't mention anything about receiving a call from a killer."

Jessica put a hand on Lizzy's shoulder. She looked at Jimmy and said, "Are we done here?"

Mitchell kept his gaze on Lizzy. "We would appreciate it if you could take a look through Jared's things . . . a calendar with an unfamiliar number scribbled in the margins, a notebook, anything that might stand out or stir a memory."

"I'll see what I can do," Lizzy said as Jessica stood.

They all came to their feet. Jimmy walked them to the door. Lizzy realized then that her hands were shaking and her knees felt weak. She needed to get out of there.

Box after box of Jared and Lizzy's life together were brought into the house. Tommy had borrowed a friend's truck, driven to storage, and picked up every box with Jared's name on it.

"Unless you need anything else," Tommy said to the group, "I'm going to take off."

"Thanks for your help," Lizzy said.

"No problem." He pointed a finger at Hayley. "I'll see you tomorrow night, five o'clock."

"Why so early?" Hayley asked.

"It'll take us a couple of hours to get to San Francisco, and I want to beat the crowds. I'll see you then." Before Hayley could protest, he gave a backhanded wave and made a quick exit.

"Where are you two going?" Kitally asked.

"Some sort of concert."

"Wow," Kitally said. "A real official date."

"It's not a date."

Lizzy took a box cutter and sliced through the tape on the biggest box. "He's picking you up. Taking you to a concert. Definitely a date." Without opening the box, she went to the next and cut that one open, too, and then the next, and so on.

Hayley must have noted Lizzy's reluctance to look inside. The girl knew her well. Hayley opened the first box and began sorting through Jared's things, carefully, methodically, without making a big deal about whatever was inside.

Lizzy knew she wasn't emotionally prepared to do this, but there was a serial killer on the loose and he needed to be stopped. She tried to look at it like any other investigation.

"What exactly are we looking for?" Kitally asked.

"Anything that stands out," Lizzy said. "Any object that might make you wonder 'Why is this here?' or 'What does this mean?'"

"Got it. Where's Jessica?"

"She had to return to Virginia for a few days. She'll be going back and forth for a while."

"What's this?" Kitally asked, pulling a tiny collar out of the box. "It says Rumpelstiltskin on it."

Hayley looked at Lizzy. "Isn't that the name he first gave Hannah when he brought you the kitten?"

Lizzy nodded and looked away. "I didn't know he had a collar made."

"And he kept it, too."

"Look at this," Hayley said, pulling out a T-shirt that said, "Don't forget to smile."

Lizzy smiled. "Jessica gave him that for his birthday. She always teased him about being too serious."

It went on like that. Kitally or Hayley would pull out something that would make them all remember a particular moment in time. By the end of the day, they had laughed and cried and laughed some more. It was a powerful, emotionally exhausting exercise. However cathartic it might've been for Lizzy, they'd unearthed nothing of use for the Strangler investigation.

After Hayley and Kitally disappeared, Lizzy closed each box and stacked them against the wall away from the high windows. The last box she picked up was filled with clothes. Lizzy's sister, Cathy, had ended up packing Jared's things for her. Jared's favorite suit was on top of the pile, zipped up tightly in a garment bag. Lizzy pulled the suit out and brushed her fingers over the lapels before putting the luxurious fabric against her cheek, breathing him in. Tears rolled down her cheeks as she recalled the last time she'd seen him wearing it at a dinner party. They had snuck out early and then stopped at some dive that ended up serving the best hot pastrami sandwich she'd ever tasted.

As she put the suit back into the bag, she felt something crinkle beneath her fingers. She reached into the inside front pocket of the jacket and pulled out a piece of paper. It was a note, folded twice. She set the suit aside for a moment and opened it up.

Three words: *We must talk.*

There was a telephone number scribbled below the message. It was a 916 area code. She glanced at the clock. It was too late to call the number now. She would wait until tomorrow.

CHAPTER TWENTY-TWO

After he finished setting up his easel, he readied his palette and then selected a few basic colors to start: titanium white, ivory black, cadmium red, permanent alizarin crimson, ultramarine blue, phthalo blue, cadmium yellow light, and cadmium yellow. He would be using oils and a preprimed canvas.

He peeked through the metal slot in the door.

"What are you looking at now, you disgusting pig? Are you going to drug me again so that you can have your way with me? I know what you do when I'm out cold, you sicko."

"My little Claire. You have not the tiniest clue of what I do to you when you're unconscious. Trust me when I tell you that whatever your imagination conjures up is nothing compared to the cold hard truth. I like to experiment and play. Your flesh is as soft and smooth as a newborn baby's. I like to take my time with you, Claire."

"Shut up!" She squeezed her eyes shut—all there was for her to do, since her hands and feet were bound with tape.

"I like to take my time with you," he repeated, louder this time. "I know every curve of your body. I know the scent of you . . . every bit of you." He breathed in, sucking air through his nostrils as if reliving the moment.

"I hate you!" she shouted, trying to spit at him, but only making a mess of her little bed. "You make me sick."

"I've tasted you, too." He smacked his lips. "Your every secret has been exposed, Claire."

"Stop it! Stop it! Stop it! You're the most grotesque and disgusting monster on earth." She shook her head wildly back and forth.

If she kept that up, she was going to pass out all on her own.

He let the flap clank shut.

Little Claire was getting on his nerves with all her name-calling over the past few days.

Even so, the excitement was building. He took in a deep, cleansing breath.

It was time to get her image on canvas.

This would be the first time he would paint a portrait of one of his victims while she was alive, right here in the flesh. His insides hummed at the prospect. Everything he'd done to her over the past few days was nothing compared to this.

His magnum opus.

As he pondered which brushes he would use, his phone vibrated in his pocket and he pulled it out. The name that flashed across the screen squashed every bit of thrill humming through his body.

Gillian.

The only woman he knew who could kill a buzz in the blink of an eye. *Why did she have to call today?* She'd always had excruciatingly bad timing. It often seemed as if she had a sixth sense. And yet he knew he must answer the call. To do otherwise would only prove pointless—she would not stop calling until he answered.

"Hello," he said, failing miserably at hiding his disappointment.

"Thank goodness you answered. I've been worried about you."

"And why is that?"

The poor, nervous female always sounded as if she were standing on a cliff, ready to jump. "Oh, you know me," she said. "Why don't you tell me what you've been up to?"

He wanted nothing more than to tell her he'd just been about to walk out the door and had to get off the line, but that would never work. She often talked about paying him a visit, and that was the last thing he wanted to happen.

His gaze fell upon the painting that had been hanging on the wall of the cellar when he'd first moved into the house. The artist had used oils. The artwork was layered, which could mean the painting dated back to the nineteenth century, at least. It was merely a fisherman on a boat, but there was something very dark about the painting. Perhaps it was the bloated grayish clouds or the tumultuous waters. *No*, he thought, *it's the fish*. A single fish at the end of the line, its tail whipping upward in vain as it tried to escape, instinctively knowing death was near.

"Are you there?" Gillian asked, pulling him back into the real world. She'd been talking nonstop, and he had no idea what she'd said.

He forced himself to answer. "Yes, I am here."

"Your classes are going well?"

He nodded, then remembered he was on the phone and said, "Yes," letting the *s* out in a long, drawn-out hiss.

"Are you taking your medications?"

He placed a finger on a pressure point near his left temple, trying to stop an irritating twitch under his eye, because if he didn't stop the twitching, he might completely lose it and then he wouldn't be able to speak at all. "I am taking my medication," he lied. "I am doing everything you've suggested I do, and I am feel-ing quite well. Thank you for asking. I no longer think it's neces-sary for you to keep checking up on me—"

"Does that mean you've been journaling?"

"Of course," he said. Journaling wasn't a new idea. But, of course, Gillian believed she'd dreamed up the idea of writing down one's thoughts as a form of therapy.

"The last time we talked, you mentioned that you had invented a new coping mechanism for when you're feeling a high dose of anxiety. You told me you had written it all down in your journal and that you would read me a bit of it next time we talked. Do you think you could do that now?"

"No. Now is not a good time." His attention was back on the painting, back on the fish. Something about the picture—the frantic movement of the water and the trout—made him shiver with anticipation. It was a speckled trout. The fear in its eyes was palpable. He could almost feel the sting of the hook and the bite of the barb cutting through his own soft flesh just inside his mouth.

"Well, I'm disappointed. Have you at least been trying to meet people?"

"Not really. No need."

"What about the woman you told me about . . . Lola, wasn't it?"

"We still talk," he lied. Lola was merely a figment of his imagi-nation, thought up to make Gillian happy. How stupid could she be to think that he actually knew a Lola, a name he'd come up with after listening to a song on the radio?

"Wonderful news. When can I meet her?"

"I don't know why you try so hard to pretend we're friends," he announced, already at his wit's end. "We're not."

"We've been over this. You know I'm only trying to help."

She made him feel as if he were suffocating. *Who does she think she is?* He could feel his anger building, starting at the arches of his feet, ready to work its way up to his core and burst into outrage.

To make matters worse, Claire shouted something from within her small confines. Despite being bound, she also managed to make a loud thumping noise against the floor.

"What's going on over there? Are you having work done?"

"It's the neighbors," he said quickly. "They're always in the middle of one renovation or another."

"Why is it always so difficult for you to talk to me?"

"Do you want the truth, Gillian?"

"You know I do."

"Because I don't like the way you make me feel."

"How is that?"

"Small and insignificant."

"If that's true, then there must be others who make you feel small and insignificant."

Endorphins rushed to his brain. *Only you, Gillian. Only you.* "Gillian," he said through clenched teeth, "do I need to remind you that, thanks to my parents naming you trustee, you control my finances, my wealth, and now you're trying to control my personal life, too? So, no, you're not like anyone else."

"I'm sorry. You're right. I shouldn't have upset you."

"I'm fine."

Finally, after a string of awkward apologies, she allowed the conversation to end. The moment he disconnected, he was overcome with relief. He felt a tremendous desire to sag against the wall and take a moment to collect himself. Instead, he pulled the key from the hook on the wall, opened the door to the wine cellar, and headed straight for Claire, eager to set her straight on who was in control around here.

And this time when she screamed, it was a shrill sound filled with fear and anxiety. It was downright primal, instantly filling him with heavenly rapture. In that instant, he found himself wishing he could keep Claire here with him forever.

CHAPTER TWENTY-THREE

Hayley had been surprised to hear from Kitally that Salma was still in the hospital after having a caesarean. Standing right outside Salma's room, she waited for a young man to exit before she headed inside. Salma looked over at her and gave her a sheepish smile. "Sorry about making a mess of your car."

"No big deal." Hayley gestured toward the exit. "Was that your boyfriend?"

"No. That was my brother. He wanted me to know that my family will not accept my baby unless I agree to never see my boyfriend again."

"Their loss," she said. "I saw your daughter in the nursery. She looks healthy."

Salma's eyes welled with tears. "I don't know why I'm getting all emotional," she said, clearly embarrassed, "but I want to thank you guys for everything you've done for me and my baby."

"Not a problem," Hayley said, antsy now. Too much praise and way too many emotions. Back to solid ground. "Have you chosen a name?"

"Not yet. I'm going to wait until the perfect one comes to me. I know you're not a mom, but how old was your mom when she had you?"

"My mom?" Hayley had to think. "She was young . . . maybe seventeen."

"What was it like for the two of you?"

Snippets of her life with her mom came flooding into her mind's eye, but Hayley stopped the flow. "You know what?" she said. "I loved my mom more than anyone in this world, but if you're looking for advice, all I can say is think of your kid when you make decisions. She didn't ask to be brought into this world. It was you and your boyfriend's doing. Don't be selfish. Put your daughter first."

"I'm going to do everything I can to make sure my daughter has the best life possible."

Hayley wished her mom had vowed to do the same and hadn't let outside forces intervene, but such was life. "I know you must be scared," she said. "As a single mom, it's not going to be easy for either of you, but the best thing you can do for your daughter is to be there for her when she needs you."

"I think that's good advice."

Kitally came into the room just then, out of breath. "You didn't give her the gift yet, did you?"

"Nope."

Kitally snatched the bag from Hayley's hand and gave it to Salma.

Salma reached inside and pulled out a pink frilly baby dress. There were other clothes in the bag, too—soft cotton bodysuits and booties. "Oh, the dress is darling. Thank you so much for everything."

"So," Kitally said, "are we ever going to meet the father of the baby?"

Salma blushed. "I can't say. In my culture, women don't really even date men, let alone men outside their religion. And they definitely don't get pregnant by them."

"Did he know you were pregnant?"

"Of course. But I haven't told him where I'm staying. My brothers have threatened to do him harm if they find out who he is, so I'm not telling anyone his name, either."

"I see. That's too bad."

Silence hovered over them like a dark cloud until Kitally said, "Have you named your daughter yet?"

"She doesn't want to force it," Hayley said.

"I feel as if I'll know what her name is after I've spent more time with her," Salma said. "Does that make sense?"

Kitally screwed up her face. "Not at all. I think Lucy would be a cute name."

"God no," Hayley said, "not Lucy." Then again, what did it matter? After looking through the wall of glass at all the babies, Hayley didn't understand why women gushed over them. With their big heads, nonexistent necks, and wrinkly skin, not one of them was the least bit attractive.

Kitally kept at it. "How about something different, like Hermione or Minerva?"

Hayley rolled her eyes.

Salma merely ignored her, and then said, "Have you two had any luck locating the Ghost?"

"Not so far."

"I tried calling the girl I lived with, the one who was evicted from her apartment, but she hasn't returned my calls. I wish I could remember her name."

"If it comes to you, let us know," Kitally said. "I'll be back tomorrow to visit."

"We better go," Hayley told Kitally. "We have work to do."

"Yeah, we need to hurry so we can get back in time for your date."

"You have a date?" Salma asked Hayley.

"No. I'm just going to a concert with Tommy. He's just a friend."

Kitally looked at Salma and winked.

Hayley couldn't remember the last time she'd been inside a mall. The Fashion Plus store where Miriam Walters worked before she disappeared was lit up with fluorescent lights so bright she squinted.

Halfway across the store, she lost Kitally to a striped sequined dress. The mannequin had drawn her as if it were a magnet. Leaving her behind, Hayley walked to the back of the store where customers could pay for their merchandise. Apparently it was a slow night. There were three people behind the counter, shooting the breeze.

"My name is Hayley Hansen. Is there anyone here I can talk to about Miriam Walters?"

A tall girl with black hair and straight-cut bangs looked Hayley over before she asked, "Why?"

"I work for Lizzy Gardner Investigations. We're looking for Miriam."

"Is she missing?" another girl asked, this one wearing a purple leather miniskirt and boots.

The other cashier, a skinny guy with a long pointy nose, said to Hayley, "She's new here. Don't pay her any mind."

"Hey, don't be rude. Is Miriam the short geeky girl with—"

"That's Monica. She quit. This lady is talking about Miriam, a tall gorgeous girl who sold tons of clothes just by wearing something in the store."

"Oh."

"Miriam and I were close," the black-haired girl said. "What do you need to know?"

Kitally joined them, and Hayley introduced her before continuing. "We need to know if Miriam ever talked about going away for a while."

"You think she might be hiding out somewhere?" the skinny boy asked.

Hayley shrugged. "Anything's possible."

"She liked her life here," the black-haired girl said. "She was a hard worker, and she was excited when she got into that program for brainy teenagers, whatever it's called."

"Opportunity Knocks," Kitally said.

The boy nodded. "Yeah, that's true. After she was accepted into the program, that's pretty much all she talked about. I don't remember hearing one word from her about leaving the area." He saw a group of girls enter the store. "Excuse me while I help these people."

The other employee, the one in the miniskirt, pulled her cell out of her pocket and wandered into the back room, texting as she went.

The black-haired girl leaned forward and said in a low voice, "There is no way Miriam left town without kicking and screaming."

"Why do you say that?"

"Because Miriam was pregnant and in love with some ultra-hot guy she'd just met."

"Pregnant?" Kitally asked. "Are you sure?"

"I don't have any proof. I just know what she told me."

"So, you never saw an older man named Wayne Bennett come around here?" Hayley asked.

"Oh, sure," she said. "You already know about him? He came around for Miriam before the hot young guy. The old guy would pretend to be shopping around for his wife. We all knew it was a lie. I never understood what Miriam saw in him. I don't care how much money he had—the man was way too old for her, and there was something skanky about him, too."

"So when did the other man—the hot guy—come into the picture?"

She tilted her head as she thought about it for a second. "I would say she met the hot guy about six weeks before she disappeared. They were perfect for each other. They were both good-looking and smart—a perfect match."

"So you think Miriam was pregnant with the hot guy's baby?"

She nodded. "Miriam told me it was *definitely* hot guy's baby."

"How could she be so sure?"

"With the old guy, she used protection with a capital *P*."

"So you don't know the hot guy's name?"

"Sorry. No idea. I don't even know if she ever told me his name."

"Did the police ever question you about Miriam?"

She shook her head. "I heard they came in to the store, but I only work here three days a week, and I certainly wasn't going to go out of my way to call them."

"Could I get your name and number in case we have more questions later?"

The girl found a business card, scribbled down the information, and handed the card to Hayley. "There you go."

"Thanks a lot."

As they exited the store, Kitally said, "I wonder if Bennett was jealous and so he killed her?"

"Who knows?"

As they walked, every store window with a set of four-inch heels or a gaudy jewelry display sidetracked Kitally. It was like a disease. Hayley was dying for a smoke, but she really did want to quit, so she tried to think about something else. And that's when she saw a girl with white spiky hair walk into the shoe store across the way.

It was the Ghost. It had to be.

"Kitally, come on."

"Just a minute, I want to—"

"We've got to go *right now*. I just saw the Ghost walk into that shoe store over there."

Kitally turned and looked to see where she pointed. "Are you sure?"

"Yep."

"What should we do?"

"Let's make sure it's her first, then we'll call the cops. After that, I'm not letting her out of my sight until they get here. I'll make a citizen's arrest if I have to."

They walked over to the store, Hayley leading the way. "Pretend you're looking for a pair of running shoes," she said.

"I would never buy a pair of running shoes. They're ugly."

"This is pretend, Kitally. Pretend you love running shoes for two minutes. Do you think you can handle that?"

"OK, OK. Chill."

They headed inside. The store wasn't very wide, but it was deep. For a second or two, Hayley worried that the girl had already escaped unnoticed.

Kitally picked up a shoe on the display rack and pretended to admire it. "This is the ugliest sneaker I've ever seen."

Hayley looked around. A mother and her son were rummaging through shoes nearby, left to their own devices by the gaggle of teenage clerks gathered at the back of the store.

The tall spiky-haired girl they were looking for was hard to miss. She wasn't anywhere in sight.

"I like that shoe over there," Kitally said as she headed to another display and then picked up one of the shoes. "Genuine leather, and look at the cool zipper on the side."

"Those are men's shoes," Hayley pointed out.

"Cool." Kitally's smile disappeared. "I see the Ghost," she told Hayley. "It's definitely her, straight across from us, right along the far wall. Don't turn around."

"Can I help you?"

Perfect, Hayley thought. Now *you take an interest in us.*

"No, thanks," Hayley said, using the clerk's appearance as an excuse to turn toward the Ghost. There she was, just as Kitally had said. "We're just looking around."

The Ghost looked up just then. There was a flash of recognition in her eyes, and then she was tearing for the front of the store.

"Shit!"

Hayley took off after her. No way would she let her get away. She'd tackle the skinny bitch if she had to and then grab her wallet and take a look at her ID. At least then she would have a name. Maybe an address, too.

"Hey, you!" Hayley shouted as she ran out of the store and down the middle of the mall. "Stop right there!"

The Ghost could fly; Hayley had to give her that. She took an escalator up, two stairs at a time. Hayley did the same.

The Ghost disappeared inside a dimly lit shop, the kind that sells lava lamps and posters.

Kitally caught up to Hayley before she stepped inside and muttered something about needing a pair of those running shoes she'd just been looking at. Gasping for breath, Kitally told her she'd wait outside the store in case the Ghost got by her.

Hayley stepped inside. The shop was dark and had long strings of neon-colored beads hanging at the start of each aisle.

It was annoying. She'd made her way down two aisles when she heard a woman scream and then a string of curses right outside the store. She ran that way. A couple of people were helping Kitally and another woman from the floor.

"She shoved this lady right into me," Kitally said. Then she pointed to her left. "She went that way!"

Hayley took off again, running at full speed, weaving in and out of shoppers.

She almost knocked a kid over. Someone shouted at her to slow down. Up ahead, she caught a glimpse of white hair right before the girl cut to the right.

The moment she made the same right, she spotted the Ghost standing at the railing, looking down to the bottom floor of the mall.

Finally. Hayley had her right where she wanted her.

The Ghost turned toward her.

"It's over," Hayley said.

The Ghost smiled, gave her the finger, then swiveled around and leaped over the barrier. She flew out of sight with her arms extended outward as if she had wings.

Stunned, Hayley ran to the railing and saw what the Ghost had done. That chick had balls. The clever piece of shit had easily landed on a giant Easter Bunny display that should have been taken down long ago. It was made of soft, squeezable foam and yellow fur. When the Ghost got as far as the bunny's hind leg, she jumped to the floor and disappeared.

By the time Kitally caught up to her, Hayley was livid.

"It's OK," Kitally said. "We almost had her. We'll find her again."

"That bitch flipped me the bird. I should have jumped on her ass the moment we walked into that shoe store." She threw her arms up in disgust.

"Don't be so hard on yourself. That girl has obviously been making herself scarce for a very long time. She's good at this."

"I've been chasing criminals for a while myself."

"Well, I guess you've finally met your match."

CHAPTER TWENTY-FOUR

Dinner had been a quick affair at Skip's Kitchen, where Tommy and Hayley both ordered big juicy hamburgers and sweet potato fries. The concert didn't start until nine o'clock.

The burgers proved to be the evening's high point. By ten thirty they were walking out to the fairgrounds parking lot in search of Tommy's car. They weren't the only ones leaving early. The band was a new one called Poetic Justice, and apparently they still needed some seasoning. At this point, they were basically a thunderous set of drums with some occasional screeching feedback whenever the lead singer tried to sing. Hayley could still feel the drummer doing his thing through the soles of her shoes as they crossed the blacktop.

Tommy opened Hayley's door for her and then went around the front of the car and climbed in behind the wheel. She clicked her seatbelt into place. When she looked over at Tommy, he made a face and said, "Sorry about that. Epic fail."

"It wasn't that bad," she said. And then they both burst out laughing.

"That was the worst band I've ever heard," Tommy said.

"Agreed."

He looked over his shoulder as he backed out of the gravelly parking lot. Once they were on the road heading home, he said, "Those were some bizarre sounds coming off that stage. My ears still hurt."

"The best part," she said, "was when they finished the first song and the lead singer gave his ten-minute rant about politics and everyone threw their glow sticks at him."

"You're right. That was the highlight of the night. I am so sorry."

"Don't be. I had fun."

"Seriously?"

She nodded. "I really did."

"I'll do better next time. I promise."

"Next time?"

He shrugged, keeping his eyes on the road as he talked. "I like you, Hayley—you know that. I always have."

She said nothing.

"What's going on inside that head of yours these days?"

She snorted. "A whole lot of nothing."

"I don't believe that for a minute. You're always up to something. Do you ever think about the future?"

"No."

"Why not?"

"The future is for dreamers."

"You don't have dreams?"

"I can't say that I do. How about you?"

"I have a few."

"Tell me."

"All right." He took a deep breath as if gathering himself, then let it out. "In my future, I imagine my girl and me living in a quaint house far from the city life. When you step outside the back door, you can hear the lazy trickle of the river. We have two wooden chairs that we keep by the river's edge. Sometimes you—I mean, my girl—watches me fish and makes fun of me when I finally catch a trout and manage to let it slip right out of my grasp when I go to remove the hook. We watch the fish swim down the river, happy, glad to be free to live another day." He grinned at her. "Should I go on?"

"Go for it."

"On occasion, we share a glass of cabernet after dinner and talk about having kids someday, but we're having too much fun living day to day to make it a reality just then. If it's meant to be, it will happen."

The long stretch of silence was too much. Hayley turned his way. "And then what happens?"

Tommy laughed. "And then we live happily ever after."

"That's it?"

"What else do you want to know?"

"The ending. I need to know what happens to you and your girl at the end."

"Seriously?"

"Seriously."

"We go on to have four children. Two boys and two girls. It's not easy raising four kids, especially after the economy spirals downward and my business goes under. My girl and me aren't asking for much, but we refuse to give up our home by the river. So we start a little farm. You know, one of those organic farms, because we want to be together 24-7. At first, she's a little worried about that arrangement, being that she's sort of a loner and likes her space, but it isn't long before she realizes how easygoing I am."

"So, that's what you and your girl do all day? Grow fruit and vegetables?"

"Well, my girl, it turns out, has quite the green thumb. People come from all over to pick up some of her amazing banana peppers and lemon basil. Over the next few years, organic everything grows wildly popular. It's crazy. My girl and me work hard enough to put all four kids through college, and those kids all go on to live amazing lives of their own. You want to know the best part of it all?"

"You can't stop now," Hayley said.

"The best part is that through it all, we always take time to sit on the porch or go down by the river and talk. Before you know it, we're in our nineties, and that's when you lean close and tell me for the very first time that you love me. And guess what I say?"

"I don't have a clue," she said.

"I say, 'I know.'" Tommy glanced her way. "And that's it. That's the end."

"Hmm."

"So what do you think?"

"I think you're a starry-eyed dreamer."

"'I may be a dreamer,'" he sang, "'but I'm not the only one.'"

She rolled her eyes and then laid her head back and listened to him sing John Lennon's "Imagine." His voice had a nice tone. She had no idea he could sing. Tommy, she realized, was turning out to be full of surprises.

CHAPTER TWENTY-FIVE

It was ten o'clock when Kitally tapped on Betty Ackley's window. As she hunched down behind a bush to wait for the old lady to make it over from her bed, she noticed a yellow pill within the soil. And then a white one and a blue one. She broke off a small branch and began to dig in the dirt around the pills. There had to be at least a dozen different sizes and colors of pills, some broken, some half-dissolved in the soil.

Using the stick, she dug a hole, and then brushed all the tablets inside and smoothed the dirt over them. When she was done, she dropped the branch, looked back through the window, and tapped again.

Would Betty even remember she was coming?

In answer to her question, there was a click and then a whoosh as the window was opened from the inside.

Kitally jumped to get her upper body over the windowsill, then used her arms and legs to pull and kick the rest of the way in.

Betty shut the window and then gestured frantically, pointing under the bed and motioning without words for Kitally to get under there and make it quick.

Kitally didn't ask questions. She got down on the ground, her body flat to the floor, and shimmied her way beneath the bed. It was a tight squeeze, but she managed.

She lay there in the dark and wondered what was going on. Betty looked downright fearful. Before Kitally could question her from her hiding place, the door opened and she heard the flick of a switch. Bright light lit up the room.

"What are you doing awake, Betty?"

"I'm having a difficult time falling asleep."

Heels clacked against Formica tiles. Kitally heard the curtains over the window being shut tight.

"Did you take your pills?"

"Why do you ask me that every time you come in here? Of course I did."

"No reason for you to get all worked up. Just doing my job."

"I don't like being treated like a child," Betty said. "My insurance company pays a large sum of money for me to be here. I deserve to be treated with respect."

"Of course you do. But we have rules around here. You know that. If we let every patient run around here willy-nilly, can you imagine the chaos? Nobody in this place would ever get any sleep at all. And would that be fair to your friend Cecil? Or what about poor Mrs. Potter?"

"What do you mean 'poor' Mrs. Potter? Did something happen to Madge?"

"Never mind." Drawers were opened and then shut.

"What are you doing?"

"Just taking a look around."

"Why? Stay out of my personal belongings. I'm going to report you. Do you hear me?"

The orderly marched across the room. The tension between the two women sucked the oxygen right out of the room. Kitally could see the tips of well-worn shoes beneath the bed. Then she felt the mattress press down on her back. *What the hell is going on?*

"Open your mouth."

"No."

"Do it or I'll be forced to call Patrick to do the honors."

"OK. OK."

It was quiet for a moment and then the staffer said, "Where are you hiding the pills, Betty?"

"I've taken every bit of medication you've ever given me. You've just given me a double dose. Here's hoping you haven't done any damage."

The orderly walked to the window, yanked back the curtains, and opened the window.

If the orderly leaned too far down, she might see Kitally under the bed. And then what? What would she do? Kitally really didn't want to think about it. The woman's voice was deep and raspy, as if she smoked three packs of cigarettes a day. She sounded intimidating. No wonder Betty looked scared.

Once the orderly finished, she closed everything and went back to the door. Before she left she said, "I've ordered a clean sweep of your room to be done first thing in the morning. I don't know what you're doing with your pills, Betty, but I know you're not taking them. If you were, you would be sleeping like everyone else in this place."

"I have a very high tolerance for medication," Betty argued. "You should know that by now."

"We'll see about that." The light clicked off and the door opened and closed.

Kitally didn't dare move. Not for another five minutes at least.

"Are you awake?" she asked as she finally crawled out of her hiding place.

"I am. Perhaps tonight isn't the best night to do this, after all."

Betty's hunched shoulders and dejected expression gave Kitally chills. The old woman really did need her help. "This is bullshit, Betty," Kitally said.

Betty looked up at her then.

"Excuse the language, but something doesn't smell right around here. I don't know what's going on, but we're going to get to the bottom of it—do you hear me?"

Betty nodded.

This was Kitally's chance to make a difference, and there was no way she was going to let Betty or Cecil or any of these people down. "I'll be back. We're going to find something to prove these people are up to no good. I'm more sure of that than ever."

"I believe you," Betty said with a smile. "I really do."

Lizzy stared out the window. It was dark outside. No moon or stars as far as she could see. But she'd lived here long enough to know where the mossy rock sat beneath a crowd of gangly-limbed oaks. She didn't need to see either to know they were there. Just as she knew Jared was always near. She wasn't a sixth sense kind of person, didn't believe in ghosts or reincarnation, but Jared was here with her. She could feel his presence as if he were standing next to her. She thought of him with her first waking breath and again with every breath that followed until she finally fought her way to sleep at night. She had no idea how many days had passed since she'd last kissed him or held him in her arms. Since his death, each day came and went as if nothing had changed. The world kept turning. Trees still danced in the wind. The birds squawked and chirped. Everything was exactly as it always had been.

And yet nothing would ever be the same again. And that particular fact fueled her rage.

Anger twisted and turned within her, its long crooked fingers wrapping around every muscle and tendon, squeezing, suffocating. The anger she felt started at her toes and worked its way up, heating the blood in her veins, making it hard to breathe. The moon, stars, and trees might all be the same, but her anger and resentment continued to grow like a cancerous cyst inside her.

The house was quiet. Salma was gone, and Hayley and Kitally were out doing who knew what.

Lizzy unfolded the piece of paper she'd found earlier. She had called the number half a dozen times today, but she picked up her cell and decided to try again.

"Hello?"

The voice startled her, so she spoke all in a rush. "Hi, this is Lizzy Gardner. I'm a friend of Jared Shayne's. I found your number on a note scattered among his personal belongings." She forced herself to slow down. "The message on the note says, 'We must talk,' and I was hoping you could tell me who the note might be from."

"I don't recognize that name," the woman said after hesitating for too long. "And I certainly never passed on any note with my number."

"Jared Shayne worked for the FBI. He was killed recently."

"I'm sorry."

"Is there anyone else at this number?" Lizzy asked.

"No. Just me."

"And who is this I'm talking to?"

"It's late. I must go. Good night."

There was a click, and the call was disconnected.

Lizzy was calling bullshit.

She had already looked up everything on the woman. She grabbed her laptop, sat on the bed, and pulled up the information she'd found earlier.

Kathryn Church.

She lived approximately thirty minutes away, in Newcastle. Satellite maps revealed a country road with lots of trees and rolling hills.

Who was she really, though? And why had she wanted to talk to Jared?

Earlier in the day, she'd put the woman's name into every database available. The basics were easy enough to find: Caucasian, thirty-six years of age, born on May 26, 1978, brunette, brown eyes. She grew up in Sacramento, went to college at UCLA, where she studied psychology, and then moved back to the area and started her own practice.

As Lizzy searched further, she found an article written by Kathryn Church two years ago. The subject matter was repressed childhood memories. Apparently, the woman believed, like other psychologists, that repressed memories could be recovered through therapy. Colleagues argued that prolonged therapy in many of these cases only served to create false memories. But Kathryn remained adamant, convinced that her own repressed memories had come back to her more than a decade after the incident. According to the article, Kathryn had been hesitant to talk about the event she'd suppressed, but once she became an advocate for others in her position, she'd come forward with details of her trauma.

Lizzy scanned the article for some mention of those details.

Proponents of the existence of repressed memories believed that these traumatic events could be recalled decades after the event, usually triggered by something as simple as a particular song or taste. Skimming over endless citations and references, Lizzy finally found what she was looking for: as an adult, Kathryn Church had been watching her best friend's child by the pool. A rubber ball rolling into the pool set off alarms and the memories came rushing back. Without warning, Kathryn was ten years old again. Her family had just moved into a neighborhood in Sacramento.

Left to admire her new bedroom on the second floor, she peered out the window, which happened to give her a bird's-eye view of the neighbors' backyard. They had a pool with a diving board. Excited at the possibility of new friends, Kathryn watched a little girl and an older boy, who turned out later to be the girl's brother. The girl pointed to the red rubber ball that had fallen into the pool. They were on the far side, which gave her a clear view. The boy nodded his approval, and Kathryn's heart raced as she watched the little girl go to retrieve the ball. After she fell in, the boy stood at the edge, watching as her little arms and legs flailed, churning the water's surface. Finally, her head popped up out of the water, and her fingers grasped the edge of the pool.

Kathryn's relief was short-lived. She watched in horror as the boy got down on his knees, pried the girl's tiny fingers off the ledge, and then, with the palm of his hand flat on her head, pushed her under and held her there until her legs no longer kicked and her arms went still.

Frozen in terror, Kathryn had watched, along with the boy, as the little girl sank slowly to the bottom of the pool.

Lizzy sucked in a breath.

Had the woman truly witnessed such a horrific event?

Once again, Lizzy wondered why Kathryn Church wanted to talk to Jared.

And why was she lying about it now?

Lizzy came to her feet. She didn't look at the clock, didn't give a rat's ass what time it was. She was going to pay the woman a visit.

CHAPTER TWENTY-SIX

He stood behind his easel and canvas, paintbrush in hand, palette ready. "Open your eyes, Claire."

Instead, she screamed at the top of her lungs, a high-pitched noise that pierced his skull.

He clenched his teeth tighter.

After drugging Claire, he'd spent most of the day yesterday setting up the room, screwing in toggle bolts and chains that could easily support a heavy load. Claire weighed approximately 110 pounds. He had to drill holes big enough to accommodate the toggles.

The chains and cuffs seemed to be working nicely. They would hold her in place while he painted. The metal cuffs might cause her some pain, but that was the effect he was going for.

She was naked. Her arms were outstretched, above her head. Same for the legs, spread downward and apart. Despite being drugged, she'd managed to fight him every step of the way. He was exhausted. "Open your eyes. This is the last time I'm going to ask nicely."

He waited, but she didn't move a muscle. Her head hung low, her chin resting against her collarbone.

He placed his paintbrush on the table he'd set up to his left. Then he made a tsking noise as he reached into his pocket, pulled out a small plastic bottle, and unscrewed the lid. Calmly, he walked over to her, placed the palm of his hand against her forehead, and firmly pressed her head upward, holding it none too gently against the wall.

She tried to wriggle her head. "Stop it! Let me go! What are you doing?"

"I'm going to use some of this amazing wonder glue to hold your eyelids wide-open."

"No! No! No! Please. I'll do what you say!"

"Too late."

More frantic wriggling.

"If you don't hold still, you're going to get glue in your eyes, Claire, and then you'll be blind. Do you want to be blind?"

"Stop. Please. I'll do what you want. I promise."

He growled as he let her go. He put the glue away, his every movement jerky as he pointed at her. "Next time you disobey, there will be no second chance. Understand?"

She nodded.

"I want to hear you say it, Claire. Say it loud enough that I can hear you."

"I understand. I will not disobey. I swear."

"Better."

He went back to his position behind the easel. He picked up his brush, dabbed it in paint, and then set his eyes on Claire's face. "Give me a crazed look, Claire."

Her eyes narrowed.

"Not angry. I said crazed."

Her eyes widened. She stuck her tongue out and frantically moved her head from side to side, her tangled hair flying in front of her eyes, her nostrils flaring.

"Wonderful," he said. "Keep your eyes just like that, but stop thrashing about. Look at *me*, though, right here into my eyes, and don't look away until I say so."

She did as he said. Her eyes were steely glints of raw fear, like the fish in the painting.

He turned up the music as loud as it would go. A full orchestra began to play, starting with the silky keys of a piano, then gradually adding in strings, climbing unhurriedly, and then *boom*, hitting the emotions with throbbing oboes and powerful brass drums.

The girl was beyond terrified, her soul aching, her every emotion rooted by fear. With each stroke of the brush, he felt as if he were transferring her inner being to the canvas. He couldn't remember the last time he'd felt so alive.

Kathryn Church's house in Newcastle was set on a quiet road—a one-story on a good-sized lot.

Lizzy knocked on the door and then looked around. Had Jared come to see this woman? Had he walked this same path?

After a while, she knocked again, harder this time.

The porch light came on. "Who is it?"

"You know damn well who it is. I don't like being hung up on."

There was no response.

Lizzy calmed herself and said, "It's Lizzy Gardner. I called you earlier. It's very important that I talk to you."

"It's late. Go away, or I'll be forced to call the police."

"People are dying, Ms. Church, and there might be something you can do to stop it."

No response.

"Jared Shayne was my fiancé," Lizzy went on. "You talked to him, didn't you? He was close to identifying a serial killer, a killer who has begun to strike much more often. We need to stop him."

The door opened. "Come inside," the woman said, "before you scare the neighbors."

After Lizzy stepped inside, the woman quickly shut the door behind her, making sure to lock it.

The pictures Lizzy had seen of Kathryn Church on the Internet didn't do her justice. Even barefoot, she appeared elegant and graceful. Tall and long-limbed, she possessed a heart-shaped face, long neck, and well-defined cheekbones. Her black silky curls brushed against the top of her shoulders.

"I hope I didn't interrupt anything important," Lizzy said.

Kathryn's smirk told Lizzy she wasn't buying it.

And she was right. Lizzy really didn't care. She glanced around the house, taking it all in: a baby grand in the living area, antique dining table and chairs, a crystal chandelier. She strained to listen, wondering if anyone else was in the house.

Kathryn gestured for her to follow her into the living area. "Why don't we have a seat in here?"

Lizzy's gaze settled on the woman's blouse and pencil skirt. "Were you going out?"

Kathryn waved the comment away with a hand. "I haven't bothered to change. Once I get started working in my office, I can't stop. I do my best work at night, right here at home."

"You're a psychologist—is that right?"

She gestured for Lizzy to have a seat across from her. "Yes, that's correct. I have my own practice. I also teach at the local college. Insomniacs like to keep busy."

Deciding to cut to the chase, Lizzy looked the woman in the eyes and held her gaze. "You talked to Jared, didn't you?"

She hesitated but not for long. "Yes. We were to meet first thing Monday after your wedding."

"Why did you lie?"

"Why do you think? Because I am afraid."

"Of what?"

"Of what might happen if he ever found out that I spoke to you."

"If who finds out?"

The woman fidgeted in the high-back chair, clearly out of sorts.

"Are you talking about your next-door neighbor?" Lizzy asked. "The boy you saw kill his little sister?"

Kathryn closed her eyes and gave a subtle nod. "I thought I had managed to get rid of any trace of the paper I wrote."

"Is that why you wanted to talk to Jared? Because you thought your neighbor might've grown into the killer the police have been looking for?"

"Yes. My plan at the time was to tell Mr. Shayne what I had seen." She swallowed and cast her eyes around the room, as though the killer might be hiding behind the couch or the heavy living room curtains.

Lizzy fought to hide her disappointment. "But now you're having doubts about what you saw?"

"Not doubts, exactly. It just all began to seem so farfetched. The incident by the pool happened a long time ago. I was going with my instincts. I guess I was hoping that Jared, with his train-ing . . ." She faded off.

"He could work wonders," Lizzy said. "But yes. Something more tangible would be helpful."

"Something tangible." Kathryn sighed, then straightened in her seat. "I have something. It's not much, but it is, at least, that."

Lizzy followed her across plush carpet, past the kitchen, and down a long hallway that led them through open French doors into a massive study. The room was dimly lit. A desk, front and center, was covered with papers.

As Kathryn opened the top drawer, Lizzy noticed the oil painting hanging on the wall behind the desk. The female in the picture was done in a Picasso fashion with an arm where the leg should be and three eyes instead of two. The hair appeared to be stalks of wheat. Earrings decorated enlarged ears, and a melted clock dripped through the woman's fingers.

Kathryn handed Lizzy a piece of paper.

After reading the note, which appeared to be nothing more than instructions on how to take care of some pets while the person was away, along with quite skillful sketches of a cat, a dog, and a bird in the margins, Lizzy said, "What is this?"

"It's from the same boy who drowned his sister."

"What's his name?"

"Zachary Tucker."

The name didn't mean anything to Lizzy. "Why would you save this?"

"Because of the drawings, I think. And because Zachary did them."

Lizzy lifted her eyebrows, telling her to go on.

"As you know, we were neighbors. When my mother offered to drive Zachary to school every morning, I was afraid of him at first."

"Did you tell anyone what you had witnessed?"

"No. I was young, I was scared, and at first I thought he would kill me, too."

"And then?"

"And then I met him face-to-face, and I decided he was just a normal boy. He was funny and cute, and little by little I convinced myself that my eyes had merely played tricks on me the day his sister drowned."

Lizzy stared at the note. "I still don't understand why you would save this."

"I did what most girls do when they have a mad crush on a boy. I saved every little thing he gave me."

"You had a crush," Lizzy said, "on the boy you might've seen drown his sister."

"Like I said, I had put that memory away by then." She drew in a deep breath and then let it out. "I wasn't very popular at school, but Zachary always made me feel special. I kept every note and letter in a shoe box I decorated with wrapping paper. As the years passed, I all but forgot about the box."

However Kathryn might explain it, Lizzy was surprised the woman could feel anything for the boy after what she'd seen—or even suspected she *might* have seen. But just as she'd said, she'd been a child at the time, so Lizzy kept her thoughts to herself.

"I was an adult by the time the memories came back to me so vividly," Kathryn continued. "It wasn't until I attended a fund-raiser for families of murder victims that I saw Jared Shayne being interviewed about a killer in Sacramento and felt compelled to talk to him."

"Why?"

"I felt a tremendous need to tell someone what I had seen." She rubbed her temple. "There were other things, too, little things that Zachary would say and do."

"For instance?"

"A few years after the death of his sister, dogs and cats were being slaughtered in our neighborhood. For months, people kept their pets inside. When I talked to Zachary about it one day, he had a smirk on his face that I'll never forget. His reaction was nothing more than a shrug. And that's not all. Once he had his driver's license, he would drive me to school. I was looking for a pen in his glove compartment, and I saw a newspaper clipping about the murder of a little girl at a rest stop."

"Did you question him?"

"No." She sighed. "I didn't begin to connect the dots until I heard Jared Shayne talking about the rash of killings in

Sacramento. That's when I began to wonder if there could be a connection to Zachary. I felt a sudden need to talk with Mr. Shayne. I wanted to do what I could to find out if Zachary could possibly be the killer."

"So you gave Jared your number?"

She nodded. "That night I slipped Mr. Shayne a piece of paper letting him know I needed to talk with him. We talked once, but I didn't feel comfortable giving him Zachary's name over the phone."

"You grant this Zachary a great deal of power, don't you think? Worrying that he might somehow hear you whisper his name into the phone?"

Kathryn didn't blink at this. "Zachary's never needed me or anyone to grant him any power," she said, her voice low and charged. "You forget. I've seen what he can do." She licked her parched lips. "And he was just a little boy then."

CHAPTER TWENTY-SEVEN

Today, Kitally decided to help Lizzy at the downtown office. They had files at both the house and the office on J Street. This particular office was a mess, and Kitally figured she was the only one who cared enough to bother with straightening up the place. But that wasn't the only reason she had wanted to come to the office today. She needed to talk to Lizzy about Salma, let her know she had taken a taxi from the hospital and she and her baby were moving in for a while. Before Kitally could start up a conversation with Lizzy, a man popped his head inside the door and waved a colorful flyer at them. "Mind if I hang this on your window?"

"I don't know," Lizzy said. "What is it?"

He stepped inside and let the door shut behind him.

Kitally guessed him to be in his late thirties. When he looked at her, it was his intense-looking eyes that struck her first. He was cleanly shaven—a preppy-looking guy with neatly combed hair, a crooked nose, and a square jaw.

He handed the flyer to Lizzy. As she read it over, he picked up a handcrafted pencil holder made of pottery and painted in fine detail and said, "This is striking. Exquisite, actually. May I ask where you found it?"

Although he was clearly going overboard with the praise, Lizzy decided to go with it. "My niece made that years ago. You're right, though, she's a creative genius." Lizzy held up the flyer. "In fact, she might enjoy visiting some of these galleries. Go ahead and hang it up, and maybe we'll see you there."

"I appreciate it." He looked around. "Do you mind if I hang it inside the window, so it doesn't blow away?"

"Not a problem."

He had to lean over Lizzy's desk to get the flyer on the window. When he was done, he apologized for interrupting their workday. He was about to head out when Lizzy said, "Are you one of the artists who will be exhibiting?"

"How did you know?"

"You've got paint on your elbow."

He looked at the spot and then laughed. "You're very perceptive."

"So I've been told. What's your name?"

"Jake Polly."

"Lizzy Gardner."

"I know," Jake said and then pointed at the etching on the door.

After he left, Kitally continued to watch Lizzy. That was the most normal she'd seen her boss since Jared's funeral. It felt sort of good to see Lizzy carry on a conversation with a stranger. Her gaze fell to Lizzy's stomach. She had on a baggy shirt, but still, she didn't have an ounce of flab on her. There was no way Lizzy was pregnant.

"Do you want something, Kitally?"

"Who me?"

"Yes, you," Lizzy said. "Nobody else is here, and I can feel your eyes boring a hole through the side of my head."

"Sorry. It's just nice to see you interacting with people again."

"You worry too much."

"Maybe you're right. My mom says the same thing."

Lizzy swiveled her chair around. "Out with it. What else is on your mind?"

"Jake Polly was right. You are perceptive, aren't you?"

Lizzy said nothing. Instead, she waited for Kitally to spit it out.

"It's about Salma," Kitally finally said.

"Is her baby doing OK?"

"The baby is fine. The thing is, I did a little snooping around when she was living at the house, and it turns out her boyfriend is a guy named Joey Rich."

"And?"

"And her family does not approve of him. Like, at all. She's worried he'll be harmed."

"It's not your problem, Kitally. Stay out of it."

"Well, it is sort of my problem because she's back at the house."

"And what do you propose to do about it?"

"I'm not sure. That's why I thought I'd ask you."

"She's young. She should be with her family. I refuse to make it my business. You should do the same. She needs to go home."

"You're probably right. I'll talk to her." Kitally stood. "I have something I want to show you." Kitally ran to the back room and returned with a broom and a dustpan.

"Good job," Lizzy said without enthusiasm. "I appreciate you keeping the place spruced up."

"You think I'm just sweeping?"

Lizzy crossed her arms and sighed.

"A*ha!*" Kitally twisted the handle and the bristly part of the broom popped off onto the floor. Then she tripped a hidden lever and a lethal-looking spear point sprang out where the bristles used to be.

Lizzy leaned back in her chair, her hand at her heart. "That looks dangerous as hell."

"That's because it is. I made it myself. Pretty cool, don't you think?"

Apparently Lizzy had no words to express her excitement for Kitally's invention.

"About a month ago, I came up with this idea, and I couldn't sleep. The next day I called this guy who works for my dad and asked him to put this prototype together. We have another one, too. We'll keep one here in the office and one at home, just in case we ever get a surprise visitor."

"I don't have any plans to stop carrying a gun, but I'll keep the broomstick in mind."

"Absolutely works fine as a broom, too," Kitally said proudly.

"Outstanding."

There was a tap on the door. Through the glass, Kitally could see an old man. He was stooped over, and he held tightly to a cane. She put the broomstick back together and set it aside, then hurried over to the door and held it open for the man.

He grunted as he walked inside. When he looked as if he might trip over his own feet, Kitally put out a hand to help him.

"Leave me be," he said.

She did as he said and backed off.

His hands shook as he pulled out the chair in front of Lizzy's desk.

"Hello, Gus," Lizzy said.

"I haven't gotten a call since I was here," the old man said. "We had a deal. I'm here for an update."

Kitally kept waiting for Lizzy to tell the old man off. Since Jared's death, she had zero patience. But she nodded and gestured toward Kitally with her chin. "Gus," she said, "meet my assistant, Kitally. She's the one working your case."

Kitally pulled up a chair and offered Gus a hand. He ignored it. "Your wife was Helsie?"

"That's right."

"I'm sorry for your loss," she said. "I've heard nothing but wonderful things about her. I wish I could have met her."

He looked uncomfortable. His eyes glistened.

"I've been to the Shady Oaks Nursing Home twice now," Kitally told him.

He wore a short-sleeved brown shirt and khakis. His shirt had two big stains on the front. "Go on," he said.

"I met Betty Ackley," Kitally said, speaking loud enough for him to hear. "She told me she knew you. Do you remember her?"

"Stop shouting," he said. "I'm not deaf. And of course I remember Betty," he said angrily. "How could I forget? Everyone's heard of that loudmouth woman. She's always getting into other people's business. She's also the noisiest little bird I've ever met."

"She's the one who sent you the note."

His mouth was open, ready to spit out more venom, no doubt, but he swallowed his words.

"You look surprised," Lizzy said.

"I am," he muttered. "We never had a nice word to say to each other. Why would she help me?"

"Because she loved Helsie and thought of her like a sister," Kitally said.

His Adam's apple bobbed, and then his eyes got all misty again.

"Betty is sure that something fishy is going on at Shady Oaks," Kitally continued. "She believes the answers we need are in the file room at the nursing home, which is why I snuck through Betty's bedroom window the other night."

Lizzy frowned.

"Why did you do that?" Gus asked.

"Because Betty said nobody would be around at night."

He shook his head. "She's addle-brained, I tell you . . . a few clowns short of a circus."

Kitally decided to let that one go. "After I climbed through the window, someone was coming, so I had to hide under Betty's bed. I could hear the exchange between the orderly and Betty. The woman forces Betty to take a handful of pills every day, whether she wants to or not."

"I think that's a common practice," Lizzy said. "And it's not unusual for the elderly to try to avoid taking their medication."

Gus waved off whatever Lizzy had to say, his full attention now on Kitally. "Go on."

"Well, the orderly, or whatever the staff people are called, got very upset with Betty. She wanted her to take her sleeping pill like everyone else in the place. Betty told the woman in the green smock that she had, in fact, taken her medication, but I know that's not true."

"How do you know?" Lizzy asked.

"As I was hunkered down in the bushes waiting for Betty to open the window and let me in, I saw a bunch of tablets scattered about the ground. On my way out, I picked up all the pills I could find and brought them home with me. I thought maybe we could take the medication to a lab and find out what they are."

Lizzy tapped the eraser end of the pencil against her chin. "I think that's a good idea."

"I'm going to go back to see Betty later today to talk about how we can get into that file room."

Gus struggled to get out of his chair. "Don't just sit there," he told Kitally. "Help me up."

"You're leaving?"

He poked the ground with his cane in frustration and said, "You're coming with me."

Kitally helped Gus to his feet and then handed him his cane. "Where are we going?"

"To the nursing home," Lizzy said.

He pointed a crooked finger at Lizzy. "Maybe you should come instead." He tilted his head toward Kitally. "Seems like the chimney's clogged in this one."

"Hey," Kitally said, pretty sure he was making fun of her. "This is my case."

"Well, then start paying attention."

Kitally rolled her eyes.

"I saw that," he said.

"We'll take my car," Kitally told him as they made slow progress toward the door.

"Not in my lifetime. We'll take my car."

Kitally winced. "Maybe I should follow you."

"Maybe you should learn to follow orders."

Kitally looked over her shoulder at Lizzy, but she wasn't even paying attention. Her expression already grave, her thoughts had wandered to a different place and time.

CHAPTER TWENTY-EIGHT

The first thing Kobi Millard noticed when she returned home after a long day filled with meetings and phone calls was that the door was unlocked. With her fingers clasped around the doorknob, she slowly pushed open the door. "Valerie?" she called as she stepped inside. "Val, are you here?"

Usually the television was on and she would find her ten-year-old daughter eating a pudding or some other snack she wasn't supposed to eat before dinner. Her pace quickened as she made her way to Val's bedroom. Her gaze fell on the backpack lying on the bed. "Val!" she said again. She unzipped the backpack. Val's lunch had been eaten. Her papers were crumpled; everything appeared as it should.

Kobi's heart dropped to her stomach. Valerie walked home from school every day. Though sometimes, if it rained, she would catch a ride with their neighbor, Gretchen Myers, downstairs.

Kobi whipped around and sprinted out of the apartment, almost tripped over her feet as she ran down the stairs and to the apartment beneath hers. She knocked on the door, didn't stop until someone opened it.

"Kobi, what's wrong?"

She stepped inside, looked around the kitchen, ignored all the surprised faces looking at her as if she'd lost her mind. "Is Val here?"

Gretchen followed her inside. "No. I haven't seen her today." She looked at her kids on the couch. "Have any of you seen Val today?"

Head shakes and grunts. None of them had.

"Her backpack is on the bed," she told Gretchen as she headed for the door. "She ate her lunch." Kobi willed herself not to fall apart. "Oh, God, where is she?"

"Take a breath," Gretchen told her. "Remember that time when she went to the park on the corner without asking, and you just about ripped her to shreds after you—"

Kobi didn't let her finish. She took off running again. Tears made it hard to see clearly as she ran down the street. "Val!" she shouted. "Where are you? Val!"

"Mom! I'm over here."

Kobi wiped her eyes as she headed for the swing set. And then she saw him. Wayne Bennett was sitting on the bench, watching her daughter swing. He had a self-satisfied smile on his face.

She walked over to her daughter. "Get off the swing now. We're going home."

"What's wrong? Have you been crying?"

"Why would you leave the house with a perfect stranger?"

"He said he knew you and that he was a friend of the family. He said he offered you a job with lots of money and that you were still thinking about it."

Wayne Bennett joined them. He put a hand on Valerie's chin and said, "Your daughter is so damn beautiful."

Valerie blushed.

"Do you want to do that again sometime, Valerie?" Bennett asked her daughter. "We can go shopping and I'll buy you some brand-new shoes or a pretty dress . . . anything you want."

"Can I, Mom?"

"No. You can't."

"Stay on the swing for a moment, dear," Bennett said, "and give me a minute to talk to your mom in private."

Valerie looked at her mom.

"It's OK," Kobi assured her. "I'll be right by the bench."

"Next time you talk to someone," Bennett told her when they were out of earshot, "you won't ever see your daughter again."

"I didn't talk to anyone."

"Not even in the parking lot at Grocery Mart?"

"Lizzy Gardner came after *me*, followed *me* from work. I told her to leave me alone and never come near me again."

"What did she want?"

"She wanted me to testify against you in court. She also wanted to know what you did to me."

"Did you tell her?"

Her mouth tightened, and she did everything she could to hold back the tears as she replayed bits and pieces of that night in her head. God, why had she risked telling Lizzy Gardner about Bennett's planned interview with that girl from the program?

Because he was a psycho, and he needed to be stopped.

"How could I tell her anything," she told him, lifting her chin and looking him straight in the eyes, "when I don't recall ever going anywhere with you at all?"

He stood tall. "I hope, for your sake, she believed you. Your daughter is a pretty, pretty girl. If I were you, I would keep a closer eye on her."

Shivers crawled up the back of her neck.

Kobi watched him leave, knowing there wasn't a damn thing she could do to stop him from coming back. She walked back to her daughter and took Val's small hand in hers.

"I'm sorry," Val cried. "I never should have gone with him."

"You and me both."

Hayley sat on the couch, going through the videos from Bennett's rental homes, while Tommy held the baby and made silly noises. Salma was in the kitchen, making a dish called Lahori beef karahi. It didn't smell too good, but Hayley decided to keep that to herself. Although she had to admit she was a little worried that Lizzy might walk through the door, take one whiff, and then kick Salma and her baby right out of the house. Everything seemed to annoy Lizzy lately. Maybe she really was pregnant.

But if she were pregnant, why would she keep it a secret?

Or maybe she didn't realize it herself.

Hayley did some quick math in her head. If Lizzy had conceived within a week or two before Jared was killed, she could or would be almost four months along.

But how could she not know?

Hayley minimized the video application so she could do a quick Internet search instead.

It didn't take long to find what she was looking for. The stats were insane: one in every 450 pregnant women didn't know they were pregnant until week twenty. Approximately one in every seven thousand pregnancies was unknown to the mother until the moment she delivered her baby. And there seemed to be a lot of reasons for this: the position of the placenta, no morning sickness, denial, irregular periods, weight gain or weight loss, and stress.

But Lizzy Gardner wasn't like most women. She would know. Hayley decided to drop the notion altogether. She looked at Tommy and said, "Could you stop that?"

"What's the problem?"

"That noise you've been making with the kid for the past ten minutes is annoying as hell. I'm trying to concentrate."

"You don't have to be a bitch about it."

She held back a smile. It was the first time he'd called her out. Ever. And for some reason, she liked it. The two of them had spent most of the day driving around looking for the Ghost. They were both tired. She clicked the video back on. After another five minutes, a room popped up. There was a couch and an end table with a lamp. Hayley sat upright as a woman appeared on the screen.

She fast-forwarded through the video, unable to believe what she was seeing. Once she got to the end, she hit Rewind until she was at the beginning and hit Pause. She looked over at Tommy and said, "We got the bastard."

Tommy leaned over so he could watch.

Salma had stepped out of the kitchen to check on the baby, and now she hovered over them, too.

"We've got a hit," Hayley said, "and it's not pretty." She moved the cursor to the arrow and started the video over.

There was no sound.

A young woman of about eighteen years of age, wearing a fuchsia dress and black heels, walked into the living area. She appeared to be alone. The camera had a full-bodied picture of her as she took a seat on the couch. She sat on its edge, her fingers entwined in her lap. She looked around the room. Her legs were drawn tightly together.

"She looks so nervous," Salma said.

The girl looked to the right, to a place inside the house that they couldn't see because of the angle of the camera. She smiled then, a nervous, tentative smile.

That's when a man came into view. He was dressed in a dark fitted suit, and he stood directly in front of the girl, his back to the camera. He handed her a drink. They couldn't see his face, but he had the same salt-and-pepper hair and big ears as Wayne Bennett. *Turn around*, Hayley thought to herself, *and show us your face.*

"Are they talking?" Salma asked.

"It's hard to tell at this point," Hayley said. "But I already scanned through the video. You'll get the complete picture of what's going on in a few minutes. You might not want to watch this."

The man caught on tape walked out of the room, leaving the girl sitting alone on the couch once again.

"I'm going to fast-forward through part of this," Hayley said. "The girl basically sips the drink as she looks around, her eyes darting from side to side. She definitely appears to be concerned about what's happening. It won't take long before you'll see a change in her demeanor. I think it's pretty clear she's been drugged."

Hayley moved the cursor on the bottom of the video, speeding through the video. When she stopped fast-forwarding, the young woman was slumped back onto the couch. The back of her hand went to her forehead. Her other hand grasped at the arm of the couch as if she was trying to pull herself upright.

The man with the salt-and-pepper hair entered the room again.

Only this time he was naked.

As he did the first time he'd entered the room, he came to stand directly in front of the woman. They appeared to be talking because you could see the woman using her hands as if she was explaining something to him. Her fingers then grasped the edge of the couch, and she again tried to raise herself to her feet. At that moment they had a clear shot of her face. She said the word *no* more than once and then tried to push him out of her way, but she looked confused and dizzy, clearly losing control of her motor skills.

The man placed his hands on her shoulders and pushed her back down on the couch. He then used those same hands to grasp the back of her head and pull her to him.

"Oh, my God," Salma said, "he's not going to—"

The woman was struggling now, still trying to push him away. She used her fingernails to claw at the back of his thigh, drawing blood. His right hand curled into a fist, and he drew back and punched her in the face.

Salma gasped and then scooped her baby out of Tommy's arms and hurried away.

The woman in the video was lying on the couch, crying. Wayne Bennett looked toward the kitchen, giving the camera a full view of his face. He wiped his brow, turned back to her, and proceeded to undress her.

Hayley stopped the video there. "I think we've seen enough. I need to call Lizzy."

Kitally hung on tightly to the grab handle and prayed for her life.

Gus could drive about as well as he could walk. He'd already gone through two yellow lights and had been honked at by three drivers. By the time they pulled into the Shady Oaks parking lot, she was just glad to be alive.

Kitally climbed out of the car and waited for Gus to do the same.

The trunk popped open.

"Don't just stand there," he said. "Get my walker."

"Make up your mind," she muttered.

"What's that? Are you being difficult?"

She pulled out his walker, unfolded the metal legs, and made sure it was ready to go before she placed it in front of him. "I'm not being difficult, Mr. Valentine. I just think you need to decide whether you want help or you don't want help."

He grunted. "Right now I want help."

"There you go."

The way he shook made her wonder if he had the onset of Parkinson's. Her phone vibrated. She pulled it from her pocket. There was a text from her mom asking Kitally to give her a call when she had time.

"Just what the world needs," he said as he took short, gingerly steps.

"What are you talking about?"

"Those contraptions that young people hold so dear to them. Everyone is attached to machines all day long. Nobody wants to stop and enjoy the sun in their face or sit on a bench and just look around for a bit, maybe do a little people watching. People need to take a minute to breathe without worrying about that Internet nonsense."

"It's sort of fun being connected to the world," Kitally told him. "You can play games with your friends in another country if you wanted to."

"It's nothing more than a tracking device. They're watching you. Right now. Everyone knows what you're doing."

"So, what's the plan?" Kitally asked him, trying to change the subject. "You do have one, don't you?"

"We're going to use the oldest trick in the book."

"What's that?"

"I'm going to distract them while you run into the room where they keep the files and get whatever it is you need."

Kitally walked ahead and opened the door for him. "We need to talk to Betty first," she said as he walked inside without so much as a grunt or a dirty look. "She's the one who needs to tell me what exactly I'm looking for."

"Fine. We'll get the old badger first, but if she starts flirting with me, I'm gonna have to put a stop to it. All the old ladies in this joint like to follow me around as if they've never seen a man before."

"Well, you are an incredibly charming man," Kitally said.

"Is that sarcasm I'm noting?"

"Are you kidding me? If I were thirty years older, I'd be chasing after you myself."

He chuckled at that.

Kitally followed him inside and let the door swing shut behind her.

Two hours after Hayley had called Lizzy with the news that they had video images of Wayne Bennett assaulting and sexually abusing a young woman, Lizzy walked into the office of Prosecuting Attorney Grady Orwell.

The man was short, with fiery-orange hair. His suit was wrinkled and his face was pale, probably due to too many hours behind a desk.

Grady shook Lizzy's hand with a strong grip, then gestured for her to take a seat in the leather chair in front of his desk.

"Thanks for agreeing to meet with me on such short notice."

"Not a problem," Grady said. "I've heard a lot about you. When I was told you had some damning evidence against Wayne Bennett, you can bet I was interested to see what you had."

"You sound passionate about this case," Lizzy said.

"And you sound surprised."

"I guess I am. Bennett has managed to get a lot of very important people in Sacramento to side with him. I thought maybe you might be one of them."

"I think it's safe to say I was as pissed off as you were when I got the news that the bastard was released on some absurd technicality."

Lizzy decided she liked Grady Orwell. "Let's get to it, then." She handed him a file along with a flash drive. Then she set up her laptop on his desk and played the video.

Together they watched Wayne Bennett drug a young woman and ruin yet another person's life. After the screen went black, Grady leaned back in his chair and took a quiet moment to think about what he'd just seen. "I've talked to a lot of people who dislike Wayne Bennett for one reason or another," he said matter-of-factly. "I knew what he was capable of, but seeing him in action leaves an extremely bad taste in my mouth. Do you know the name of the young woman in the tape?"

"I do. It's all in the file."

"I am assuming you obtained this video illegally."

"The file was left at my doorstep, and so, of course, I have no way of knowing how the video was obtained or who is responsible."

"Of course."

"My plan," Lizzy went on, "is to make contact with the woman in the video and see if she's willing to appear in court and swear before the judge. I have no plans to tell her about the tape."

"I do need testimony to build my case," he said approvingly.

"If you look in the file, you'll see a handwritten declaration signed by Olimpia Padula, another young woman who was assaulted by Bennett. Not only is she willing to tell her story in front of a jury, she's eager to do so."

Grady opened the file and read through the woman's statement. "This is good. We both know the judge will rule out the use of the taped video as 'tainted' and therefore inadmissible in court, but I'm going to show it to the judge anyhow. It won't hurt for him to see Wayne Bennett as the monster he truly is. But this," he said, tapping Olimpia Padula's declaration, "is a gold mine."

"Is there any way you can persuade the judge to place Olimpia Padula in some sort of protection program to prevent possible retaliation or further intimidation?"

"Not a chance."

"That's what I was afraid of." Lizzy gathered her things, including her laptop, and then stood and looked Grady square in the eyes. "He must be stopped."

"You're preaching to the choir. I've been working to put Bennett away for years."

"At the very least, he should be arrested and locked up for threatening witnesses."

"I agree."

"But your hands have been tied," Lizzy stated.

"I think you know why."

"He's bribing the whole lot of them."

Grady Orwell's silence said it all. He thanked Lizzy and walked her to the door. "We'll get him eventually. In the end, good will triumph. It always does."

"You believe that?"

He didn't answer, but before Lizzy could disappear completely, he called her name.

She stopped and turned his way. "What is it?"

"Don't stop."

She lifted a questioning brow.

"Don't stop looking. Don't stop pushing. If we're ever going to get this guy, it's going to be because you never stopped pushing for answers. Just don't stop."

CHAPTER TWENTY-NINE

Claire woke to the sound of a woman's voice. At first she thought she was hearing things, but then she heard it again. Someone was there, and they were calling out, asking if anyone was home.

"I'm in here!" Claire said, her voice raspy and hoarse. "I'm down here! Please let me out!" It was no use. They would never hear her. She grabbed the piece of wood she had finally dislodged from the wine rack last night and used it, along with her fists, to pound on the door.

It felt like forever before the metal slot creaked open. The eyes looking through the opening did not belong to the lunatic who had brought her here.

"Who's in there?"

"It's Claire Kerley. Help me, please. Get me out of here."

"Why are you in there?"

"I've been kidnapped," she said, her voice struggling to be heard. "I want out! Please!"

Claire saw the doorknob moving. Her breathing quickened at the thought of escaping. "There's a key somewhere in that room," Claire said, her body pressed against the door. "Maybe on the ledge above the door."

"It's not there. Let me check—oh, here it is, on a hook. I found it!"

Claire stepped back.

The door opened. A stream of light spilled in through a tiny window at the bottom of the stairs.

The woman entered the wine cellar and staggered back, gagging at the smell. Her gaze fell on all the bruises covering Claire's legs and arms. She wore a dirty T-shirt and nothing else. "What is going on? Did Zachary do this to you?"

"I don't know what his name is, but he's crazy and we need to get out of here!"

Claire pushed past the woman and made her way to the stairs. Her legs wobbled, forcing her to use the wall for support. "Get out of here while you can," Claire told the woman as she made her way up the stairs. "He could be back any minute now."

Confused, the woman heeded her advice and followed close behind.

As soon as Claire made it to the landing, the front door opened.

He's home.

As soon as he'd pulled his car into the driveway and seen a car he didn't recognize parked in front of his house, he'd known something was wrong, especially since nobody was sitting inside the vehicle.

He hurried up the walkway toward the house. When he came through the front door he found himself face-to-face with Claire. She stood at the top of the stairs, frozen in place. Her hair was tangled, her eyes big and round and filled with panic.

He shut the door, slid the extra dead bolts into place, and then slipped the padlock through the chain and clicked it into position. "Where do you think you're going?"

She screamed at the top of her lungs, but the sound that came out was a whimpering cry at best.

He had to stop her. He pounced, wrapped his arms around her waist, and pulled her close to him, her back to his chest. He clamped his other hand over her mouth to keep her quiet.

Just then, a woman appeared at the top of the stairs.

"Gillian," he said, struggling a bit to hold Claire still, "what a surprise. What the hell are you doing here?"

"After our last conversation, I was worried about you. Reasonably so, it appears. Let the girl go, Zachary."

The woman's ability to stay calm under fire wasn't lost on him. She was a rock. Sadly for her, she had a rock for a brain as well. "How did you find me?"

"According to files your parents kept on you, this was your last known address. I should have paid you a visit years ago. Your refusal to open a bank account should have raised a red flag."

He sighed. "Having you make yearly deposits to Jake Polly's account in the Cayman Islands should have also given you pause." He shook his head in wonder. "I will never understand why my parents left you in charge of their trust."

"They trusted me to look after you. Now, please," she said, "let the girl go."

"I can't. She's mine."

"What do you plan to do with her?"

"What do you think?"

Claire had continued to thrash annoyingly in his arms, and now she managed to bite his hand. He squeezed her so hard, she gasped for air.

"When we first met," Gillian dumbly persisted as if he actually gave a fuck what she had to say, "I asked you if you ever had dark thoughts about killing."

"I remember every word."

"I asked you if you ever entertained thoughts of killing your parents."

"And I said *never*."

"But you were lying."

He grinned.

"Everything you told me that day and since was a lie."

"Of course they were all lies." He released one of his hands from Claire now that she was docile and used it to pull his hair in frustration. "Yes, Gillian, I killed my parents and every woman I could get my hands on. You are the worst fucking psychologist in the world. I killed a few children and an old man, too. I killed my own sister, and I can't wait to kill you."

Gillian's eyes widened as if she finally understood her fate. The woman gave dimwits a bad name. She ran past him toward the living area. He couldn't have her screaming from the balcony. Tossing Claire to the side, he went after Gillian, grabbed her by the hair, and whirled her to him, driving his knee into her stomach. She crumbled to the floor, and he dragged her toward the kitchen.

Claire, he noticed, had given up on getting out the front door. A smart move, considering the number of dead bolts, not to mention the padlock that would need a key to unlock.

He heard her clattering down the hallway. He wasn't worried. She no longer had much of a voice. All that screaming had destroyed her vocal cords. She would have to jump nearly fifteen feet out the window if she wanted to get away.

Gillian wasn't a big lady, but she was tall, which made her quite an unwieldy load. She clawed at his hands and arms, doing her best to get away, but frankly, she had no muscle and no drive. All in all, she was a bit of a dud.

He knew Claire wouldn't jump, but he didn't like the idea of her running loose in the house. Picking up his pace, he dragged

Gillian to the kitchen. She surprised him when she twisted her body and pulled free, leaving a massive clump of hair entwined in his fist. Dropping the hair, he went for the sharpest knife he could find.

"Your sister and your parents have forgiven you," Gillian cried as she staggered out of the kitchen and careened toward the front door.

She tried to open the door, gave up, and turned toward him. "It's time to put a stop to this madness, Zachary."

Knife clutched tightly in his hand, he walked toward her.

Before she could say another word, he plunged the blade into her chest.

He took one glance at her eyes and then guided her, by the knife's handle—she was holding it with him now, gently, with both her hands—toward the kitchen, where her mess would be easier to clean up. He didn't care about Gillian. He never would have gone after her at all if she hadn't come for a visit.

The woman took her sweet time dying, standing before him in the middle of the kitchen, both hands still clutched around the handle of the knife. But the poor girl didn't have the strength to pull the blade from her chest. Bored, he watched her until she fell almost gracefully to the floor.

He released a long laborious sigh, leaned over her, and removed the knife with a good, sturdy yank. "You never should have come. If it weren't for you, Gillian, my parents would still be alive. As much as I wanted to kill them over the years, I refrained. They were my parents, after all. But then you came along and stuck your nose into my affairs."

With the bloody knife in hand, he turned back the other way and made his way down the hallway. "Claire, my dear, come out, come out, wherever you are."

He stopped to listen.

Silence. Not a peep.

He walked quietly into the master bedroom.

The window was open, as he suspected it would be. He poked his head out and took a moment to breathe in the fresh air and enjoy the lovely view. If his finances hadn't been controlled by Gillian, he would own the house. He would have added on to the balcony off the main room, so it swept around the entire house. A shame really, to waste such a beautiful view with one useless window. If he did a good job of disposing of her body and car, it occurred to him, he might just have that balcony, after all.

He looked straight down at the hard-packed soil directly below the window. No sign that Claire had jumped. Turning about, he made his way into the bathroom. His fingers curled around the shower curtain. He jerked it back, expecting to find Claire, shivering in fear.

No such luck.

"Claire," he called again. "Come out now and I won't punish you for trying to run off. It was Gillian's doing. We both know that."

He crossed the room. Blood dripped from the sharp blade of his favorite carving knife.

"Don't make me search for too long. I've had an exhausting day."

Before opening the mirrored closet doors, he stopped to admire his reflection. He was quite a good-looking fellow, if he did say so himself. His teeth were straight and white, no stains at all. His eyes were piercing. His nose, although crooked, was not too big, not too small. He had yet to paint a self-portrait, but he could not lie, the idea intrigued him.

His fingers touched the edge of the closet door and slowly, almost lovingly, he slid it open. Anticipation filled him with excitement.

But then his heart sank.

She was sitting in the corner. And she wasn't even going to bother putting up a fight. Instead, her arms were wrapped tightly around her knees, which were pulled up close to her chest.

"Claire," he said. "Did you really think you could get away from me?"

Her head was bent forward, and she seemed to be sniffling like a baby.

"This was the best you could do?" He'd expected more from her, his little fighter. "Don't be a coward, Claire. The reason I like you so much is that you're a bit sassy and unconventional."

He nudged her with the tip of his shoe. "Come on," he urged. "I feel a second wind coming on. I think it's time to paint another portrait." He reached down and touched her arm.

Her head snapped up, her expression fierce. She reached out and slashed his arm with something sharp. A goddamn hanger.

Blood trickled down his arm.

The little bitch didn't stop there. She lashed out, again and again, hitting flesh every time, across his arm and then his neck. But he felt no pain. He welcomed it. Simply put, he would never allow little Claire to get the best of him. He lifted the knife in his hand and slashed her across the right shoulder, rendering her arm useless.

End of story.

She fell back.

He tossed the knife and then took hold of her good arm and dragged her out of the closet and down the hallway. "Big mistake, Claire."

She kicked and hissed, growled like a dying wildcat. Even if she'd been able to muster a scream, she'd come to accept it would be pointless. He dragged her all the way to the front entry, where Gillian's corpse lay. The bitch had managed to crawl out of the kitchen, making a mess of his front entry, after all. He took a handful of Claire's hair at the back of her head and shoved her face closer to Gillian's. "In case you didn't realize it, she's dead."

Claire let out a whimpering cry.

"Yes, yes, I know. So very sad."

He shoved her face closer until her lips touched Gillian's. An electric current charged through him. "The kiss of death," he said, holding her there. "That's the title of our next painting. I like it, don't you?"

CHAPTER THIRTY

Gus had told Kitally to give him ten minutes before heading for the file room. That was exactly how much time passed before Gus walked by. Kitally and Betty stood in the doorway of Betty's room and watched him.

He was pushing the woman in the wheelchair, the one who liked to caw like a bird, down the middle of the wide corridor. She was in fine voice today.

Behind them trailed a rising cacophony.

Not only had Gus rounded up the bird lady, he had gathered more than a dozen residents, all of them squawking, banging forks against plates, and stomping canes against the floors and walls like a parade accompanied by a marching band. One lady used candleholders as drumsticks. A tall fellow kept leaning over and grabbing handfuls of all the women's butts. Some liked it and some didn't, but the old man didn't seem to care either way. He was having the time of his life.

Bringing up the rear was a hunched-over woman with an amazingly loud voice who kept shouting, "No more pudding! We want cake! We want cake!"

Betty shook her head. "She doesn't like cake, either, but she always wants whatever they don't give her."

"Which way to the file room?" Kitally asked.

Betty looked both ways and then took off in the opposite direction Gus and his posse had gone. The woman was spry, and Kitally had to hurry to keep close to her side. Whenever someone in a green smock ran past, she pretended to be helping Betty along, but that wasn't easy considering the woman didn't need any help.

"Damn," Betty muttered, pulling back from peering around a corner. "The file room is down that hallway. But it looks like Dixie is guarding the post."

Kitally moved ahead of her. "I'll take care of her."

"Hello," Dixie said as they approached the nurses' office. "Glad to see you have your badge on this time."

Betty brightened. "I told you she was a good girl."

"I don't know if someone else has taken care of it," Kitally said, "and I hate to be a tattletale, but I just saw Cecil sneak out through the back door. The one that leads right out to the parking lot."

"Oh, lord." Dixie huffed past them. "Thanks for telling me," she called back, then disappeared around the corner.

"It worked," Kitally said before she realized Betty had already grabbed the file room key from the nurses' office and was making her way down the hall with it. She had the file room open and had disappeared inside before Kitally could catch up.

"Here," she said when Kitally entered the room. "Put the key back on the little hook just inside the nurses' office door and then hurry back."

Kitally did as she said. The file room was exactly that—a twelve-by-twelve room with wall-to-wall filing cabinets. According to Betty, they were looking for any document or file with the names of any of five residents she believed had died under suspicious circumstances: Helsie Valentine, Dennis Turner, Jade Ross, Mary Branham, and Sandy Hutchins.

Kitally came up with something almost immediately, in a basket labeled "To Be Filed" atop the nearest file cabinet. "Well, here's something strange," she said.

"What is it?"

"This is a bill for Helsie Valentine, but the date stamped on the form is for just two days ago. Shady Oaks charged over three hundred dollars for bringing Helsie special meals and delivering packages, and another five hundred dollars for administering medication."

Betty scampered her way and hovered over her. "See if you can find anything on Marty Balch."

Kitally dug through the basket. "Yep, here it is. There's a file for Marty. He was charged for a bed, food, and medication. When did Marty pass away?"

"Nine months ago," Betty said.

"Are you thinking what I'm thinking?"

"Absolutely," Betty said. "They're killing Shady Oaks residents and then filling the beds and collecting double the money."

Betty nudged Kitally to the side and rifled through the files herself. She gasped when she pulled out a file.

"What is it?"

"Lisa Coriell. She died three years ago."

"This has been going on for a while."

They both froze when they heard a voice. It sounded as if Dixie was on the phone.

"Dixie must have returned."

Kitally looked at Betty. "What are we going to do?"

"Put this file inside your pants, and button your sweater up."

There was no time to question the idea. Kitally did as she said.

Betty gestured toward the door. "Come on. Let's go."

Kitally locked the door from the inside and pulled it shut after them.

"Act natural," Betty whispered. "Tell Dixie I kept insisting the bathroom was this way."

The minute Dixie noticed them coming up the hallway, she marched up to them and grabbed hold of Kitally's arm.

"Ouch. What are you doing?"

"That's what I want to know. I'm taking you straight to the director. Betty Ackley hasn't been any trouble for us until you started coming around."

"Betty told me there was a bathroom down the hall," Kitally said in a firm voice. "I've done nothing wrong."

A sniffling and then a mewing cry sounded as Betty began to weep. It was the most pitiful sound Kitally had ever heard. She yanked her arm out of the woman's grasp and turned toward Betty. "What's wrong?"

"I need to go to the bathroom. Why won't any of you take me to the bathroom?"

There was a distinct trickling noise, and something splashed against Kitally's ankle.

Dixie and Kitally looked down and saw a yellow puddle spreading on the tile between Betty's feet.

"Look what you've done," Kitally said. "You scared her. If you don't let me take care of Betty and get her cleaned up and back to her room, I'm going straight to the police to report you, along with the rest of the staffers in this place!"

"You take her back to her room and clean her up," Dixie said through clenched teeth, "but if I see you inside Shady Oaks again, I'm going to make sure you get thrown out of here. Do we understand each other?"

"That's fine. But you better be ready to do just that, because I'll be checking on Betty from here on out."

Dixie and Kitally stared each other down until Dixie finally gave in and turned away.

Kitally took hold of Betty's elbow and ushered her back to her room, leaving a trail of urine for Dixie to clean up.

"Are you OK?" Kitally asked, her voice low.

"Never been better. I really did have to go."

He stretched out the tarp he'd dragged from the garage and then rolled Gillian's body onto it until she was faceup. He then took a breath and plunked his hands on his hips. She was deadweight, and she was heavy.

He looked around. So much blood had seeped into the cracks and crevices of the stone floor. "Look at this mess you've made, Gillian. Everything was going perfectly until you came along and complicated matters. Are you happy? Huh?"

He kicked her in the side. It felt good, so he did it again.

She just looked at him with that blank, lifeless stare of hers.

Dead or alive—it didn't matter. She looked the same. He'd never once seen any fire in her eyes. Even when she was dying, she'd shown all the animation of a carp.

The nosy bitch had gotten what she deserved. He hated her more than he'd ever hated anyone. For a while there, Gillian had a small semblance of control over him, and he hadn't liked it one bit.

A knock on the door jolted him. His heart rate soared.

Judging by the silhouette, it was a small boy. It was the neighbor, Landon. The boy used his hands to cup both sides of his face as he tried to see through the decorative glass.

"Go away, kid," he said in a loud voice. "I'm busy."

"What are you doing? Are you having a party in there?"

With a sigh, he walked over to the door, unlocked the dead bolt and padlock, then opened the door just an inch or two so he could see the expression on the boy's face, see if the kid knew too much. "Why do you ask?"

"I heard some loud noises. And then just now I heard you talking to someone."

"I had my music on really loud before. And after that you must have heard me singing to myself." *Nosy kid.*

"Oh. Are you painting another picture?"

"Not at the moment."

Landon pointed at his chest. "You've got some red paint on your shirt."

"Oh, well, would you look at that. You're right. I do." He thought about inviting the kid inside and finishing him off, but he had enough on his plate as it was. In any event, his mother chose that moment to call her son back home. "Your mom's calling you. You better skedaddle."

"Skedaddle?"

Get lost, kid. "It means hurry home."

"Oh." The kid turned and ran a few feet before he turned around and said, "I'll see you later, sir."

He shut the door and locked it. He had work to do. And he didn't have much time if he planned to be at the gallery in time for the showing.

Lizzy pulled up in front of her sister's house, turned off the engine, and sat there for a moment in the quiet. The last time she was here, Cathy and Richard had been fighting. Had her sister really left him?

It was time to find out.

She climbed out of the car and was halfway up the walkway when the door opened. Brittany stood there with a grin on her face.

Seeing her niece gave her a burst of energy.

"I can't believe you're here," Brittany said. "I feel as if I haven't seen you in years."

Lizzy took Brittany into her arms, and for the first time in the longest while, she felt a bit of life creep into her. "I've missed you so much," Lizzy said close to her ear.

"I've missed you more."

Taking a step back, Lizzy took a good look at her. She reached for her hair, let the silky strands brush through her fingers. "Your hair is getting so long. You look so grown-up."

"I've been so worried about you, Lizzy."

"I know. I'm sorry. I should have come sooner or at least called. Is everything OK?"

"Everything is good. Dad and Mom are getting divorced. They don't belong together, but you already know that."

Lizzy said nothing.

"And don't worry about not coming around lately. I know you're sad. I just don't want you to ever feel like you're all alone."

Lizzy swallowed a lump in her throat.

Brittany glanced around. "Mom had to go to work today, but if you want to come in for a bit first—"

"No, I'm good. Are you ready to go?"

Brittany grabbed her things, and it wasn't long before they were on the freeway, heading for Midtown.

"So," Lizzy said, "I heard that you started art classes. How's that going?"

"I love it. We have more than one instructor teaching the class. The teachers are inspiring, and the students are talented. I can't believe I was accepted."

For the next twenty minutes, they chatted, catching up on Brittany's life. Lizzy enjoyed listening to the sound of her voice. It was like hearing a song she'd forgotten she loved.

It wasn't easy finding a parking spot since many streets had been closed off from traffic, but they managed. The crowds were thick and the music was loud, a different musician on every other street corner. The first gallery they visited was the Phoenix Art Gallery. The art was interesting, and they had fun exploring. Lizzy noticed one particular painting where a magistrate in ancient Rome was carrying a bundle of rods with a projecting axe blade. "Look at that," Lizzy said. "A fasces."

"Good job," Brittany said. "I just took a test on symbols in art. A fasces is commonly used as a symbol of power."

"I knew it represented power, but I had no idea it was used in art."

"Yep," Brittany said.

This tidbit of information got Lizzy's mind working overtime. "What are some other symbols?"

"Oh, gosh, there are lots of them. For instance, a book could symbolize learning or transmitting knowledge. A clock might symbolize the passing of time."

Lizzy couldn't help but wonder if the objects being left on the Sacramento Strangler's victims could have anything to do with art. "What about a piece of coral?"

"Definitely. The red of coral often represents the blood of Christ. Since when are you so interested in art and symbolism?"

"It has to do with a case I'm working on."

As they moved through the gallery, Brittany examined the artwork and paintings at close range while Lizzy examined each painting for something more. The idea that a piece of red coral could represent the blood of anyone hit an investigative nerve. They were on to something here. Her niece stopped and pointed at one particular painting and said, "See the distaff, the wooden tool right here?"

"What does it mean?" Lizzy asked.

"The distaff could represent the domestic role of women," Brittany explained. "And this picture over here has a mirror lying on the bedside table. The mirror often signifies truth or vanity."

It felt as if every molecule in her body were tingling as Lizzy followed her niece along, listening intently as she talked.

"The cool thing about symbols is they can evoke powerful emotions without the beholder even realizing it."

"Really? That's amazing," Lizzy said. "So, what about a wreath of red roses around a young man's head?"

Brittany took a moment to ponder before she said, "I don't know if that's a common symbol in art, but are you talking about Picasso's *Boy with a Pipe*?"

"I don't know. What does it look like?"

Brittany pulled out her phone, clicked away, and then showed her an image of a boy with a garland of roses around his head. "It's oil on canvas," Brittany explained. "It's actually a painting of a local boy who used to visit Picasso's studio. The painting went for one hundred million dollars at auction in 2004."

Lizzy could hardly contain her excitement. It couldn't be a coincidence. Maybe it was a long shot, but right now it seemed more than possible that the Sacramento Strangler could be involved in the art world.

After visiting the Phoenix Art Gallery, and then checking out some handmade jewelry being sold by local vendors on the sidewalk, they stopped in Ginger Elizabeth's for some gourmet chocolates. Some of the other galleries they visited were devoted to photography. Although, after learning so much about symbolism in art, it was hard to concentrate on anything but the killer running loose in the area, Lizzy did her best to focus on her niece and their time together.

Their last stop before they headed off for dinner was the largest gallery they had been to so far. While Brittany admired two extraordinary Peter Max paintings, Lizzy found herself mesmerized by a contemporary picture of a woman stretched out on a raft, the fingers on her left hand brushing against clear blue water. Everything about the picture seemed to express a feeling of relaxation, and it might have done just that if not for the eyes. The eyes spoke volumes—enormous and round and frozen in terror. The woman on the raft was anything but tranquil. She was—

"That's intense," Brittany said as she stepped close to her side.

"I would say so."

"Brittany," a male voice called out, "so happy to see you here. And exploring one of my paintings, no less."

The voice was familiar. Lizzy turned to see who was talking.

"And you," he said, wagging a finger at Lizzy. "Don't we know each other?"

"This is my aunt, Lizzy Gardner."

He snapped his fingers. "Of course."

"Lizzy, this is Jake Polly. He taught one of the classes I was telling you about."

Lizzy looked at him sideways. "You put up the poster in our window. This is your painting?"

"It certainly is. What do you think?"

Lizzy's gaze fell on his hands, where she saw deep scratches that disappeared beneath the sleeves of his shirt.

"I don't know anything about art," Lizzy told him, "but your painting is definitely interesting. There's so much going on, and yet it's the woman's eyes that draw me in."

"I agree," Brittany said.

"Is this lady on the raft supposed to be relaxing, or is she scared?"

"She's having the time of her life," he said. "She's in heaven."

"I'm not seeing that."

Brittany touched Lizzy's shoulder, trying to stop Lizzy from embarrassing her, no doubt. "I don't think he wants us to critique his work, Aunt Lizzy."

Lizzy didn't pay her any mind. "Do you have models you work with, Jake, or did you use a photograph?"

"It's OK," he told Brittany. "I believe everyone should make up their own mind about art. *The Lady on the Raft* could be telling a story or making a statement. But none of that matters. It's all about how it makes you feel, Lizzy."

They spoke for some time about how he'd gone about painting the picture before them. No, he'd used neither a model nor a photograph, conjuring the woman out of whole cloth—"Except for the eyes," he said, his own eyes gleaming. Lizzy never lost her feeling that there was something very odd about the man, and yet he was kind enough to answer her questions, and he seemed genuinely interested in explaining things to her.

"Well," Lizzy said at last, "it's certainly a powerful piece."

"Well, art *is* powerful. Isn't that right, Brittany?"

"Definitely," Brittany answered. "There's nothing like the emotion I feel when I look at paintings I love."

Jake Polly beamed at her, then turned to Lizzy. "She's very bright," he said. "It's all about what you feel inside here." He put a hand over his heart. "The beauty of artwork is that it can challenge preconceived ideas."

"I didn't realize looking at a painting could be so thought-provoking."

"Well, maybe not a still life. A bowl of lemons might not have a deeper meaning." He winked at Brittany. "But who am I to say?"

"You do amazing work," Brittany told him, blushing.

"Nice of you to say." He looked at his watch. "Time has gotten the best of me. I need to meet up with friends. But first I must thank you, Lizzy Gardner, for letting me put the flyer in your window."

She nodded, but she couldn't help it—she didn't like the man and didn't appreciate the way he ogled Brittany.

"See you in class," he told Brittany before sauntering away.

CHAPTER THIRTY-ONE

Olimpia Padula turned on the bathwater and then went to the bedroom, where she sat on the edge of the bed and removed her heels and stockings. She had worked a ten-hour shift today, and her feet were throbbing. She massaged the arches of both feet and then removed the rest of her clothes before heading back into the bathroom.

She adjusted the temperature of the water as the tub filled, then readied her towel and made sure she had everything she needed for a long, hot bath. Soaking in the tub was better than enjoying a glass of wine while watching the sunset. It was her favorite thing to do.

She rushed back into the bedroom when she realized she'd forgotten her mask that she liked to put over her eyes. She turned the radio on, something soothing, a little classic soul. Last, she added some lavender oil to the water. She shut the faucet off and then dipped her toes in first. *Perfect.*

After settling fully into the tub, she slid her mask over her eyes and laid her head back on the bath pillow. Her only thought was how lucky she was to have found a full-time job. In three months' time she would have full benefits. Life was turning around for her. She was going to be all right.

A noise in the other room lifted her out of her thoughts. She slid her mask up to her forehead. "Is anyone there?"

Wayne Bennett stepped into view. He stood within the door frame, his expression grim. "I told you not to talk to anyone. Did you think I was kidding?"

How the hell did he get inside her apartment? Nobody had a key but her. "I think you should leave," she told him, unwilling to stand up while she was unclothed. He'd seen it all, but he wasn't going to get another free show. When he failed to listen to her demands, panic set in. "Get out of here right now, or I will scream."

"I don't think you should do that," he said as he stepped closer. "Do you know what I think you should do?"

Bewildered, she shook her head.

"I think you should die." He knelt swiftly beside the tub and, his big hands covering her face, shoved her under the water and held her down. She thought she could fight him, but he was too strong, and he was right . . . she was gonna die.

After dropping Brittany off, Lizzy made a call to Jessica.

"Hey," Jessica said when she answered, "what's going on?"

"Are you in the middle of something?"

"Just packing and getting ready to fly back to California."

"I wanted to call and see if you found anything on Zachary Tucker, the name I gave you after talking to Kathryn Church."

"If you have time," Jessica told her, "I'll grab my notes and tell you what I've found."

"I've got time. I'm driving home, and you're on speaker."

When Jessica came back on the line, she said, "This is what I know so far. Zachary H. Tucker was born to Phil and Patty Tucker on September 20, 1977, and his little sister drowned in July of

1985. There is nothing that even hints at the possibility that Zachary was responsible for his sister's death. Besides, he was eight years old at the time."

"You said yourself that there are serial killers as young as ten years old."

"I did, didn't I? Anyhow," Jessica went on, "as you mentioned last time we talked, if Kathryn Church saw Zachary kill his sister, it seems farfetched. She was in another house altogether. Her view could have very easily been distorted, and she was very young at the time."

"Maybe I can visit the house where they used to live and see what Kathryn's view would have looked like. Where were the Tuckers living at the time? Do you know?"

"It's right here. They were living at 3500 Canyon Road in Sacramento at the time of the incident, but after Zachary turned eighteen, they moved to Florida. After that, it gets fuzzy."

"What do you mean?"

"On paper, it looks as if he disappeared off the face of the earth. I cannot find a Social Security number for this particular Zachary Tucker. That'd tell me a lot. As you know, a person is required to apply for an SSN when they start their first job. But it doesn't appear as if his parents ever applied for Social Security numbers for their children. Before 1986, many people didn't bother obtaining an SSN until somewhere between the ages of fourteen and sixteen. Perhaps Zachary Tucker never worked a day in his life. If that were the case, he could have stayed under the radar if he changed his name and got a driver's license using his new name."

"How about a picture of a young Zachary Tucker?"

"That's where it gets even weirder. Five years ago, Patty and Phil Tucker were killed during a robbery. According to the reports, jewelry was taken, but the only person they could rely on for that information was Gillian Winslow. It looks like Zachary's parents hired Winslow to take care of everything. Their will even stipulates that she's to be Zachary's trustee until the day he dies. She's a psychologist. It seems strange that these people would hire a psychologist for their son and then put her in charge of everything. I don't get it. I called Gillian Winslow's office. Her secretary said she should be back to work next week."

"Are you saying there is absolutely no paper trail or anything else for this man?"

"That's exactly what I'm saying. We need to talk to Gillian Winslow. And that's not all—it gets even more bizarre."

"How so?"

"It was easy enough to find out what elementary school Zachary Tucker attended. Every classroom in every school I've ever heard of takes a class picture, and the school he attended was no exception."

"But?"

"But somehow Zachary managed to miss picture day every single year from kindergarten through the eighth grade."

"That is curious."

"Unquestionably."

"It sounds like our only hope is the psychologist."

"That's right." There was a shuffling of papers on the other end before Jessica said, "Anything else on your mind?"

"As a matter of fact, there is. Brittany and I just returned from a Second Saturday Art Walk near Midtown."

"I'm glad you had a chance to spend time together."

"So am I. She's definitely passionate about art. But the reason I'm bringing this up is because I learned a lot about symbolism used in artwork, and I think you're going to find it all very interesting."

"Go on."

"This might sound like a crapshoot, but the objects in those pictures Kenneth Mitchell showed me might actually mean something when it comes to symbolism and art. According to Brittany, books, mirrors, you name it—even the fasces—all have special meaning."

"Are you suggesting the killer we're looking for could be an artist?"

"Yeah, that's what I'm thinking . . . maybe a painter. It might be wise to zero in on the art world in general. He might be a curator or an art dealer."

"This is good, Lizzy. I'll talk to Mitchell."

"Get your things packed and get back here so we can find this guy."

"Will do," Jessica said, "but there's one more thing."

Lizzy waited.

"Did you hear about the missing girl?"

"I believe so. Claire Kerley?"

"That's right. Seventeen-year-old girl missing for quite a while now."

"You're thinking there's some connection to the Strangler?"

"I think it's a possibility, though Mitchell has his doubts. As far as we know, the Strangler's never hid his victims before, and there's no trace of this girl. Just based on the last three homicides, it's clear the killer is acting randomly, but what if that's his plan? To make it look random and throw everyone off the track with all the recent killings so he can grab a girl and keep her for a while before he kills her? He's escalating all along, and that could be the next level."

"He must know with all the budget cuts there aren't enough investigators to go around."

"Exactly. He's spreading us thin investigating the rash of killings, which is why they called me in to help in the first place."

"Anything I can do?"

"Just be careful, OK? If Jared was close to naming this guy, you could already be in his line of fire."

"I haven't noticed anyone watching me," Lizzy said. "No hang-up phone calls."

"If the Sacramento Strangler is the same guy who took the girl, then he's not going to be hiding behind trees watching you."

"Well, that's a relief."

"No," Jessica said. "It's not. This killer is getting increasingly brazen. He wouldn't be hiding at all. He would be watching you up close and personal. Just be careful. That's all I'm asking."

"I always am," Lizzy said, although she didn't like what she was hearing. "I'll see you tomorrow."

Lizzy disconnected the call as she pulled into the driveway of Kitally's house.

Hayley was sitting on the curb, smoking a cigarette.

Lizzy got out of the car and headed that way. "I thought you were quitting."

"I am." She took another drag off the cigarette and then stamped it out in the gutter.

Lizzy took a seat next to her, and they both stared out into the woods across the street.

"Life is so fucked up."

"It's hell," Lizzy agreed.

"People are stupid and selfish."

"I hate people."

"Sometimes I don't know why I even bother getting out of bed."

"Wasted energy, for sure."

Hayley sighed. "Salma is back."

"I heard."

"What are we going to do with her?"

"It's Kitally's house. I guess it's her problem."

"Good point."

"Has she named the baby yet?"

"No. I don't think she's going to, either. Is it a law?" Hayley asked. "Does everyone have to have a given name?"

"No idea."

"I can't imagine they would lock her up for not naming her kid."

Lizzy shrugged. "It wouldn't surprise me."

Hayley snorted. "You are so right. They would lock Salma up, but not one of the many rapists running around town."

Kitally drove up and pulled her car into the driveway next to Lizzy's. She exited the car, hit the lock, and then joined them on the curb.

Kitally didn't say a word, which was unusual. She looked worn-out.

Through an open window, they heard the sound of a baby's cry.

It was going to be another long night.

CHAPTER THIRTY-TWO

Donna Smith, it turned out, was the name of the young woman they had seen on the video being sexually assaulted by Wayne Bennett. She lived with her family in a tiny apartment in West Sacramento. The apartment building was dingy. Garbage and cigarette butts littered the ground. The elderly woman who opened the apartment door and peeked out was a tiny thing. She had a deeply wrinkled face and dark eyes that peered just above the chain. Lizzy assumed she was Donna's mother.

"Who is it?" the woman asked.

"Lizzy Gardner and Hayley Hansen. We're investigating the Wayne Bennett case, and it's very important that we talk to your daughter."

The woman unlatched the chain and opened the door. "Get in here before anyone sees you."

They both stepped inside and then watched as the woman locked the door and hooked the chain back in place. The place was dark. It smelled like old socks and rotted food. It was times like this that Lizzy was glad she carried a gun.

The woman pointed a crooked finger at Lizzy. "I'm going to get Donna. When she appears, you will have five minutes to talk." She put out a hand, palm up. "It'll cost you one hundred dollars."

"To talk to your daughter?" Hayley asked, confused.

This wasn't the first time Lizzy had been asked to pay to get answers. She reached into her purse. "I have sixty-two dollars."

The woman snatched the money out of her hand and then looked at Hayley. "We have to eat, and you want information. Pay or get out."

"I never keep more than a twenty on me, but you can have it." Hayley reached into her back pocket and handed the woman a folded twenty-dollar bill.

The woman took it and then disappeared.

Lizzy and Hayley stepped from the entryway and found a small, well-populated living room. A young girl, about thirteen, stood off to the side, leaning against the wall and watching them warily. She looked just like her eighteen-year-old sister, Donna, who Lizzy had seen on the video with Bennett. Three kids Lizzy guessed to be between the ages of ten and sixteen, all boys, sat packed together on a couch in front of a television turned to a sports channel. From his chair next to the couch, an older man with black hair, tipped with gray, watched Lizzy and Hayley closely. No one said a word. A minute passed before Donna's mother entered the room with her older daughter in tow.

"Here she is. Your time starts now."

The girl didn't look anything like the young woman they had seen on the video. She was badly bruised. Her left eye was nearly swollen shut, and her lip was purple and yellow.

"I'm sorry this happened to you," Lizzy said. "It's terrible."

"Why are you sorry? You didn't do it."

"Because he's not in prison where he belongs."

"What do you want?"

"Will you testify against Wayne Bennett?"

The girl shook her head, but she didn't deny that was the man who did this to her. "I can't."

"Why not?"

"Kobi Millard is a good friend of mine. In case you haven't heard, shortly after you talked to her in the parking lot, Kobi came home to find her ten-year-old daughter missing. Guess where her daughter was?"

Lizzy exchanged looks with Hayley and said nothing. Waited.

"At the neighborhood park with Mr. Bennett. Apparently they'd had a nice couple of hours eating ice cream and playing on the jungle gym. The little girl enjoyed herself so much that she asked her mom if she could do it again. Wayne Bennett just smiled at Kobi and told her how goddamn beautiful her ten-year-old daughter was."

Donna paused for a breath. "It was a warning. Not just for Kobi, but for all of us. Which one of us here do you think is going to pay for this little visit of yours?" She gestured toward her little sister and then to her brothers on the couch. "Because one of us will pay—I guarantee it. Maybe we'll all pay."

Hayley stepped in front of Lizzy. "Before you continue on with that holier-than-thou tone, maybe you should stop and think about what you're saying and who you're saying it to. Lizzy isn't getting paid to spend her days on the street, doing everything she can to see that fucker Bennett locked up behind bars. She spends her time working cases like this for one reason only. To help people like you. She doesn't want your little sister over there to get assaulted by some asshole entrepreneur who thinks he owns the world. He's already got you because you're choosing to live in fear for the rest of your life. So fuck you." Hayley looked around the room. "Fuck all of you. And, yes," Hayley said, looking at Donna's mother, "I'm pretty sure I just took an extra minute of your time, and I'm not paying you shit."

Five minutes later, Lizzy and Hayley were in the car heading home.

"That went well," Hayley said.

Lizzy's hands were clenched tightly around the steering wheel. "Wayne Bennett is never going to stop, and there might not be anything we can do about it."

"There's only one way to stop him for good."

Deep down, Lizzy had a horrible inkling that Hayley was right.

CHAPTER THIRTY-THREE

Five o'clock the next day, Hayley heard a knock on the door. Since she was on her way to the kitchen for chips for her bean dip, she stepped to the door and looked out the peephole. "Who is it?"

"Joey Rich."

"That's the father of Salma's baby," Lizzy said from the kitchen table, where she was sitting with her laptop.

Hayley opened the door. "What do you want?"

"Is Salma here?"

"Maybe. What's your business with her?"

The guy looked as if he'd come straight out of business school or maybe accounting. Total geek. His hair was gelled and combed a little too neatly to one side. He wore the standard long-sleeved button-up white shirt, khaki pants, and a belt that looked cinched one notch too tight.

"A girl named Kitally sought me out and told me where Salma was living. I need to talk to her. I would like to meet my daughter."

Hayley looked over her shoulder.

"Let him in," Kitally said.

No sooner had she shut the door than another knock sounded.

"Are you kidding me?" Hayley returned to the door and peeked out. "It's another guy," Hayley said, "only this guy looks a lot like Salma." She opened the door.

"I was told that my sister, Salma, is living here. I would like to speak to her, please."

"Do you have a name?"

"Badar."

Kitally rushed to Hayley's side. "Come in," she said.

Hayley shook her head. What the hell was Kitally thinking by telling everyone where Salma was living?

Kitally ushered Badar into the living area across the room from the other guy, and then she let out a long sigh before disappearing down the hallway. They could all hear her arguing with someone. That someone was Salma, and it wasn't long before Kitally returned with the girl at her side.

Lizzy stood off to the side, her arms crossed. She was not happy.

"Have the two of you met?" Hayley asked Joey.

"No."

"Well, great. Joey, this is Badar, Salma's brother." Hayley then turned to face the brother. "Badar, this is Joey, Salma's boyfriend, and the father of her baby girl who has yet to be named."

Neither of them looked happy or showed any sign of being gentlemen and shaking hands.

Salma looked at Joey. "Why are you here?"

His face turned red. "You're kidding, right?"

She crossed her arms to let him know otherwise.

"I thought we had something good going, and then one day you disappeared from my life, and I haven't heard from you since. You weren't going to ever tell me that we have a daughter?"

Badar puffed out his chest. "You need to shut up," he said. "Look at her! She's much too young to be having babies, much less one of *your* babies."

"Leave him alone, Badar."

"Come on," her brother said, gesturing toward the door. "I'm taking you home. Mother is ready to take you back. She's worried sick."

"If she was so worried, why did she kick me out of the house?"

"Because she was angry. She's been disgraced." He looked at Joey with hatred in his eyes. "And as I told you before, if I ever found out who dishonored our family's name, I would do something about it."

The asshole, Hayley realized, was threatening to hurt Joey, just as Salma had feared.

Salma stiffened. "I would like you to leave."

His nostrils flared. "It makes me sick to know you have given birth to this man's baby. I do not know why Mother will allow you into her home, but it is because of her that I cannot leave without you."

Hayley wanted to drag his ass right out the front door, but she decided to wait and see how this played out and hopefully discover what Salma really wanted. Ultimately, it was her decision to make as to whether she returned home. No matter what happened, Kitally was going to get an earful from both Lizzy and Hayley.

"Is this why you left?" Joey asked Salma. "Because you were afraid for my life? Or because you no longer loved me?"

Her eyes glistened. "I love you, Joey. But this," she said, gesturing between him and her brother. "I cannot live with this."

Badar marched toward his sister and grabbed hold of her arm. "Come on. Let's get the baby and get out of here."

"Let go of her," Joey demanded.

Badar pivoted and took a swing at Joey.

Joey ducked, then threw a good right and an even better left into Badar's gut, doubling him over.

Salma's brother recovered quickly, though, and lunged for Joey, sending them both onto the coffee table and breaking it in half. Hayley's bean dip went flying, splattering the television screen and the floor with brown goop.

Salma and Lizzy shouted for them to stop, but it was too late for that.

They could hear the baby crying in the other room.

The two men wrestled around the room, knocking into furniture and walls as they went. When one of Kitally's favorite decorative vases went flying and crashed to the floor in a million pieces, Kitally put her fingers in her mouth and let out an ear-piercing whistle.

Nobody cared.

"That only works in the movies," Hayley told her.

"Thanks," she said. "I can see that."

Joey finally managed to push Badar off him, sending him staggering backward across a good portion of the living area before he found his balance. If he had any decency at all, he would have stopped right then and left the premises, but, like he'd said earlier, his family had been dishonored and apparently he was ready to fight to the death.

Lizzy didn't care if the two man-boys killed each other.

She'd followed the baby's cry and found her wrapped up and left atop a makeshift bed of blankets. Her tiny legs were stiff, and her face was red from crying. Lizzy picked her up and held her close to her chest. "Everything's going to be all right," she said, although she had serious doubts that would prove true.

Through the bedroom window, she saw Detective Chase walking toward the house.

What the hell? With the sounds of the living room battle still raging, she walked with the baby to the front entry and opened the door to find the detective just reaching the steps.

"What are you doing here?" Lizzy asked.

"Whose baby is that?"

"Nobody you know," she said. "What do you want?"

"You're not going to invite me in?"

Glass shattered in the other room.

He stiffened. "What's going on in there?"

"Do you really want to know?"

"Shoot."

"A young girl and her boyfriend had a baby." She tipped her chin toward the baby in her arms. "Her family strongly disapproves of the boyfriend and have threatened to do him harm." She tipped her head toward the sound of chaos. "Boyfriend and brother are inside duking it out."

"How do you get yourself into these messes?" he asked her.

"Trouble follows me wherever I go. You know that."

"Maybe I should put a stop to it."

"It's your call," Lizzy said, "though you're probably a lot safer right here. Why are you here?"

"Your neighbor called in to complain about the noise. When I heard the address, I decided to swing by and make sure you were OK."

"I appreciate it."

As the male shouting inside built to a crescendo, he took a closer look at the baby in her arms. "She's a cute one." He put his finger in her little hand, and she gripped it tightly.

Chase turned to her. "I also wanted to tell you that I've authorized two of my best men to check out the area in and around Bennett's vacation home in Lake Tahoe."

That bit of news surprised her. Chase was letting her know he'd listened to her concerns about Bennett . . . and that he had her back. "Thanks, Detective. That means a lot."

"Don't get too excited. I'm not doing it because I think you're right about the man. I'm doing it for peace of mind."

"Got it."

With nothing better to do, they both headed into the living room to see what was going on.

Badar would not let up, and he finally had to be dragged out in cuffs by Chase. Once Badar was secure inside the back of Detective Chase's sedan, the detective walked over to where Lizzy stood a few feet away.

"What about the girl?" Chase asked Lizzy.

"What about her?"

"I don't think her brother is going to let it go, and I'm not sure how long I can detain him."

"I don't know what to do," Lizzy said. "Can't you threaten the boy with jail time or something?"

He shrugged. "I'll see what I can do. The kid's running pretty hot. I'll let him cool down, then see if I can put the fear of God into him."

Lizzy watched Chase walk back to his car and said, "You'll keep me updated on the Bennett matter?"

"Do I have a choice?"

No, you don't, she thought as she watched him get in his car and take off down the street. Lizzy looked at the baby wrapped in her arms and brought her tiny face next to hers. She smelled like sweet innocence mingled with baby powder.

When Lizzy stepped inside the house, Salma and Joey were waiting for her.

Lizzy handed her the baby. Before she could talk to them

about what had just transpired, she felt the vibration of her cell phone in her back pocket. The caller ID told her it was the prosecutor, Grady Orwell.

"I have bad news," he told her when she answered.

Lizzy walked through the house, weaving around overturned furniture and broken pottery, making her way toward the office at the end of the hallway, away from everyone else. "What is it?"

"Olimpia Padula," he said. "She was found dead in her apartment. Drowned in the bathtub."

Lizzy stopped walking. "Jesus."

"They're calling it accidental."

"That's bullshit."

"I'm sorry."

"Me, too. Thanks for letting me know." Lizzy disconnected the call and then swallowed hard. Her fingers gripped the phone until she thought it might break.

"What's wrong?" Hayley asked. "Who was that?"

Lizzy walked into the office.

Hayley followed behind and shut the door.

"Olimpia Padula is dead." Lizzy took a seat at the desk and let her head fall into the palms of her hands. A few seconds passed before she gathered herself and looked up at Hayley. "I should have parked my ass in front of Olimpia's apartment 24-7. Fuck that man!" She took a breath. "Bennett might very well have gotten away with murder . . . again. That asshole has been captured on video drugging and assaulting a woman, and yet it's inadmissible in court." She stabbed a finger in the air. "Nobody will speak out against the amazing Mr. Bennett. But guess what? I don't give a shit. I refuse to let that man continue on his merry little way. That man will not lay a finger on anyone else."

"What do you propose?" Hayley asked.

"Bennett isn't the only one with eyes in the back of his head," Lizzy said flatly. "His wife is in Europe. Mr. Bennett sent her away to spend time with friends until the media circus died down. Tomorrow night, when he comes home from work, we'll be waiting."

CHAPTER THIRTY-FOUR

They had parked the car blocks away and then made their way into Bennett's backyard via an undeveloped greenbelt. Lizzy watched behind a thick shrub and signaled to Hayley and Kitally that Bennett had arrived.

As she had seen the man do many times before, he parked his car near the fountain in front of his mansion. As he busied himself with unlocking the front door, Lizzy moved swiftly and silently after him. When he'd stepped inside and disabled the alarm, she rushed up from behind, put the TASER to his neck, and hit the switch.

He collapsed to his knees; fell flat to the marble floor, his body twitching. His face, turned to one side, contorted as he grimaced in pain and shock.

Kitally, Hayley, and Lizzy all wore black. They also wore dark full-faced ski masks just like the one Hayley was now sliding over Bennett's head as he writhed on the floor.

Lizzy shut the door and locked it while Kitally wrapped duct tape around Bennett's neck, securing his mask in place. Lizzy and Hayley stripped his clothes off. Hayley injected him with Dilaudid to help keep him under control.

They dragged him through the house, to the side door leading into the garage. His head knocked into the door frame and then clunked against the doormat covering a small section of the cement floor.

"Watch his head," Kitally said.

They ignored her.

There was only one other car, an expensive BMW, inside the five-car garage, leaving plenty of room for them to do their work.

As soon as he stopped twitching, Lizzy hit him with the TASER again, giving him a good jolt. "How does it feel to be naked and powerless, Mr. Bennett?"

He grunted, tried to say something, but had a difficult time getting any words out. "You . . . will . . . pay . . . for . . . this," he finally managed.

Lizzy held out her hand toward Hayley. "Give me the baton."

Hayley did as she said.

Lizzy extended the stick and cracked it hard across the pale flesh of his thigh.

His pride did not allow him to scream out in pain. Although most of his face was covered, she could see the agony in the clenching of hands and teeth.

"Get on all fours," Lizzy told him. "I want to see you walk around on the cold cement floor like the pig you are. Do it now or I'll zap you with the TASER."

He didn't move.

She swatted him again, swinging harder this time, hitting him across the chest and then the stomach.

His knees rolled up to his chest in pain, but then he did as she said. He rolled over and pushed himself to his hands and knees.

"Move around in circles and squeal like a pig. We're getting this on tape, so make it good."

"You will die," he said between pathetic squeals, his voice muffled beneath the mask.

She swatted him on the buttocks, leaving a red welt against his skin. "Squeal louder. We can't hear you."

He shrieked more than squealed. Pathetic. After a few seconds, he stopped, came to his knees, and put his hands to his neck. His fingers pulled and clawed at the ski mask covering his face.

Lizzy whipped his right arm and then his left. She swung out wide and came back hard, lashing his chest and then his side. Blind with rage, she whipped him across the shoulder. Blood spurted. An intricate network of red welts appeared.

He fell to the ground.

He was on his side, his knees curled close to his chest.

She couldn't see through her fury, couldn't stop whipping him, gaining no pleasure from what she was doing, just intent on stopping him from ever hurting another human being. He had been molesting young women for years. He raped and murdered and paid people to turn the other way.

Her arm was sore, her palm blistered from holding so tight to the baton, but she refused to stop.

She would put an end to this now.

She continued lashing out until, out of the corner of her eye, she saw Kitally.

The horror she saw scrawled across her face prompted Lizzy to stop and take a step back. Her arm fell to her side, and the baton dropped from her hands, clanked, and rolled across the cement floor.

She turned her palms upward and saw a new blister forming. And then she looked at Bennett. He was a bloody mess. He was no longer moving. She had no idea if he was breathing.

Have I become one of them?

Her stomach turned. Was she now a clone of the monsters she'd been trying so hard to get off the streets? When had this happened? What had she done? "We're finished here," she said, trying to catch her breath. "Let's go."

Hayley grabbed hold of her shoulder. "You two get out of here. I'll take care of the rest."

"No, you won't. Leave him be."

Hayley frowned. "You know he'll just do it again. How many young lives is he going to ruin before you regret this decision?"

Silence. It took all she had to keep the bile from coming forth.

"He's the devil," Hayley said. "We need to finish this . . . right now."

Lizzy couldn't bring herself to look into Hayley's eyes. She was responsible for these girls, and look what she'd done. She'd brought it to this.

She thought of Jared then. He'd seen evil in all forms, and yet he never would have bent down to the criminal's level. Never. There was no excuse. "I said let him go, and I mean it."

She went to the side door that led out of the garage, held it open, and waited for both Kitally and Hayley to come.

Kitally didn't waste any time getting out of there.

Hayley took a little longer. She looked from Bennett to Lizzy. "This isn't right."

"We never should have come," Lizzy told her. "I made a mistake."

"Your hormones are all fucked up."

"Let's go," Lizzy said again, refusing to leave without her.

Once they were outside, Lizzy shut the door and looked at Hayley.

She'd never seen Hayley direct her anger at her before, but she was seething and there was no doubt who she was pissed off at. Hayley got right up in her face, their noses an inch apart. "I know why you can't do this. But you don't have a clue, because you're too wrapped up in all those distorted thoughts of yours to see the sky through the clouds."

Lizzy opened her mouth to respond, but Hayley shut her down. "I shouldn't have to tell you this, Lizzy, but you need to get your ass to the doctor. You're fucking pregnant."

Jessica greeted all three of them when they returned to Kitally's house in Carmichael. She had Salma's baby positioned atop her shoulder. Awkwardly, she tried to create a rocking motion and pat the baby on the back at the same time. "Where have you all been?" she asked. "I've been calling you for the last hour. I left messages on all of your phones."

Kitally swept right by without saying a word.

Hayley grunted and disappeared.

"What's wrong with everyone? What's with the black outfits?"

Lizzy headed inside.

"I really need to talk to you, Lizzy."

"I need some water first," Lizzy said. "When did you get in?" She grabbed a glass from the cupboard, filled it with tap water and gulped it down.

"I arrived this morning," Jessica told her, "but I've been at the office all day. Jimmy dropped me here at the house a couple hours ago." She stepped closer. "What's wrong with everyone?"

"Don't ask. What do you need to talk to me about?"

Jessica asked Lizzy to follow her to the dining room table where pictures were spread out from one end of the table to the other. Lizzy had seen most of the pictures when they met with Jimmy Martin and Kenneth Mitchell downtown. There were new pictures as well.

"You're a genius," Jessica told her.

"Why is that?"

She poked a finger at a picture at the far left of the table. "This is one of many cold cases now linked to the Sacramento Strangler. See the pearl earring on the woman's ear?"

Lizzy nodded.

"The killer used the earring to pierce his victim's ear. Her other ear was not pierced. One pearl earring."

Salma entered the room and took the baby from Jessica. She was wearing a robe and had a towel wrapped around her head. "Thanks for letting me take a shower."

"No problem," Jessica said, not missing a beat as she continued with her line of thought. She turned the photo around. There was a smaller picture taped to the back of it. "Look at this. I did an Internet search and printed off some famous paintings. The copies I made are black and white so you can't see that the band around the woman's head in the painting is blue, which is very close to the blue-colored band that was wrapped around the victim's neck. Guess what the picture is called?"

"I have no idea."

"*Girl with a Pearl Earring*, by Johannes Vermeer."

Lizzy listened, waited.

"Here's another one." Jessica handed her one of the pictures she'd seen when they met with Jimmy and Kenneth Mitchell. It was the male victim—the one with the wreath of red roses around his head. "Although you won't see it in the picture, crime scene technicians found a smoking pipe buried close by. That picture is in the files at the bureau." Again, Jessica turned the picture around and showed her another copy of a painting taped to the back. "This painting is called *Boy with a Pipe*, by Pablo Picasso."

Lizzy tried to pay attention, but her mind was still back in the garage with Wayne Bennett. She'd lost control. She could have killed the man. If she hadn't seen him twitch before she left, she might have believed he really was dead. And where would that have gotten her or any of them? And yet maybe Hayley was right. Maybe it would have been better if she'd finished him off. If he knew who was responsible, they were all in danger. Her heart raced, and her mind whirled. What should she do? Talk to Detective Chase? No. Not yet.

Her hand went to her belly. A slight bump perhaps, but more likely she felt something because Hayley had put the idea in her head. It was true that she hadn't been feeling well lately. She'd thrown up more than a few times in the past few months, but she'd put it all down to stress. The truth was she couldn't recall the last time she'd felt so-called normal. She would make a doctor's appointment first thing in the morning.

"What's wrong?" Jessica asked.

"I've had a rough go of it today, but I'll be fine. Go on."

Jessica didn't look so sure. "You look pale. Maybe you should lay down for a bit."

"I'm OK. What about the victim found covered with irises? Did that mean anything?"

Jessica shuffled through the photographs, picked up the one showing the victim covered in flowers, and turned it over. "*Irises*, by Vincent van Gogh. It goes on and on, just like this. Mitchell is impressed, Lizzy. It looks like you might have found the missing link."

Lizzy blindly sorted through the pictures, her mind still reeling. *A baby?* She couldn't raise a baby amid this crazy life of hers. Was it possible she could be carrying Jared's child? She grabbed hold of the edge of the table.

Another worried look from Jessica.

"I'm fine," Lizzy said flatly. "Go on."

Jessica had known her long enough to know it would do her no good to argue. "We have a suspect," Jessica blurted. She reached over the table and retrieved another picture from the bottom of the pile. "His name is Jovan Massing. He's an art dealer who did time for hiring master forgers and selling fake paintings for millions."

The man was short and stocky. He looked like a bulldog, with pinched nostrils and baggy jowls. The only thing missing was a drool-slathered tongue hanging to one side. *This* was the man who'd killed so many? It just didn't compute. Not just because of the way he looked, but . . . "A master forger suddenly becomes a serial killer?"

"He also did time for attempted murder."

All right. That was something. But still, it didn't fit. Something niggled at the back of Lizzy's mind although she couldn't pinpoint what it was. "What about Zachary Tucker?"

"Nothing has come up. It's as if he never existed."

"What about the house on Canyon Road where the Tuckers used to live? Did anyone visit the current home owners to see if they knew anything?"

"Yes, of course," Jessica said. "Mitchell sent one of his agents to talk to the owners. They said they did, in fact, buy the house from the Tuckers, but they never met them face-to-face. They know nothing about Zachary Tucker."

Lizzy thought about Kathryn Church and what she'd seen as a young girl. It might be time to pay her another visit.

"Lizzy, I've put Zachary Tucker's name through every available database. There's *nothing*. But Jovan Massing is promising as hell. The years he spent in prison fit the gap where no victims at all turned up in the Sacramento area. At the time, investigators figured the Sacramento Strangler might be dead or in prison, which could very well be exactly what happened."

"Where is Massing now?"

"They have yet to find him, but they're confident they're closing in and will have him in custody soon."

"What about Kathryn Church seeing Zachary kill his own sister?"

"Think about it, Lizzy. There's really nothing to link Zachary Tucker to any of this. You said yourself that Kathryn was just operating on a hunch. A 'feeling.'" Jessica shook her head. "The woman obviously has some issues. And maybe for good reason—if she really saw what she thinks she saw, that would be a hell of a thing to witness when you were a little kid, and a hell of thing to keep to yourself all these years. But what did she expect Jared to do for her? It all happened thirty years ago."

Lizzy scratched the back of her neck as she tried to think clearly.

"Lizzy, I understand your frustration. Maybe, just maybe, Jovan Massing was Kathryn's neighbor. Maybe he *is* Zachary Tucker."

"You would have checked that out already. You have Massing's whole history, his every address."

Jessica lifted her hands in question. "What else would you have me do?"

Hayley had been waiting in a recliner in Donald Holmes's living room for over an hour when she heard the rattle of a key in the front door and slipped out of sight into a hall closet.

Just as she thought—he'd brought home the young woman she'd seen him talking to at the club earlier. The girl's words were slurred but clear enough to be heard. "This isn't my apartment," the girl said. "Where are we?"

"It's all right, sweetheart. I thought we could have one last drink and watch a movie."

"You said you would bring me home."

"Come on, baby—don't be a drag."

"I want to go home. Now."

A scuffle ensued. The sound of a chair toppling over and then a grunt before all went quiet. Hayley readied the TASER and sauntered out to the front room.

Yep. It was the same girl she'd seen at the club. Holmes was standing over her where she lay on the couch, her body twisted at a weird angle, her face a bloodied mess. She was out cold but clearly breathing.

Holmes turned her way. "What the fuck?"

Hayley smiled. "You took the words right out of my mouth."

He pointed a stubby finger her way. "You're that chick. The one who was in here with that other girl. You bitches broke my damn nose. In my own damn house!"

"Terrible thing," Hayley said, walking toward him. She ducked when he took a swing, then stung him with the TASER— once, then again. He fell to the floor with a thunk. She worked quickly after that while the girl from the club sawed logs on the couch. After driving his car into the garage, she dragged him out there and hauled his heavy ass into the trunk. She was breathing hard by the time she climbed in behind the wheel.

The girl on the couch had a strange awakening ahead of her in the next hour or so, coming to bruised, bloodied, and memory-free in a strange, empty house. But she was safe, and that's all that mattered.

Nora Belle Castor, also known as the Ghost, paced the bathroom floor, back and forth, in front of the mirror. Ever since being chased by that dyke bitch at the mall, she'd been antsy to release some of her frustrations. She spent most of the night on the street, waiting and watching. And then she'd made her move, but she hadn't seen it coming: one of the homeless assholes got a jab in after she jumped him. Got her right in the eye with his dirty, disgusting finger. Made her look as if she had fucking pinkeye.

She leaned over the sink and tried to open her infected eye as wide as she could, but it was no use. The dirty asshole had done some damage.

She looked down.

The fucker had also soiled her shoes.

The stupid goon she was living with didn't have shit for a washer and dryer, but his crappy appliances would have to do. She took off her sneakers and headed into the main room. Asshole was asleep on the couch with a can of beer still in his grasp.

She wasn't sure how long she would be able to live with the douche. His dick was long and thin, like a fucking wand but without the magic fairy dust. Fucking the man meant going through the motions without ever knowing if there was anything inside her. A waste of time. A shitty five-minute workout, at best.

She opened the closet in the hallway, swept all his dirty clothes to the floor, put her sneakers in the wash, added bleach and detergent, and turned on the machine. Before she could take more than a few steps back the way she came, she saw a little girl standing in the hallway watching her, a thumb shoved in her mouth.

"Who the fuck are you?" Nora Belle asked. And then she remembered Michael telling her he had a kid and that he swapped weekends with his ex every once in a while. She hadn't paid much attention at the time because, hell, she didn't give a shit about Michael. He was merely another idiot to take advantage of for a few weeks, maybe months, if she could stand him for that long.

"Take that thumb out of your mouth," she told the kid. "It's disgusting."

The kid kept sucking away, looking at her with big round eyes as if she really were looking at a fucking ghost. She hated the nickname she'd been given, but it was better than any of those assholes using her real name. The funny thing was, the police didn't seem to give a shit about what she did to those people. And they weren't the only ones. A lot of people didn't give a shit, which made all those homeless losers easy targets. She liked beating the crap out of those stupid people. Her mother was homeless, and God only knew where she'd ended up. Being raised among an endless string of deadbeats had made Nora Belle angry. Going after these people gave her something to do and helped release some frustrations. Mostly, it was just plain fun.

She walked up to the little girl and yanked her thumb out of her mouth. "What's your name?"

"Leah."

"How old are you?"

"Four." She held up four fingers as if that fucking confirmed it.

"OK, Leah, what do you want? Why are you staring at me like that?"

Thumb went back in her mouth. Tiny shoulder came up in a half shrug.

And then Nora Belle got an idea. "Hey, want to play a game?"

Suck. Suck. Suck.

That's all the kid knew how to do.

Fucking idiot, like her father.

She clamped a hand around the kid's shoulder and said, "Come on—we'll get something to eat and then go in the other room and play some games. It'll be fun. I have all night."

CHAPTER THIRTY-FIVE

It was the next afternoon, and Kitally had just had another door slammed in her face. Not exactly the friendliest neighborhood she'd ever visited. After heading back to the car, she climbed in behind the wheel and drove farther down the road looking for Hayley until she caught sight of her talking to a teenager playing basketball with a friend.

Hayley was still pissed off at Lizzy for doing a half-assed job with Bennett. Kitally, on the other hand, wasn't angry with Lizzy at all. She was just relieved that she hadn't stepped over the line. It was true that they would need to keep a vigilant eye on Bennett—make sure he didn't know who his attackers were and keep him from doing any more harm before justice was served. But as far as Kitally was concerned, that didn't include killing the man.

Right now, though, here they were, back in West Sac, looking for the Ghost. They had driven back to the neighborhood Salma said the Ghost used to haunt. They were going door-to-door, hoping someone would know something about her whereabouts.

Kitally was losing hope. But not Hayley. After being so close to nabbing the Ghost and then losing her in the mall, Hayley was more determined than ever to find her.

After Hayley finished talking to the teenager, she climbed into the car and said, "Let's go."

"Did you get a name?"

"Nope, but I have an idea."

Kitally didn't like the look in her eye. "What is it?"

"Me and you," she said, "are going to be homeless for a while."

"Seriously?"

"It'll be fun," Hayley said. "Like camping out."

"It could take weeks to catch her. Maybe months."

"I don't think so. The Ghost seems to make an appearance at least twice a week. I don't think she does what she does because she wants whatever these people have. I think she has a problem with homeless people. If we put ourselves in her path, she'll find us."

"How will you know where she'll hit next?"

"I got another call from the shopkeeper who keeps me updated on what's happening on the streets. Oftentimes, he mentions a homeless woman named Naomi Griffiths. I've talked to the woman before. She says the Ghost has it in for her. Our best bet will be to stick close to Naomi."

Kitally scratched her head where a bullet had grazed her scalp during the shooting the day of Lizzy's wedding. The wound had healed, but it still itched. "There's got to be an easier way to catch this person."

"Well, I'm moving out there tonight. You don't have to come."

"No, I'll come. I'm not going to let you go out there by yourself."

Hayley was searching through the garage at Kitally's house for a sleeping bag and anything else she might find useful on the streets when Lizzy approached her.

"I know you're pissed off at me," she said, "but I need your help with something."

"Why don't you ask Kitally or Jessica?"

"This is something only you can do. I've seen how well you can draw. It has to be you."

"How long will it take?"

"The woman lives in Newcastle. So I'll need you for a couple of hours at least."

"When do you plan to do this?"

"Right now."

Forty-five minutes later, they were sitting at the kitchen table inside Kathryn Church's house. Hayley had a sketch pad and pencil ready to go. The woman made everyone hot tea and then took a seat at the head of the table. Her hair was pinned high on her head. Dark circles framed her eyes. She looked as if she hadn't slept in a week.

"Where should I start?" Kathryn asked.

"First of all," Hayley said, "how old was Zachary the last time you saw him?"

"He was eighteen, a senior in high school. I was seventeen."

"Great. It would be helpful for me to start off with the shape of his face."

"Normal," she offered.

"How about this," Hayley said. "I'll give you a few choices, and then you pick the closest thing to how you picture him in your mind's eye."

"OK."

Lizzy was sitting at the table, too, but she appeared to be far, far away. Hayley found herself feeling bad for giving her shit, and yet she wasn't sure why she should feel bad about it. Lizzy had needed to make a decision and stick to it for once in her life. She liked to ramble on about how they needed to be safe and not get caught, and yet they had all put themselves in danger of being exposed last night. And for what?

The clink of a teacup pulled Hayley back to the matter at hand. "OK," Hayley said, "would you describe his face as round, square, thin, or heart shaped?"

"Heart shaped, I guess. Or maybe more like an egg. Yes, he had an egg-shaped face."

"That's great." Hayley began to sketch. When she was done with that, she looked up at Kathryn again. "Do you remember anything about his eyes?"

"Oh, yes. They say the eyes are the windows to the soul, and his certainly were. His eyes were gray-blue. Intense-looking eyes. When he looked at you, it was as if he were sucking you in. Pure seduction. When he looked at me, I couldn't look away. Magnetic. That's the word I would use to describe his eyes."

Wow, Hayley thought. She wondered if Lizzy realized Kathryn had feelings for Zachary Tucker. "That's really great," Hayley told her, "but now I need some details. For instance, were his eyes set far apart or close together? Were they deeply set?"

She shook her head. "None of those things. All in all, he had a very symmetrical face. Nose where it should be. Eyes, too—not round or narrow, either, but normal," she said with a sigh. "I'm sorry. I'm no help at all."

"No, this is good. I won't make his eyes too large or too small. Let's talk about his nose. Was it crooked or straight—"

"Straight," she blurted out before Hayley could finish. "And he had generous lips. And firm. A handsome face, overall; no doubt about it."

"What about his ears?"

She tilted her head as she thought about it. "He had a good amount of thick dark-brown hair that covered his ears, but his hair wasn't too long when I knew him. It touched low on his neck and had a slight curl to it. I never saw his ears peeking out, so I would guess normal-sized ears that were flat to his head."

Hayley sketched as the woman talked. More details shook loose as she went—a wide jaw, a sharp chin. Bright, even teeth. The image that was appearing on paper would certainly be considered by most to be a good-looking man, but the guy in the picture could be just about anybody. At last she handed the drawing to Kathryn and said, "What do you think?"

The woman put a hand to her chest right over her heart. "My goodness. It looks like Zachary."

Lizzy examined the picture. It clearly bummed her out that she didn't recognize him. "He looks nothing like Jovan Massing," she told Hayley.

"Who is Jovan Massing?" Kathryn asked.

"He's the FBI's number one suspect at the moment." Lizzy handed the picture back to Kathryn and asked her to make sure there was nothing else that needed to be tweaked, and then she looked at Hayley and said, "Great work. This was no simple crush you had on Zachary," Lizzy said to Kathryn. "You're *still* in love with him, aren't you?"

That took Hayley completely by surprise. She hadn't thought Lizzy was paying any attention at all.

Kathryn's eyes brimmed with tears. Unable to find her voice, she nodded instead.

"Why didn't you mention this before?"

"Because if he did kill his sister," she managed, "what would that make me? Over the years, I tried to convince myself that my imagination had gotten the best of me. As I came to know Zachary, I chose to believe he could never harm anyone. He was good to his family pets, and he doted on his parents. He was good to me, too."

"Did he know you were in love with him?"

"I don't know. Probably. I think Zachary knew all the girls at school were in love with him. Like I said, he had magnetism. He could have had any woman he wanted."

"Did he date anyone?"

"No. Not that I know of."

"Do you think he preferred the same sex?"

"I don't think so. It never once crossed my mind. I think he liked the girls to know he was single and yet they couldn't have him. I don't know for sure; it's just the feeling I got back then."

"Sorry to break things up," Hayley said, "but if we're done here, I need to get going."

Lizzy thanked Kathryn, and they all walked to the door.

When Lizzy got to the car, she looked back at Kathryn with a flash of concern, hoping the woman would stay safe until they found Zachary.

CHAPTER THIRTY-SIX

Hayley and Kitally found Naomi Griffiths searching through a Dumpster outside a grocery store off Ahern.

"Naomi," Hayley called out. "I brought you some food."

The woman turned, and recognition lit up her face. "Thank you, Jesus. I'm starved." She might've been in her forties or early fifties, but she looked much older.

As they watched her eat a hamburger from a fast-food chain, Hayley told Naomi their plan. They wanted her to do exactly what she always did each evening, but for the next few nights they were going to stay close by and keep an eye on her.

After Naomi finished eating, she spent most of the night talking, telling them her story. It was, no surprise, a sad one. It all started in 2009 when she was laid off from her job as an administrative assistant. She was working for the state, and she had all kinds of great ideas about retiring someday, putting her face to the sun and watching her grandkids a few times a week. But the state budget had become strained, and she was one of the first to be laid off. She hadn't been worried, though. She'd saved some money and was confident she'd be able to find another job quickly. But it didn't happen that way. A week became a month, and a month became years. She lost her apartment. Her daughters lived in other states and had problems of their own.

And yet Naomi still had hope that someday she would find a way to get out of this mess and find a job. Most of the women she knew on the streets had been abused and had nowhere to go.

At a little past eleven, Naomi had fallen asleep in a doorway down the alley from them. It was one in the morning now, and the sky was lit up with stars.

"I'm freezing," Kitally said.

Hayley sat up in her sleeping bag, pulled her sweatshirt off over her head, and handed it to Kitally.

"Are you sure?"

"I'm not cold. Take it."

"Thanks." Kitally slipped it on over the rest of her clothes. Then she rubbed warmth into her arms and snuggled deep into her sleeping bag, trying to get comfortable.

Hayley hunkered down. It wouldn't do any good if the Ghost came by and saw them chatting.

"Any sign of her?" Kitally asked.

"Nope."

"Any sign of life at all out there?"

"Just the stars and the moon."

Kitally peeked out. "It's pretty, isn't it?"

"Hmm," Hayley said with a nod.

"Are you still mad at Lizzy?"

"Yeah, a little. She put us all in danger without any thought to what she was doing. Her actions were shortsighted and she acted on emotion. Big mistake."

They were quiet after that, lost in their own thoughts until they both drifted off to sleep.

It was after ten the next morning when Lizzy made her way downstairs to the office. Nobody was around.

She opened the blinds to let the sunlight in, then took a seat at the desk. It wasn't the thought of being pregnant that was at the forefront of her mind, although she figured the notion certainly should top her list of concerns. Instead, it was the name Jake Polly that kept repeating itself over and over inside her head. There was something right there within her reach, something that could tie everything together.

But what was it?

Jake Polly was an artist.

He had scratches on his hands.

She found the picture Hayley had drawn and took a closer look. Kathryn was certain Zachary Tucker matched the image to a tee. Other than the nose and longish curly hair, Lizzy guessed Jake Polly did look a little like the man in the drawing. Maybe more than a little. Noses could break and hairstyles could definitely change over the course of twenty years.

Could Zachary Tucker be Jake Polly?

Lizzy doodled on her notepad while she stared at the picture. She wrote the name *Zachary Tucker* and then *Jake Polly*. She then scribbled *jp* and *zt*. She repeated the process using capital letters.

Nothing.

There was nothing particularly "magnetic" about either the man in the picture or Jake Polly in person, but Kathryn had been or still was in love with him, so of course she would think he was magnetic. Hell, the woman hadn't seen Zachary in twenty years, so how would she know any longer?

Lizzy's instincts hollered at her to drive to Kathryn's house and take a closer look at the note and the rest of the letters Zachary Tucker had given Kathryn. She should have asked for the shoe box full of goodies the last time she was there, but she'd really had no reason to do so at the time.

Before Lizzy could decide whether or not to make the drive to Newcastle, Jessica entered the office. A stream of sunlight sliced through the window and made a line across the floor between them. "Good morning," Jessica said. "Or should I say good afternoon?"

"Either one works," Lizzy said. "The house was so quiet I thought you had left. What have you been up to? Did you just get up?"

"I spent most of the morning helping Salma with the baby, but then her boyfriend showed up. Joey's helping her now. I can't believe she hasn't named the baby yet. I tossed out a few suggestions, all of which were nixed. After that, I called in for an update on Jovan Massing, left a message for my brother, and then I talked to Magnus."

"How is Magnus?"

"The same. Stubborn as hell. He thinks he's holding me back, ruining my life because I chose to live with him and be with him. He calls himself a cripple." She sighed, shaking her head. "He's way too hard on himself. It's difficult to watch at times. He told me he couldn't do anything on the list I left him, which isn't true."

"You left him a list?"

"I do it all the time. The doctors want him to keep active and busy. They want Magnus to challenge himself. And it's not like the lists are that daunting. Things like getting the mail, watering a few plants, feeding the hamster."

"You have a hamster?"

"Squeaky wheel and all. It's supposed to be therapeutic, keep his mind off the pain, but I think the little rodent is mostly just annoying."

Lizzy did her best to give Jessica her undivided attention, but wasn't succeeding since she was unable to stop picking at the idea of Jake Polly and Zachary Tucker being one and the same.

"I wonder how Hayley and Kitally are doing out on the streets?" Jessica asked.

"Kitally has her machete and Hayley has her badass attitude. They'll be fine."

"Why is Hayley so angry with you?"

"We don't always see every situation eye to eye, that's all."

"What was that list of names I saw, the one you snatched away before I could get a good look at it?"

"Why do I feel as if I'm being interrogated?"

"Maybe because the questions are making you feel uncomfortable."

"I don't remember any list."

Jessica shook her head. "You're lying."

Lizzy said nothing.

"Your eye twitches when you lie. It's the craziest thing, but it happens every time."

Lizzy shrugged.

"I know you're all up to something, but I have yet to figure out what it is. I hope you and Hayley haven't gone and done something irreversible."

"You worry too much."

"No, I don't. You've been acting strange, and before I went back to Virginia, you blurted out 'she's not a killer.' Who were you talking about?"

"I don't remember that particular conversation."

"I think you're holding back."

Lizzy sighed. "There's nothing going on, Jessica. You have a lot on your plate right now, so don't try to sniff out trouble where there isn't any."

Before she could say another word, Jessica's phone rang. She snatched it from her waistband and picked up the call. She paced the floor near the door while she listened. The minute she hung up, she said, "I need to borrow your car."

"Why, what's going on?"

"They found the Massing fellow, and they're bringing him in for questioning."

"I'll go with you," Lizzy said. "I want to talk to Jimmy."

"OK, grab what you need, and meet me at the car."

When Lizzy went to find her purse and coat from the other room, she saw Joey and Salma sitting on the couch playing with their baby girl. They made a cute couple. "Hope," Lizzy said. "You should name your baby Hope."

They both looked up at her, but she didn't have time to stick around. She fished out her keys as she ran through the kitchen. Out of the corner of her eyes, she saw the note Kitally had left her in case she went to the store for groceries.

And it hit her like a brick to the side of the head.

The note. The note Kathryn had shown her had drawings of his pets in the margins. Next to each drawing were the names of the pets scribbled in hard-to-read writing. The name next to the bird, though, had looked a lot like Polly.

Lizzy pulled out her cell phone and punched in Kathryn's number as she headed back for her office.

Kathryn answered on the third ring.

"Kathryn, it's me, Lizzy. I have a question for you."

"What is it?"

"What were the names of Zachary's pets? The ones he asked you to care for while he and his parents were away?"

"Oh, gosh, I don't remember off the top of my head. Let me get the note from my office."

As Lizzy waited she glanced at the scribblings she'd made on her notepad. Jessica was already in the car, probably antsy as all hell.

"Here it is," Kathryn said. "Polly, Peter, and Jake."

"Polly," Lizzy said. "Jake Polly."

"What?"

"I think Zachary might have changed his name to Jake Polly." Lizzy's gaze fell on the *ZT* and how the letters, when overlapped, looked a lot like the symbol left on many of the Sacramento Strangler's victims. "You said that you saved every letter and note he ever gave you."

"I did."

"Did he ever sign his name with his initials? With the *Z* and the *T* overlapping?"

"Almost always. How did you know?"

"I'll explain later. Stay safe, Kathryn. Lock your doors, and do not leave your house."

"I won't."

Lizzy hung up the phone and then called her sister.

"Hi, Lizzy. I'm so glad you called. I was just thinking about you, and I thought it would be great if you, Brittany, and I went out and—"

"I'm sorry I have to cut you off," Lizzy told her sister, "but is Brittany there? I really need to talk to her."

"No. Remember the art class I told you about? What am I saying? Brittany probably told you all about the class herself when the two of you spent time together the other day."

"She did," Lizzy said, trying to remain calm, determined not to let on that something might be wrong. "Where is the class held? I know she told me, but I forgot."

"Although she'll be attending Sacramento State, the classes are held at Folsom Lake College. I have the paper right here. You know how I like to know exactly where she is at every minute."

"I was thinking of stopping by when class ends and surprising her. Jessica is here, and I thought it would be nice for the two of them to get a chance to see each other."

"I think that's a wonderful idea. It's in the Harris Center for the Arts building. Room 154. The class runs from twelve to three."

"You wouldn't happen to know who the instructor is today, would you?"

"No. Sorry. Why would you want to know that?"

"No reason, just being nosy. Jessica has been waiting in the car. I have to go, but I'll call you later and we'll set up a date to get together, OK?"

"Sounds good. Say hello to Jessica for me."

"Will do."

Lizzy grabbed the notepad and then ran out the door to the car. She jumped in, handed the piece of paper to Jessica, started the engine, and took off before Jessica could bitch about how long she'd taken.

"Whoa. Slow down."

"No. No. No. Not again."

"What is it?" Jessica asked.

"You guys have the wrong man. Jake Polly is the killer."

"Jake Polly?"

"Also known as Zachary Tucker. He paints and he teaches art."

Jessica didn't need for Lizzy to spell it out. "Shit," was all she said. "I hope you're wrong about this."

"I'm not. Look at that paper. That's not some crazy symbol the killer leaves on his victims. It's a *Z* and a *T*. His initials. That's all it is."

CHAPTER THIRTY-SEVEN

He unlocked the door to the wine cellar.

Claire hung from the wall in chains. He admired the clever artwork he'd done on her body, using paint and all sorts of fabulous tools. Her attempt at getting away and daring to attack him had been too much. He needed to teach her a lesson. "You're dying in here—aren't you, Claire?"

He pulled the lid from the lip balm he had brought and dabbed it over her cracked lips. She didn't fight him, hardly even moved. "You've lost all your fire. Such a disappointment. I was hoping we would spend more time together, but such is life . . . and death."

She didn't ask him to remove the chains or the metal cuffs that were clearly cutting into her ankles and wrists. She looked like a bloody mess.

"They'll find you," she said, her voice a ragged whisper.

"I hate to disappoint you, but they won't find me. Or you. It's all over the news. Their number one suspect is in custody. They'll spend the next week or so questioning the poor man, perhaps knocking him senseless until he confesses."

"You're a liar. I don't believe you."

"Well, you can believe what I'm about to tell you, Claire. Today is the day you're going to die."

It took some effort, but she lifted her head and spit in his eye. "Go to hell!"

"There's my girl," he said fondly as he used his sleeve to wipe the spittle from his face. "I'll tell you what, Claire. Why don't we enjoy these last few hours together? I'll set up the upstairs, let you sit on the couch beside me and enjoy the lovely view. You haven't had a chance to see the river and the way the water sparkles before the sun disappears in the distance. It's beautiful. You're going to love it. Any requests for your last meal?"

Again, she said nothing. "I'll be back soon. Although I wish I didn't have to, I will need to drug you first."

"No drugs. I won't fight you."

"Oh," he said with a laugh, "now who's the liar?"

Lizzy did her best to explain what was going on, but Jessica didn't seem convinced.

"I'm going to go on this wild-goose chase with you, Lizzy, because I have great respect for you, but when this is finished, you can either lend me your car or I'll call a taxi. Massing will be there by now, and I need to question him."

The tires screeched as Lizzy pulled into a parking spot of Folsom Lake College. She jumped out and sprinted up endless flights of wide stairs and then toward the buildings, with Jessica at her heels. When the Harris Center for the Arts didn't present itself to them, Lizzy asked a group gathered at an outdoor dining area for directions. It was across the small campus from them. When they finally arrived, Lizzy burst through the heavy front doors and sprinted for Room 154, threw open the door, and stepped inside. Jessica stepped in behind her.

A bearded man at his desk in the far corner stood tall and said, "Can I help you?"

"Are you in charge here?"

He nodded. All the student painters in the room were looking their way now, as well as the naked male model sitting on a stool in the middle of their small circle of desks.

Lizzy and Jessica were both panting, trying to catch their breath. Lizzy was doubled over with her hands on her knees. OK, so she needed to make a little more time for running.

Jessica told Lizzy to collect herself while she went over to talk to the instructor.

While Jessica talked to the man, Lizzy straightened and looked around, her gaze sweeping over the room. No sign of Brittany. Maybe Cathy had given her the wrong room number.

The students had gone back to their painting.

Lizzy caught the attention of one of them and said, "Do you know if Brittany Warner is in this class?"

"This is my first day," the girl explained. "I don't know anyone's name."

"Brittany was here earlier," one of the other students told her.

"Are you sure?"

"Yep. She just stepped out, in fact." He pointed to the painting in front of an empty seat next to his.

"I saw her talking to someone outside," another student chimed in.

Lizzy rushed from the room, the clicks of her heels echoing in the empty hallway. She pushed through the main exit door and then took a moment to take in her surroundings. In the middle of the campus was a parklike setting, grass and trees, where a group of kids were gathered. She could see the library behind them and office buildings farther on to the left. The sidewalks were mostly empty. She ran toward the group of students, couldn't stop tears from streaming down her face when she saw that Brittany was not among the group.

"Lizzy!"

She stopped, turned around, and saw Brittany standing on the other side of the quad, a confused expression on her face. "Brittany!" she called out as she headed her way. "Where were you?"

"I took a quick break. Why? What's going on? Is it Mom? Is she OK?"

Lizzy grabbed hold of her niece and held her tight. "Your mom is fine." She moved her to arm's length.

"Why are you crying?"

"I couldn't find you, and I thought the worst. I'll explain later, but right now you need to go home. When you get to your house, I want you to lock the doors and don't come out until I tell you it's safe. Do not open the door for anyone, including Jake Polly."

"Jake Polly? The painter?"

Lizzy nodded. "He's a dangerous man. I don't have time to explain. Just do as I say."

"You're scaring me, Lizzy."

"I know. I'm sorry. But you need to do this . . . for me."

"My things are still in the classroom," Brittany said, pointing that way.

"OK, come on. Let's get your things and then I'll walk you to your car."

Candles burned all around the house. He'd gone to the bother to pick wildflowers that grew close to the river's edge and put them in cups of water. *Quite beautiful*, he thought as he admired his handiwork.

He'd cleaned off Claire and then drugged her before carrying her up the stairs and setting her on the couch next to him. He'd also slid the doors to the balcony wide-open, hoping to see the sun when it finally disappeared behind the tall trees.

He sipped his Red Bull from a crystal glass, and then slipped his arm around Claire's shoulder. He wondered for a moment what it would be like to have a girlfriend, someone to talk to and confide in, share a few laughs and, of course, a beautiful sunset with. He thought of Kathryn then, the only girl he'd ever considered hooking up with. He'd always felt close to the girl next door while growing up. Like most females, she'd been infatuated with him from the start. But her infatuation had been different. She had loved him since she was a little girl. He'd kept track of her over the years and had been quite shocked to read her academic paper on repressed memories. Luckily, it had been stored in the darkest corner of the most obscure academic site; only someone searching out every last crumb of Kathryn-related material would turn it up, and, even then, who would be able to connect the dots to him? He hadn't been worried by the discovery. If anything, he was touched. Growing up, she'd never once given him reason to believe she'd witnessed his sister's murder. And yet she'd still loved him. Had she kept the portrait he'd painted of her just before they fell out of touch, all those years ago? She had posed all weekend for him, her back straight, her smile like Mona Lisa's while he painted her portrait. He'd barely gotten started when he'd decided to make it into a Picassoesque piece. He couldn't help but imagine an arm where her leg should be and a finger instead of a nose. He quite liked the finished product. Of course, Kathryn had been stunned when she'd taken a first glimpse of his work, but overall the painting delighted her.

A snore out of Claire made him turn to her. *Sweet, sweet girl.* Too bad he couldn't keep her.

She had to die.

It was a funny thing how his mind worked. Death fighting against life—the two forces wrestling with each other. On the one hand, life was ever changing, with no real purpose, so why keep her alive? But death was final—never again would he be able to talk to her while he painted her portrait.

He brought his glass to his lips. A knock at the door caused him a bit of a jitter, and he spilled his drink. He looked toward the door, but the way the sun was hitting the house, he couldn't make out a silhouette or see who might be there. It was probably Landon, but he couldn't be sure. He thought about leaving Claire where she was on the couch, but then he decided against it. He would lock her in the guestroom and then get rid of the annoying kid.

Leaning over the couch, he scooped Claire into his arms. "Come on, my precious Claire. I need you to hide in the back room for just a moment while I get the door."

He laid her on the bed in the guestroom. *So small, so weak*, he thought as he bent over her and kissed her forehead. Hurrying from the room, he locked the door from the outside. After bringing Claire to the house, for exactly this purpose, he'd changed the locks so the bedroom doors couldn't be opened from the inside.

Another knock alerted him to the fact that whoever it was, they were not going away anytime soon. Agitated, he headed for the front door.

Lizzy drove, while Jessica tightened her seatbelt. "Slow down, Lizzy. You're not going to be able to help anyone if you get us into a wreck."

"So how did the instructor know where Jake Polly lived?"

"As soon as I mentioned Jake Polly's name, he told me everything he knew about the man. I guess he already had his suspicions about Polly. Last month, while Polly was in the middle of this three-week series of guest workshops, the instructor tried to call him on some administrative matter, but his number had been disconnected. The address on his application was on the instructor's way home, so he drove by. It turned out to be a hair salon. The instructor was starting to get worried now—he was the one who'd hired Polly and put him into such close contact with his students. He didn't let on what he knew right away, though. Instead, just the other day, he followed Polly home after his last class. And that's how he came to have his address. The instructor has already filed a complaint with the department head and has no plans to allow Polly back into his classroom."

Lizzy sped through a yellow light and Jessica clutched the grab handle. "Slow down, Lizzy. If we get pulled over, it'll take even longer to get there."

"So what do you think now? Is Jake Polly our man?" Lizzy asked.

Jessica sighed. "Do you have any idea how routinely people lie on their résumés and employment applications? People lie about past employment, degrees, DUIs, you name it."

"Look at my notepad . . . at his initials. It's the same mark he's been leaving on his victims, for God's sake. And like you said before, he's not like other killers. He would never watch me from afar, which is exactly why he made a point of visiting me downtown under the guise of wanting to hang one of his posters inside my office."

"Jake Polly came to your office?"

Lizzy kept her eyes on the road and nodded. "It's just like you said—he wants to keep me up close and personal."

Before Jessica had a chance to respond, her phone buzzed. She pulled it from her pocket. "It's Mitchell," she told Lizzy before she hit Talk.

"Where are you?" Mitchell growled loud enough to be heard by Lizzy.

"I'm with Lizzy Gardner. We're checking out another lead."

"By whose orders?"

She didn't answer.

"I told you I wanted you here."

"This will only take a few minutes, and then I'll be on my way. Has the interrogation started?"

"In two minutes."

The call was disconnected.

"He sounds a little demanding," Lizzy said.

"Look who's talking."

"Thanks for believing in me."

"I didn't have much of a choice. Once your mind is set, there's no stopping you. And I don't like the idea of you running into some strange man's house and waving your gun around. You've done it before. With all the stress you've been under, it wouldn't surprise me to see you do it again."

"Well, thanks for the vote of confidence."

"I'm here, aren't I? I might lose my job, but we aren't leaving Jake Polly's house until you're sure he's not your man, all right?"

"OK." By the time she pulled her car in front of the address they'd been given, Lizzy felt somewhat defeated. What Jessica said was true; once again she had acted hastily, going on instinct rather than proof. But they were here now, and she wasn't going to let on that she was quickly losing faith that she had the right man.

Lizzy climbed out of the car and waited for Jessica.

The house was on a tree-lined street that might have struck her as lovely under different circumstances. The house had been built on a steep hill with a bank falling sharply into the river. She could smell the river from where she stood—damp and earthy.

"OK," Jessica said as she walked toward the front door, "let's do this."

Lizzy followed behind, decided to let Jessica do her thing, since she appeared to be much better at acting cool and calm.

Jessica rapped her knuckles against the door.

Lizzy pressed her face up close to the decorative glass and tried to see inside. She could see straight through the hallway and into the main area. The doors to a balcony were wide-open, and there appeared to be a nice view of trees and water. Then she saw a man walk past, carrying something in his arms. Her heart rate soared. "I think a man just walked by with someone in his arms."

Jessica waited another minute before she knocked again.

When Lizzy saw someone coming toward the door, she took a step back and listened to a series of dead bolts and chains being dealt with. Who kept more than one dead bolt on their door unless they wanted to keep something out . . . or in his case, something in?

Claire tried to sit up, but every part of her felt heavy. She could hardly lift her head from the mattress. When the maniac had fed her some sort of liquid drug using a teaspoon, Claire had managed to let half of it dribble out the side of her mouth after he turned away.

She was woozy, but she'd pretended to be completely out of it as he carried her from the wine cellar and up the stairs to the living room, waiting for him to leave her side for one damn minute. But he hadn't left her side. He'd carried her to the couch and then made himself comfortable. The weirdo had snuggled close and kept his arm around her as if they were boyfriend and girlfriend living in a house on the river.

It took some effort, but she managed to push her legs from the bed. She was worse off than she'd first thought. Her mind was relatively active and clear, but her body wasn't responding to her brain's directives.

She could hear the psycho talking to someone at the door. It wasn't the kid he often complained about because she could hear a voice . . . a woman's voice. They were questioning him about something, but he was playing coy, making jokes, and having a good laugh.

Adrenaline made her heart pump faster. She tried to scream, but her voice was gone. She needed to get out of there.

When she slid off the side of the bed, she bumped her hip against the wooden frame and fell to the floor. She grasped the carpeted floor, feeling the nylon fibers between her fingers, using the strands to pull herself to the door. She needed to hurry. Her body had been mutilated, and yet she no longer felt any pain. She was way past feeling anything at all. Her arms were weak, but she had to be strong.

It seemed like forever before she finally got to the door. Using the wall for support, she pushed herself upward to her knees, relieved when she managed to grasp the doorknob.

Her efforts were all for nothing.

It was no use.

The door had been locked from the other side. Bastard had thought of everything. She glanced toward the window, thankful she could still hear people talking at the door. She felt so tired. She couldn't pass out now.

Please don't leave me here. Please don't leave.

Crawling on all fours, she made it halfway across the room before she was on her belly again, snaking her way across the room. Her right leg gave out first. Whatever he had given her was just now taking effect. *No. No. No.*

Come on. You can do it. Not much farther to go.

She already knew she wouldn't have the strength to open the window. She needed to throw something at it. Break it if she could. But with what?

There was a lamp and a clock on the bedside table. There were books set within bronzed bookends on the bottom shelf. Just another foot or two to go. She headed that way.

Jessica started the conversation by pulling out her badge and asking Jake Polly straight up if he knew anything about the whereabouts of Claire Kerley.

Although the man looked sufficiently surprised by the badge and the question, he pulled himself together and said, "Lizzy, how nice to see you again."

Lizzy grunted.

"Now, who is this person you're looking for?"

"Claire Kerley." He was a creepy man, Jessica thought, no doubt about it. He had a wild look about him, and he seldom blinked. She noticed a bruise on his jaw and more than one scratch on his neck. As Lizzy had mentioned, his hands were covered with scrapes.

Restless, Lizzy stepped away. She walked along, staying close to the side of the house. It was obvious that she was trying to get a peek through a window.

"What is she doing? Do you have a search warrant?"

"Why? Do I need one?"

"I have nothing to hide, if that's what you're asking, but I must say I don't appreciate her wandering around my property without permission. Please tell me what's going on."

"I'll tell you exactly what's going on," Lizzy said as she marched back to the door.

"Lizzy," Jessica said, "let me handle this." She turned back to Polly. "Claire Kerley is missing, and we have reason to believe she's in the area. We're going house to house. Nothing personal."

The lie seemed to appease the man somewhat.

"Now that we're here, though," Lizzy said in the most cheerful voice she could conjure up, "I would love to know how long you've lived by the river."

"A few years," he answered unhappily.

"You must love it." Lizzy was obviously buying time. She took in a whiff. "The air is so pristine. I love the smell of the river. Have you heard of any neighbors planning on putting their place on the market?"

Clearly, he was not a fan of Lizzy's, but he managed to force a smile. "No, I'm sorry." When Lizzy opened her mouth to ask him another question, he turned to Jessica. "Nice as it is to chat with you two, I'm really quite busy."

"It looks like you have a dock leading to the water," Lizzy said. "Do you mind if we have a look around?"

"In fact, I do."

A loud crash sounded from inside the house.

Lizzy looked at Jessica. "What was that?"

"Is someone else inside the house?" Jessica asked the man.

"No. I have a cat, and the animal is always knocking things over."

"I hate to bother you too much longer, Mr. Polly, but I don't think my friend will be able to leave until she's had a look around."

"Not without a warrant. I have been generous enough with answering your questions. I'm afraid we're done here."

Jessica tried to stall, but it was no use. He was about to close the door.

"I know who you are," Lizzy said.

He raised one eyebrow.

"Zachary Tucker."

His forehead creased, and then he sneered at Lizzy.

And that's when Jessica realized Lizzy had been right all along.

Before he could shut the door, Lizzy shoved her foot past Jessica into the doorway, causing the door to bounce off the edge of her sole.

Another loud crash inside. One of the windows to their right had been cracked.

"It's the girl," Jessica said. Both she and Lizzy drove their shoulders with all their might into the door, knocking the man back and sending them crashing inside after him.

He took off across the living room, disappeared through the sliding doors to the balcony overlooking the river. Jessica followed after him, leaving Lizzy to run out through the front door and around the house to cut him off if he tried to escape.

An ear-piercing scream cut through the air. By the time Lizzy got to the backyard, Zachary Tucker was dragging his body toward a kayak along the riverbank. One leg was bent sharply at an odd angle, clearly shattered in more than one place. She looked up at the balcony and realized the idiot had jumped. She stepped over to him and put the barrel of her gun to the back of his head. "Please do keep crawling, Zachary. I'd love to squeeze this trigger."

He slumped to the grass and closed his eyes.

Jessica walked up from behind and cuffed the man's arms behind his back. "I'll take it from here. You find the girl."

Lizzy rushed around the house again, this time in search of Claire Kerley. She made her way back inside and down the hallway to the door of the front room where the window had been broken. It was locked. "Are you in there, Claire?"

There was a faint knock on the wall.

"I'm going to shoot the lock off this door. Knock again if you're out of the way of the door."

Another knock sounded.

Lizzy fired at the lock. The door swung open.

Inside the bedroom, lying on the floor between the bed and window, was the missing girl.

She had thrown every item in the room at the window. Glass crunched beneath Lizzy's feet as she crossed the room.

The girl's face was swollen and bruised. Her lips were cracked. She looked as if she were on the brink of death. She'd been stripped of clothes and every bit of her flesh was covered with cuts and bruises. Parts of her body had been painted. The monster had used her as a human canvas. Her wrists and ankles were raw and infected, but Lizzy did her best not to visibly react to Claire's condition.

She pulled her phone from her pocket and dialed 911. Next she called Jimmy Martin and told him they had found Claire Kerley and gave him the address. After hanging up, she pulled a pillow from the bed and placed it beneath the girl's head, then yanked off the sheet, too, and used it to cover her. "You did good," she told Claire. "I need you to hang in there for a while longer. I'm going to take a quick look around, make sure no one else needs help. I'll be right back—I promise. An ambulance is on its way."

Lizzy walked briskly through the house. She stepped outside onto the balcony and peered over the railing at Jessica and Zachary Tucker, still flat on his belly in the grass with his leg canted at its freakish angle. "I found the girl. She's pretty beat-up, but she's going to be all right. I also called it in. An ambulance is on its way."

"This one says his leg hurts," Jessica said.

"Really? That's too bad."

"Yeah," Jessica agreed. "I was thinking the same thing."

"I'm going to go back and sit with Claire."

"I should have listened to you from the start," Jessica said.

"We're here, aren't we?"

Lizzy walked back into the house, then stopped to look at a painting propped on an easel in the corner of the living room. The picture was grotesque. Claire had been chained and cuffed to a wall. Her hair fell over parts of her face, but her eyes were wild and deranged, her teeth snapping.

Lizzy wanted to rip the canvas to shreds, but she couldn't destroy evidence so she walked away. Drawn by a strong smell and afraid someone else could need her help, Lizzy made her way downstairs. It was damp and dark, and she had to use her shirtsleeve to cover her mouth and nose as she continued down the stairs. Inside a wine cellar, atop a dirty mattress and rolled partially within a bloody tarp, was a dead body. A woman. Her eyes had been carved out of her head.

Lizzy gagged as she ran from the room.

She needed to get Claire out of here.

By the time she got back to the room upstairs, Claire had crawled to the door. "Come on," Lizzy said. "Let's get you outside and get some fresh air." The girl weighed next to nothing. Lizzy propped her on the edge of the bed and fastened the sheet around her again before carrying her down the hallway and out of this nightmare.

Sirens sounded in the distance, growing louder with each step.

"I'm going to live," the girl whispered as Lizzy set her on her feet and they made their way down the walkway.

Lizzy held her close to her side. "That's right. You're a survivor, Claire."

"I need to talk to Mom."

"Let's get into the car, and then we'll give her a call, OK?"

As soon as Lizzy and Claire were sitting safely in the backseat of her car, they called Claire's mother. Lizzy told her that her daughter was alive, and then she held the phone close to the side of Claire's face so she could talk.

"I love you, Mom."

They both wept.

CHAPTER THIRTY-EIGHT

Hours later, Lizzy talked to both Brittany and Cathy on the phone. She told them what had happened and that it was safe to come out of the house. They were shocked to learn that Jake Polly might be the Sacramento Strangler. For the hundredth time, her sister talked about moving to another state. Lizzy would talk to her later, convince her to stay. They needed each other.

As soon as Lizzy said her goodbyes, Jimmy motioned for her to come with him, letting her know they had Zachary Tucker back from the hospital with his broken leg set and they were about to interrogate him. She followed Jimmy deeper into the task force offices, to an already crowded ten-by-ten dimly lit room adjoining the interrogation room.

Behind the glass, she saw Kenneth Mitchell sitting at a table across from Zachary, whose leg was in a cast and propped stiffly on a chair to one side. A wheelchair was parked in the corner. Jessica, along with three other agents, sat up front in the observation room. Jimmy and Lizzy took a seat in the back.

"How long has Claire Kerley been staying with you?" Mitchell asked Zachary.

"I don't recall."

"How did she come to be in your house?"

"She was hitchhiking, so I thought I'd give her a ride. She told me she hated her family and her boyfriend and she wanted to get high. She's a sassy one."

"So you brought her home with you?"

"I did."

"Tell us about the wine cellar."

"What would you like to know?"

"It looked as if you did some renovating. Tell us about the bolts and cuffs that were found embedded in the walls. The ones with your fingerprints all over them."

"Oh, that. It was Claire's idea."

"She asked to be hung by metal cuffs?"

"She certainly did."

"You painted her portrait, is that right?"

"Of course. Lovely Claire wanted something different than the others, so I gave her exactly what she asked for."

"Speaking of the others, let's talk about some of them. I would like to start with Lorry Jo Raciti, the woman found near the American River, not too far from where you live."

"I don't recognize the name. Never met her."

"Maybe this picture will help jog your memory." Mitchell slid an eight-by-ten color photograph of her body in front of him.

"Ahh," he said.

"You remember now?"

"Perhaps," he said, transfixed by the photo.

"So, what were you thinking after you killed her?"

Zachary didn't say anything. Merely leaned closer for a better look.

"We have your journal in our possession. No reason for you to keep it all bottled up. It's over, Zachary."

The killer had yet to take his eyes off the woman he'd killed by the river. "I was thinking how lucky she was to be one of the chosen ones." Zachary looked up and smiled at Kenneth Mitchell. "Her eyes were so blue. They flickered between wild and fearful. I could see her heart pumping against her chest. She was magnificent. My plan was to paint her next—from memory, of course—once I was finished with Claire."

Jessica looked over her shoulder and made eye contact with Lizzy.

Jimmy gave her the thumbs-up.

They had their man. He had just confessed to a murder.

There was a pause during the interrogation when Zachary asked for an energy drink, specifically a Red Bull. He refused to go on until his request was fulfilled.

The questioning went on like that for another two hours. Zachary Tucker/Jake Polly seemed more than content to talk about his victims as Mitchell held up one picture after another.

"So why did you kill them?"

"It's my calling."

"Killing is your calling?"

"Definitely. I am surprised it took you people so long to find me."

"Why is that?"

"I left you enough clues." He gestured to all the pictures scattered across the table. "It was all there, all these years, pointing in my direction."

When Mitchell asked him about Gillian Winslow, the therapist his parents had hired and assigned as Zachary's trustee, Zachary decided he'd given them enough information. "I think I'll request a lawyer now. I want the same deal as the Green River Killer."

"What deal is that?"

"I want life."

"Anything else you want to tell us before a lawyer is appointed to you?"

"Yes. I want the world to know that nobody out there really gets it."

"Nobody gets what, exactly?"

"Evil never dies."

"Can you explain?"

"Of course. You can catch a killer like me and throw away the key, but there's always someone else out there slicing and dicing, killing people just because they can. Me," he said, pointing to his chest, "I am a natural born killer. I killed my own sister, and if given the chance, I would do it again."

Lizzy could see now why she hadn't recognized Jake Polly from Hayley's sketch. Kathryn had been right about his magnetism, and that was something most artists just couldn't translate to paper. Since Kathryn had seen him last, his nose had definitely been broken, maybe more than once—by his victims, Lizzy hoped. His hair was short and straight, much different from the thick, wavy hair Kathryn had described. Zachary had no facial hair whatsoever.

But they had found him, and that's all that mattered.

"Good work," Jimmy said. "That's officially a wrap for me."

There was a mischievous glint in his eye.

"You're finally going to retire?" Lizzy asked.

He jingled the coins inside his pants pockets. "That's right. I want to learn to sail. I want to travel and spend time with the grandkids."

"Good for you. I hope you really do it this time . . . for your sake."

"What about you, Lizzy? Are you going to keep fighting the good fight?"

"Nope. I'm finished being a PI. It took losing Jared to realize this isn't the life I want to lead, and that's something I'll never forget."

Jimmy looked surprised. "No more investigative work?"

"I've had enough. And Zachary Tucker is right."

"About what?"

"Evil never dies. It never ends. Jared knew that. He got it. But me? I kept thinking I could make a dent." She shook her head. "It's impossible. For every evil person caught and locked behind bars, there's two more waiting on the sidelines."

"You made a difference, Lizzy. That counts for a lot."

"Thanks, Jimmy. I'm wishing you the best. Stay in touch, will you?"

"I'll send you a postcard. Let you know what I'm up to."

They came to their feet, smiled at each other, and then he gave her one of his comforting bear hugs.

Mitchell came out of the interrogation room. He raised his arms and tried to get a kink out of his shoulder. His eyes were bloodshot. "Lock that crazy son of a bitch up until he has a goddamn attorney. We've got what we need for now."

Jimmy and Mitchell stepped to the side and shared a few words before Jimmy headed off. Three officers brought Zachary Tucker out of the room. His arms and legs were now chained to his wheelchair.

"Hey, Lizzy Gardner," he said cheerily, metal chains clinking as he gestured her way. He looked at Mitchell. "Can I talk to her for a minute?"

Mitchell looked at Lizzy, who nodded her approval.

Mitchell motioned for the guard, letting them know it was OK to push Zachary that way.

"What? No privacy?"

"Never again," Mitchell told him.

Zachary set his wicked gaze on Lizzy. He looked as if he wanted to hypnotize her with his eyes. "Good thing you caught up to me when you did, because your niece was on my mind."

Lizzy didn't flinch.

"I bet you're thinking the same thing I think every time I have my next victim in sight."

"What's that?"

"Kill, kill, kill, kill."

"No," she said. "That's not what I'm thinking at all."

"Tell me, please."

The corner of her mouth turned up slightly before she said, "I'm thinking about you spending the rest of your life behind bars, hopefully in solitary confinement, every day alone with no one to talk to, no freedom whatsoever."

"And how does that make you feel?"

"Very happy."

"You talked to Kathryn, didn't you?" he asked.

"Several times."

"Did she show you the picture I painted for her?"

"Nope. Didn't mention it."

A flash of anger crossed over his face, and yet he recovered quickly. "She's in love with me, isn't she?"

"Not even a little bit."

His eyes searched her face for the truth. "You're lying. Want to know how I know?"

"How?"

"It takes a liar to know one."

"OK, that's enough chatter," Mitchell said. "Get his ugly mug out of here."

The guards pushed Zachary's wheelchair out of the room. Agents and security filed out after them until there were only three people left in the room: Mitchell, Jessica, and Lizzy.

"You did good," Mitchell said. "Both of you."

"Thank you, sir," Jessica said.

"Jared Shayne was right about you, Jessica Pleiss."

"How so?"

"He said from the beginning that you were going to be a top-notch profiler. Judging by what I've seen so far, he was right. Your keen assessment of the crimes and the reconstruction of events were point on. I'm going to put in a good word for you at Quantico."

"Thank you, sir."

"Now get out of here, both of you. Go get some rest."

CHAPTER THIRTY-NINE

Two days later, Lizzy walked out of the doctor's office and headed straight for her car. She had an appointment with a real estate agent in Loomis. She'd seen the house on the Internet six months ago, had even shown it to Jared. He'd liked it, too. It was run-down and not very big, but it was set on ten acres. She'd only seen the pictures online, but if the house was even half as cozy and quaint as it looked to be in the pictures, she would make an offer. Jared had left her a tidy sum, including the proceeds from the sale of his house. She would sell the business, too, and would be able to live comfortably if she stayed within her means.

She couldn't live with Kitally and Hayley forever, especially now that she knew she was going to have a baby.

After she drove up the long dirt road to the house, she stopped the car and realized the place was even better than she'd imagined. The house had been built in harmony with its natural surroundings. There were fruit trees and plenty of shade trees—a relaxed country setting. There was a pond and a rickety old barn in the foreground. It was hard to believe no one had scooped up the house months ago.

The agent greeted her at the door, took her on a leisurely tour. There were two bedrooms and a smaller room without a closet that could be made into an office if she ever felt the need. Overall it was small, just as she knew it would be, but the high ceilings and open floor plan made it feel airy and spacious. She and the agent turned on faucets and discussed water wells and the two inches of irrigation water she would get during the summer.

When they were done, Lizzy told her she wanted to make an offer. There wasn't any furniture, so they stood at the kitchen counter and drew up the papers. The agent said she would be in touch.

Lizzy's next stop was the cemetery. The place was beautiful and well kept. In the distance there was a funeral taking place—mourners dressed in black, heads down. Lizzy walked past rows of grand headstones. She stopped to view one weathered sandstone marker that appeared to be as old as time. "1892, Corrie Perrelman, beloved wife, mother, and sister."

Jared's grave marker was a good long walk from where she'd started out, but the headstone was clean and the grass around his marker had been mowed recently. She stood there, taking it all in. It was a peaceful day. Blue skies dotted with a few puffy white clouds. After a moment, she took a seat on the grass close to his marker. "I put an offer on that house I showed you," she said. "The one with the acreage in Loomis. You liked it, and you said something about how it would make a good place for our kids to run around." She hadn't meant to cry, but the tears rolled freely as she talked. "We're having a baby, Jared. You and me. Isn't that a kick in the pants?"

She used a sleeve to wipe her face. "I want to thank you for everything. For bringing me back to life and for this child I'm carrying inside me." She took a moment to breathe before she added, "I screwed up, Jared. I thought I could take the law into my own hands and dish out some vengeance, but I was wrong. I want you to know that I'm going to do everything I can to get the girls back on track. And this baby of ours," she went on, her voice wavering, "is going to be brought up surrounded by love." She brushed her fingertips over his headstone. "Everything's going to be OK."

Against her will, the image of Wayne Bennett rose up in her mind, and she prayed what she'd just said was true.

When Lizzy walked into the house a few hours later, there was lots of chatter. Hayley and Kitally had returned.

Betty Ackley, the woman Kitally had been working with at Shady Oaks, sat on the couch, fussing over the baby. Kitally and Hayley were there, too. Female names for Salma's baby were still being tossed out there, everything from Alicia to Zoey, as Salma passed around another Pakistani dish. This one was called besan ladoo. The minute Salma saw Lizzy enter the room, she rushed over to greet her. "So? When is the due date?"

Lizzy frowned. "How did you know?"

"I was the one who told Hayley and Kitally that you were pregnant. It was so obvious."

The room grew quiet until the only noise was the low rumble of a motor outside. Through the window, Lizzy saw Gus pushing a lawn mower through overgrown grass and weeds.

Hayley looked at her and said, "So, what's the verdict?"

"It appears everyone knew I was pregnant except me. Looks like we're having a baby."

They all let out a cheer of some sort. Kitally rushed over to give her a congratulatory squeeze. "When are you due?"

"September 5."

There was a lot to celebrate that day. They had all played a part in putting away the Sacramento Strangler. For now, citizens of Sacramento could breathe easier again.

And that wasn't all. Kitally, Betty, Gus, and the others, had all gathered at the house for a reason. Shady Oaks Nursing Home was going out of business. Stacey Whitmore with Channel 10 News was covering the story.

Kitally hit Pause on the remote and then ran to the back door and called Gus inside.

Once everyone was present, Hayley picked up the remote, hit Play, then turned the volume up. "Stacey Whitmore here, reporting from the Shady Oaks Nursing Home in Orangevale."

The reporting had been prerecorded.

Behind Stacey Whitmore, Shady Oaks was crawling with FBI agents.

"Look," Kitally said, "they're bringing Dixie out in handcuffs. She's being arrested along with the owners and two other orderlies."

"After the sudden death of Gus Valentine's wife," Stacey Whitmore was saying, "a tip from a resident of Shady Oaks prompted Gus Valentine and an investigator to do some snooping around. What they found prompted state officials to look into the matter. When investigators reviewed the medical records of Helsie Valentine, they determined she had died of ailments often related to poor care, including dehydration and an infected ulcer. Officials have since concluded that former resident Mary Branham's demise was hastened by the inappropriate administration of antipsychotic drugs, which can have lethal side effects for seniors.

"The owners and five of their orderlies have declined to speak. The criminal case is ongoing. Health care regulators have already taken action, restricting Shady Oak's medical license. The federal government is likely to move to fine the home's owners upwards of half a million dollars."

Kitally held up a fist and gave Gus a knuckle bump.

"You did it, kiddo."

"*We* did it, Gus. You, me, and Betty."

Wayne Bennett was hardly recognizable. Detective Chase stood at his bedside and took notes. He tried not to look at the man for too long, as it was hard not to wince at his swollen mess of a face. Bennett had been at Sutter General for days now, but this was the first time the man was able to talk.

"If you don't arrest Lizzy Gardner," Bennett was saying, "I'll have every one of your boys scrutinized. They won't be able to bet on a *Monday Night Football* game with their friends without getting written up. Do you hear me, Chase?"

"Do you have any proof that Lizzy Gardner was responsible for what happened to you?"

"I saw her with my own two eyes. Is that proof enough, Detective?"

"I thought you said your face was covered by a ski mask."

Bennett tried to give him a winning smile, but he failed miserably. One of his eyes was swollen shut. His nose had been taped, and his upper lip had been sliced through and then patched up with stitches and tape. His signature flash of straight white teeth was nowhere to be seen. "It was her! I recognized her voice," Bennett said. He pushed one of the buttons on his bed and told the nurse to get him a painkiller and make it quick.

He looked back at Chase. "I have security cameras. I'm sure I've got all the proof you need, Detective. Just don't make the same mistake you made in DC."

"What's that?"

Bennett grimaced in pain. After a moment, he said through gritted teeth, "I know everything about you, Detective. I know why you were demoted, and what good did it do? You knew Mark Falcon owned the police station, but you went after his son anyhow."

"His son was bad news."

Bennett chuckled. "Yeah, I know. So why was he let out after serving two months of a six-year sentence?"

Chase kept quiet, let Bennett have his say. What Bennett said was true, but Chase knew he'd done the right thing. He'd do it again. He'd done all he could do to make sure Falcon's rapist son got a fair trial and was put away. The kid needed to be taught a lesson. But Falcon's son was released too soon, and Chase was demoted for his efforts. He had refused to play office politics, and that had landed him here in Sacramento.

"You refused to violate your own sense of morals, and for what?" Bennett said. "You have a lot to learn, Detective. If you want to impress the higher-ups, you're going to have to impress me first. The guy with the money gets the last say. I'm that guy."

"Are you finished?"

The nurse came in and was about to ask for privacy when Bennett shut her up and told her to just give him the damn shot.

She folded the sheet over and did as she was told.

Chase saw a crisscross of deep red welts across his ribs, stomach, and legs. It appeared every part of him had been left with a mark. Even Bennett's face would more than likely be left with permanent scars.

There was something very satisfying about seeing how the creep had been brutalized, but at the same time he worried about Lizzy. If she was responsible, and even if she wasn't, Bennett was going to make her pay for sticking her nose in his business.

Chase had seen enough. He headed for the door.

"Where do you think you're going?"

"I'm going home."

"We're not finished here, Detective."

"Oh, yes we are. If you have anything more to say, you give me a call and I'll send someone over."

"Get your ass back in here," Chase heard the man call out as he walked toward the elevator.

Lizzy wasn't surprised when she heard from Detective Chase. He told her he had some questions for her, but he wanted her to meet him at his house. He told her lunch would be served, and that she should arrive prepared to eat.

She figured it was about Bennett. She didn't have to play detective to discover Bennett was in the hospital with multiple contusions, a fractured wrist, and some internal bleeding. Nothing that couldn't be fixed. Once Bennett was released, she and the girls would be on red alert. She continued to work with the prosecutor, Grady Orwell. Until Bennett was locked up, nobody was safe. Nobody.

Lizzy arrived at Chase's house right on time. When he opened the door to let her in, she couldn't help but smile at his appearance. Over a pair of beige slacks and a button-up shirt with the sleeves rolled to his elbows was a full-length white apron.

"Looks like you're doing some serious cooking."

"Cooking is serious business. Come on in."

Lizzy followed him inside. Everything looked the same as the last time she was here: single-hole golf course where the dining room table should be, television on in the other room. Detective Chase headed for the kitchen, where he slipped on an oven mitt, opened the oven, and pulled out crusty Italian bread covered in bubbling cheese and tomato sauce—operating entirely with one hand, as he still wore a sling on his left arm.

"How's the arm?"

"It's been better. It'll get there. Time to heal is all it needs."

"Smells good," she said.

"Today we're having eggplant and mozzarella melt. I hope you like garlic butter and eggplant Parmesan."

"It looks delicious."

He'd set places for them in front of stools at the kitchen counter. He poured them both a tall glass of cold milk and then sat down next to her and dug in.

She took a bite. "Delicious. Where did you learn to cook?"

"Mom. She's Italian. Best cook in all of New York City."

After she'd finished about half of her open sandwich, it had become clear he wasn't in a hurry to have a conversation about whatever he had called her here to talk about.

"So, what's this about? Why am I here, Detective?"

He washed his last bite down with half a glass of his milk and then used his napkin to wipe his mouth. "OK, I'm feeling better now. I needed that."

She waited.

"It's about Bennett."

"What about him?"

"I was called to the hospital to take the report. Apparently he was attacked after arriving home from work. He said there were three people working on him, but he only heard two voices. Both female."

"Hmm. Interesting."

"He was beat up pretty bad. Fractured nose, broken wrist, lacerations deep enough to require over a hundred stitches."

"Why are you telling me this? I can't say he didn't deserve it."

"You already know he's a very powerful man."

"He's a child molester and a rapist, and you and I both know he killed Miriam Walters, otherwise she would have turned up by now. I'm sure you've heard about Olimpia Padula? The girl in his program who drowned in the bathtub?"

"She was a drug addict. It happens all the time."

"Chase, listen to what you're saying. Did you ever talk to the girl?" Lizzy shook her head. "I did. Olimpia hadn't taken drugs since she was fifteen. She went straight. She worked hard. Hard enough to be accepted into Bennett's program for honor students." Lizzy tapped a finger on top of her head. "Use some logic. You don't do *that* well in school if you're doing drugs. And that's not all. As he did to so many others, Bennett sexually assaulted Olimpia Padula, but this promising young woman was willing to testify against him."

He sighed.

"It's your problem now, though. I'm closing up shop. I'm done."

That got his attention.

"Don't look so glum. You should be thrilled that I won't be causing you any more trouble."

"Why now?"

"Because I'm pregnant."

That seemed to take the air out of him.

"Jared and I are having a baby. I'm four months along."

Detective Chase looked dumbfounded.

"I think I might have been every bit as stunned as you look right now when I found out."

"Do I detect a note of happiness?"

"Yeah," she said with a smile, "you do. I didn't see it coming, but I'm excited about what's ahead."

Chase's surprise quickly turned to concern. "I'm glad for you, Lizzy, but the reason I asked you to come here today is because I'm worried about something."

Lizzy waited for him to continue.

"Bennett named you specifically as his assailant."

"Ridiculous." Lizzy did her best to appear untroubled. "Thanks for the warning, Detective, but you don't need to worry about me."

"He was hoping to find video footage on his high-definition security system. I have to ask you straight up. Did you set foot on Wayne Bennett's property?"

"No."

"As you know, he can be ruthless."

"You said he was hoping to find video footage . . . Did he or didn't he?"

"My guys have already checked into it. Bennett's recording was on full HD. He didn't have the required HDD storage capacity needed to keep the video loading. He's got nothing."

Relieved, Lizzy said, "Are you trying to say you think he might come after me?"

His shoulders dropped. "I'm just telling you to be careful, that's all."

"Don't worry. I always am."

CHAPTER FORTY

Tonight Hayley had decided to make the rounds by herself. Her car was still broken down and she had no plans to have it fixed, so she had hitchhiked her way to West Sacramento.

She and Kitally had spent five nights out on the streets, and they had nothing to show for their efforts. Kitally might be upset when she found out Hayley went without her, but that was too bad. She preferred to work solo.

She passed by the park and then found a spot where she could sit on the curb and watch a few people down the road setting up camp. She pulled out her cigarettes and lit one up, wondering if she'd ever really be able to quit the habit.

As she sat beneath the stars, she thought of her date with Tommy and found herself smiling as she remembered his absurd talk of his future plans. Living in a little house by the river. Tommy could be a doofus at times, but he'd stuck by her. And she couldn't help but wonder why.

She turned toward the sound of rattling wheels. A shopping cart, being pushed by a guy with long red hair and the beginnings of a beard. He stopped when he'd moved abreast of her and peered down at her.

"Got an extra smoke?"

"Sure."

He took a seat next to her on the curb, and she gave him a cigarette and lit it for him.

"Thanks." He took a long, luxurious drag and sent a column of smoke into the night air. "So," he said, turning to her, "what's a nice girl like you doing out here on the street?"

"Just enjoying a smoke," she said with a laugh. She took a hit and then looked him over. "How's it going?"

"Not too good. I lost my job six months ago. Made the rounds, spending the night with friends and family until I finally wore out my welcome. I wasn't out here on these very streets for too long before I woke up one night to some mean-as-hell monster chick beating the hell out of me."

Hayley sat up. "Skinny girl with white spiky hair?"

"That's her. Demon girl, and I'm not kidding." He shot another shaft of smoke into the night, then shook his head. "Who would have thought someone that mean would have a nice, sweet-sounding name like Nora Belle Castor?"

Butterfly wings danced in her stomach. "How do you know her name?"

"I tried to stop her from stealing my things from my cart here, and when I grabbed hold of her sweatshirt, she yanked away so fast I ended up tearing the thing halfway off her. I was inches from her bare arm, and there it was in fancy black ink—Nora Belle Castor. She lit into me after that. I spent the entire next day filling out a police report. I gave them her name, but they said there was no address for her. Not that they would have given me the information if they had it. They said I wasn't the first one to complain about the girl who everyone referred to as the Ghost." He frowned. "I guess that could have been her mother's name, now that I think about it."

Hayley stood then and handed him her entire pack of cigarettes and the lighter. "Here you go. They're all yours."

"Hey, thanks."

"I really hope you find a way to get yourself off the streets." And then she walked away.

Two weeks after Hayley had found out the name of the Ghost, she walked into the kitchen as she did most mornings after waking up, and she knew instantly that something was wrong.

It was way too quiet, for one thing.

Concerned, she went to Salma's room. The bed was neatly made. All baby accessories were gone. On the dresser was a handwritten note:

Dear Hayley, Kitally, Lizzy, and Jessica,

I can never repay you for your kindness. I hope you find it in your heart to forgive me for leaving without saying goodbye. I couldn't take any chances. Joey and I have been making plans for a while now. Sadly, I will be unable to make contact with you in the future. As you know, it must be this way. In order to live a happy life without looking over our shoulders, difficult choices had to be made. I am giving up the only family I ever knew to make a new life for myself. All of you have taught me what it means to have a family I can trust and lean on in difficult times. I will never forget any of you. Our daughter, Hope Elizabeth, will grow up surrounded by love.

All our best,
Salma, Joey, and Hope

Later that day, Hayley sat at the end of the driveway and made a call to Jessica. It had to be done.

"What's going on?" Jessica asked as soon as she picked up.

"I'm calling in a favor."

"You can't call in a favor, Hayley, unless I owe you a favor, which I don't."

"Do you always have to take everything so literally?"

"I just call it like it is."

"OK, I *need* a favor. How's that?"

"Better. What do you need?"

Hayley looked heavenward. "I need all the help I can get in locating a Nora Belle Castor. Caucasian. Young—late teens, early twenties. Last seen downtown. I've tried everything. I found a cousin, but he had no idea what she was up to or where she was living. Her parents live in New York and have yet to return my calls. I'm stumped."

"No problem," Jessica said.

"Thanks." Hayley couldn't believe it was that easy. If she had known Jessica wouldn't balk at her request, she might have called her weeks ago.

"How are Salma and the baby doing?"

"They're gone. She and Joey took off with Hope Elizabeth in the middle of the night. I found her room empty. Just a note thanking us all, including you, for teaching her what family is all about."

"Ahh, well, that's sweet . . . Wait a minute, did you say Hope Elizabeth? Did she finally give her a name?"

"That's what the note says."

"I like it. And Salma is right—we are family, aren't we?"

"That's us. One big happy family."

Jessica laughed. "Did Lizzy tell you that she's leaving the investigative business?"

"She did."

"Did she tell you she was thinking about selling the business?"

"She mentioned it, yes."

"What do you think?"

"If you're thinking of buying it, I think it's one of the craziest ideas you've ever had, and you've had your fair share."

"Wow. Don't be shy. Tell it like it is."

"You never liked the business," Hayley said. "You hate stepping over the line. You don't like confrontation. You quit the business for a reason."

"Hey, I was always good with people."

"Are you kidding me? You were shot and kidnapped, and I've never seen anyone get more doors slammed in their face than you."

"Now you're just being your usual rude self."

"You asked me what I thought. The idea makes absolutely no sense to me. You've worked hard to get where you are. Why would you even consider giving that up?"

"I asked you what you thought about Lizzy selling the business. Although I've already begun to realize that bureaucracy equals paperwork and I've never been keen on paperwork, I have zero interest in becoming a PI."

"Well, phew, that makes me feel better."

Jessica laughed. "Kitally, on the other hand, has shown some interest."

"Kitally wants to buy the business?"

"When Lizzy and I talked about it, that's what she told me."

"Well, she certainly has the money to do it," Hayley said. "Either way, you should stick with the FBI gig, Jessica. You're going to make a fine special agent someday. We all know that."

"Thanks," Jessica said.

"You're welcome. Now if you could find an address for Nora Belle Castor, I will be forever indebted."

"What did the girl do?"

"She's trouble with a capital *T*. She beats the crap out of homeless people while they're sleeping."

"So, what are you going to do with her when you find her?"

"Don't worry, I'm going to turn her over to the police." And that much was true.

There was a long bout of silence before Jessica said, "Sure. I'll call you if I get a hit."

"Thanks. Talk to you soon."

As soon as she hung up the phone, Hayley heard Lizzy's footfalls approaching. *Funny*, she thought, *how everyone has their own distinct walk*. She always knew who was coming and going based on the quickness of their movements and the noises they made. Kitally walked fast and always sounded like a deer scampering through the room. Lizzy was the opposite. Not slow, exactly, but methodical, as if she was watching everything in her path as she went along.

Lizzy sat down on the curb next to her, a cup of hot tea snug between her palms. Hayley could hear her breathe in.

"It's so quiet in there without Salma and the baby," Lizzy said at last.

"You might want to enjoy it while it lasts."

"You might be right."

"If you came out here to find out if I was still angry with you, the answer is no. If you had finished Bennett off, I don't think you could have lived with yourself, although now we all need to sleep with one eye open."

"I think it's time to call it quits."

"You can't simply forget about Bennett. You know that."

Lizzy nodded. "Not Bennett, but the others."

"There's only two more people left on the list who haven't been taken care of. Scott Shaffer and the Ghost."

"Bag it, Hayley," Lizzy said. "It was never a good idea to begin with."

"I'll think about it," Hayley said, even though she would do no such thing.

Lizzy looked at her for a long moment, then asked, "Do you remember the first time we met?"

Hayley dropped her head into her open palms. "Are you going to get all sentimental on me, Lizzy?"

"I don't know . . . maybe. My hormones are raging. Are you really going to deprive me of one little sentimental journey through time?"

"Fine. Go for it."

"The first time I saw you, I saw a little bit of me in you." Lizzy nudged her arm. "Don't make fun."

"I didn't say a word."

"You had piercings all over your face, and your hair was dark and spiky. You had a tough look to you, but there was one thing that gave you away, something that told me you just needed a friend."

It was quiet, and Hayley knew she was waiting for her to ask. "OK, I'm taking the bait. How did you know I was really this amazingly kind person with a soft inner shell?"

"All sarcasm aside, it was the angel tattoo on your collarbone."

Hayley shook her head.

"What?"

"You're grasping at straws here. I almost chose a devil with horns instead of an angel. It's just a tattoo, Lizzy."

"You're right. Who am I kidding? You made the sheriff bleed that day."

They both laughed, and yet they both knew it wasn't funny. Lizzy had asked Hayley to demonstrate for a classroom full of young girls how she might get away from someone if she were grabbed from behind. After Officer Stuckey put his arms around Hayley, she bit him so hard he bled right through the sleeve of his shirt.

"I wonder how many kids over the years really listened," Lizzy said, "really understood what they would need to do to save their own lives."

"No telling," Hayley said.

They sat quietly for a moment, each lost in her thoughts.

"Brace yourself for some more sentimental claptrap," Lizzy said.

"Oh God."

Lizzy ignored her. "I know you miss your mom," she said, "but I want you to know that I love you as if you were my own daughter. I never want you to feel as if you're alone. Not for one minute. You will always have me, and I like to think that I will always have you. Does that make sense?"

Hayley gave her a nod.

"It's hard to believe I'm going to be a mother, isn't it?"

"Not really. I saw you hold Salma's baby. You looked like a natural to me."

"Jared would have been an amazing father," Lizzy said.

"He would have been. But you will be an amazing mother, and that kid of yours will be just fine."

"And you," Lizzy said, "will be an extraordinary godmother."

"I can't be there for your baby," Hayley told her. "I want to be, I really do, but I've decided to leave town."

"I know you're angry at me for not taking care of Bennett while I had the chance, but, like you said, I couldn't have lived with it. It wouldn't have been right. And I also know I've made a lot of mistakes and I've let you down more than once. But, Hayley, you can't leave."

"You didn't let me down. Yes, I would have preferred it if Bennett had been taken out of the picture, it's true, but it was your decision to make, not mine. Besides, I'm not going anywhere until that maniac is behind bars. He's a loose cannon, and we can't leave him be."

"Agreed," Lizzy said.

"You never let me down, Lizzy. I let myself down. Sure, we might be able to put a few criminals away, save a few more lives from being ruined, but it will never stop. I get that. And, yes, there was a time when I thought I could fight evil with evil. Maybe you did, too. But I still have this rage inside me. It's deep and it's dark, and it hasn't even hit the surface. I certainly can't be around your son or daughter, a tiny person who would be influenced by my actions and words. I can't change, not completely. I don't even know if I want to change."

"If you left, I would spend the rest of my days worrying about you. Stay with me. Help me raise this baby. You know I can't do it alone."

"Nice try. You've been alone most of your life. You were born to be a mom. Hell, you'll be the best mom in the world. I know it and you know it."

"I found a house in Loomis," Lizzy went on. "It's not far from here. The property is amazing. There's a lake and an old barn. We could get a horse. There's an extra room just for you. Whether you come to live with me next month or next year, I want you to know there will always be a room ready and waiting for you."

"I appreciate it," Hayley said.

Lizzy patted her knee and then pushed herself to her feet. No sooner had she walked back into the house than Hayley's phone vibrated.

It was Jessica.

Hayley picked up the call.

"I have an address."

"Already?"

"Let's just say I got a little help from a friend."

"OK. I'm all ears—let's have it."

CHAPTER FORTY-ONE

Sitting across the street from the home of Scott Shaffer, number four on their list, Hayley looked through the binoculars and saw movement in the upstairs window.

She looked at the time. They had replayed what needed to be done over and over. It was supposed to take five minutes, seven tops. But Kitally had been inside the house for twelve minutes. "Hurry up, Kitally. Get in. Get out. That's the rule." She never should have agreed to let her handle this one, but Kitally had made it clear that she was tired of always being on the outside looking in. And besides, she was the one who knew about making bombs.

Just when Hayley thought about texting her and calling the whole thing off, she saw Kitally jump over the side gate and run across the street toward her. She jumped into the passenger seat and said, "Go!"

As they drove off, they heard an explosion. In the rearview mirror, she saw part of the roof land on the front lawn.

"I thought you said it would be a small explosion."

"That was a small explosion."

"His roof just came off."

"That was two shingles at the most. It was perfect."

"Nobody was in there, right?"

"Nobody was in there," Kitally repeated. "Not so fun sitting in the car waiting and not knowing what's happening, is it?"

Hayley didn't respond.

"When they find all of those stolen goods in his place, they are going to put Scott Shaffer away for a very long time."

Hayley could only hope. They had gone to a lot of work for this one. They had stolen Shaffer's backpack from the backseat of his car and then taken assorted debris from his garage—everything Kitally would need to make a bomb. Tonight was the night Shaffer usually went to a club or drove the streets until he found some unsuspecting young woman to get into his car. And then he raped her and dropped her off.

"I really hope this works," Hayley said.

"If it doesn't," Kitally said, "I'll go back to sharpening knives and let you do what you do best."

"Mind if I borrow your car for a while?" Hayley asked when she pulled up in front of the house.

"What for?"

"I just have one more thing I need to take care of."

"Are you sure you don't need my help?"

"Positive. This one's mine."

"And after this, we're done with all of this craziness, right?"

"Absolutely."

Hayley pulled her ski mask over her face and took out her tension wrench, worked it within the lock until she heard a click, then snuck quietly through the door. She'd been watching Nora Belle for a while now, and she knew her routine. The only thing Hayley regretted was that Nora Belle had gotten in another beating. The good news was that the man with the red hair and Naomi were able to scare the Ghost off before the old man took too many blows.

Hayley glanced at the couch, saw the Ghost's boyfriend passed out and snoring loud enough to wake the dead. She walked slowly down the narrow hallway. The boards were creaky, but the snoring would take care of that. She eased open the door to the bedroom, and there on the bed was Nora Belle, sleeping peacefully.

After locking the door behind her, she stepped to the side of the bed and watched the Ghost sleep. Hayley pushed her sleeves to her elbows, then climbed atop her on the bed and made herself comfortable.

Nora Belle's eyes shot open. "Who the fuck are you?"

"I'm the Phantom," Hayley said, and then she started pummeling her, hitting Nora Belle's face with such force and so often that very soon all she was aware of were the crunch of bone beneath her fists and the spray of blood on her face. Nora Belle bucked beneath her, but she was trapped beneath layers of sheets and blankets.

Hayley wouldn't stop. She drew back and hit her again and again until her knuckles began to hurt.

When she at last stopped to examine her aching knuckles, Nora Belle laughed wetly beneath her. A number of her front teeth were broken. Her nose would never look the same. "Not so easy, is it?"

Hayley reached over to the bedside table, grabbed hold of a lamp, and bashed her over the head with it.

That silenced her. Finally. Hayley felt for a pulse. She was still alive.

Hayley walked into the closet, gathered all the white sneakers she could find and shoved them into a duffel bag.

Finished with the shoes, she turned about to survey her work.

Satisfied, she headed back the way she came, walked past the boyfriend, and slipped out the front door. After she delivered the shoes to the homeless, she told Naomi and friends the Ghost's full name and where she lived. They assured Hayley they would take care of the rest. Hayley didn't know what that meant exactly, but it was out of her hands now.

It was later than shit by the time she made it back to Kitally's house. Tommy was sitting on the front stoop waiting for her. If not for the front light being on, she wouldn't have known it was him.

"Where have you been?" he asked.

"Out and about."

"Doing what?"

"Walking. Thinking. The usual. What's up?"

"I've been thinking a lot about you lately, and I wanted to talk. I heard from Lizzy that you were thinking about moving away."

"It's true. Once I'm sure Bennett is no longer a threat to Lizzy and Kitally, I'll start making plans." She sat down next to him, close enough to smell a hint of soap, or maybe something more. "Are you wearing cologne?"

He ignored the question, his expression bleak. "Were you ever going to talk to me about this harebrained idea of yours to move away?"

"Sure . . . eventually I would have gotten around to it."

He looked into her eyes and held her gaze. "You have no idea how I feel about you, do you?"

"Tommy, you wear your feelings and emotions on your sleeve. Of course I know how you feel. But here's the problem. You have no idea who I am. I'm bad news, Tommy. I've done things I can never talk to you or anyone else about. Things I don't even like to think about myself. And the thing is . . . I don't know if I can stop, or if I want to."

"I love you, Hayley. Whatever it is you're going through, I want to help you."

"I care about you, Tommy, you know I do. But whatever you think we've got going . . . it's over." She pushed herself to her feet and walked to the door. "I can't let you into my life."

"I know you better than you think," Tommy said. "I know you're all screwed up, but I'm never giving up on you, Hayley. You might not be able to see it yet, but I can. I can see the light shining out from inside of you. It's bright. Blinding, even. Even tonight, when you first laid eyes on me, I saw it all—your strength and goodness, your compassion, your need to help others because nobody was there to help you when you needed it."

"Go home, Tommy."

"Sure, I'll go." He stood. "But if you do decide to move away, no matter where you end up, I'll be somewhere close, waiting for you to understand that me and you are going to spend the rest of our lives together."

CHAPTER FORTY-TWO

All the girls—Hayley, Jessica, Kitally, and Brittany—had come to Lizzy's new house to paint the baby's room. The problem was, they wouldn't let Lizzy help. Sniffing paint while eight months pregnant was not advised. Instead of arguing with them, Lizzy kept herself busy in the kitchen, but she made sure to check in and bark orders every once in a while just to keep them on their toes.

As she stood over the kitchen sink, she thought she saw something out of the corner of her eye. Her head snapped up, and her gaze roamed over the property. The beat of her heart accelerated. There was nothing out there.

She counted to ten.

Calm down, she told herself. *You're safe.*

"We're finished," Kitally said before Lizzy could enter the baby's room. "Where should we put these brushes?"

"Bring everything outside. I've set up two buckets of warm water by the faucet," Lizzy said as she led the way. Once outside, she watched them walk single file out of the house. Every one of them had more paint on their faces and bodies than they had on their brushes. They dropped their brushes into the first bucket. Brittany worked on getting paint from the brushes while everyone else washed paint from their hands and faces using water and hand soap.

Lizzy put a hand on her belly, prompting one of them to ask, "Boy or girl? Do you know yet?"

"I have no idea," Lizzy said. "I told the doctor I didn't want to know ahead of time."

"Any ideas for names?" Kitally asked.

"Not yet. But don't worry. I won't take as long as Salma did to come up with a name."

"We need to hurry this along," Hayley said, "if we're going to get Jessica to the airport on time."

"When are you coming back to Sacramento?" Lizzy asked Jessica.

"I'm not sure yet, but I'll give you a call next week."

Lizzy watched the girls and found herself smiling, relieved to think that their vigilantism had been short-lived. Nobody, including Detective Chase, ever brought up the file regarding the unnamed man with the bag over his head, leaving Lizzy to believe, or at least hope, it had been a suicide, just as she'd thought. Owen Dunham, the man who'd had his balls cut off, and Donald Holmes, the prison guard, were nowhere to be found. Holmes was a wanted man. If he ever did reappear, he would be thrown in jail, since they had searched his house and discovered he had uploaded thousands of indecent images of children on the Internet. Wallace, the first on their list to be thrown in jail, would be serving the next ten years locked up. Scott Shaffer, number four on the list, had been arrested after one of his homemade bombs was detonated. They'd found five more bombs along with detailed letters on his computer of the buildings he planned to destroy, including the state capitol. Hayley and Kitally both swore they had nothing to do with the bombing incident. *Ironic* was the word Kitally had used when Lizzy asked her about it. Hayley had responded with a shrug and nothing more. Lizzy got a different response from her when she'd asked about Nora Belle Castor, also known as the Ghost. Within twenty-four hours after Hayley had delivered the Ghost's name and address to a group of homeless people, the girl had disappeared. Hayley swore she had no idea what had become of her.

Wayne Bennett was the only one on their list who was free to do as he pleased. His crutches slowed him down, and, according to Detective Chase, he would be undergoing an extensive and painful recovery. Even so, there would come a day when he was back to his old tricks. Grady Orwell, prosecutor and now friend, had a new plan he wanted to discuss with Lizzy, and she would be meeting with him next week.

Brittany and Jessica gave Lizzy a hug and headed for Kitally's car.

"We didn't hang the mobile or the pictures," Kitally explained, "because the walls are still wet and you should probably wait for Tommy. He said he would come by next week to help." She gave Lizzy a hug, told her to take care of herself, and then made her way to the car.

Hayley stood at Lizzy's side. "I really don't like the idea of you living here in the boonies," Hayley said, "without a gun to protect yourself."

"I still have my gun. I just want to get used to keeping it locked up where it belongs. I can't keep it in a drawer after this baby is born."

"I get that. But you and I both know Bennett is going to find out where you live. When that happens, you need to be armed and ready."

"He'll be out of commission for a while longer," Lizzy told her. "What about Owen Dunham and Donald Holmes?"

"What about them?"

"I haven't been able to locate either one of them. What if they decide to seek revenge against you and Kitally?"

"It's not going to happen."

"How do you know?"

"I just know," Hayley said. "Let it go, and stop worrying. It's not good for the baby."

Lizzy gazed out toward the pond. She refused to believe Hayley had stepped over the line. Instead, she thought about all the barbecues and parties they would have here on her property. She would get a kayak and have someone set up a horseshoe pit. It was easy to let her imagination get away from her because in her mind's eye, they were all here, even Jared.

Two hours after the girls had left, Lizzy stepped back, screwdriver in her hand, and wiped her brow. She took a good long look at the baby's room. They had painted the room a beautiful powder blue. On one of the walls, Hayley had painted a tree with two shades of green leaves and a bluebird singing on a branch. She was a talented young woman. The room was perfect.

Although Lizzy had promised them she would wait for Tommy to build the mobile that attached to the crib, she'd only managed to hold off for an hour. After they all left the house, Lizzy found the tools she needed, and finished the job herself.

She wasn't an invalid—she was pregnant.

Setting up the mobile had taken fifteen minutes.

She set the screwdriver on the dresser. Her feet sank into plush carpet as she walked to the crib. Reaching inside, she brushed her fingertips over the cotton blanket. She wound up the mobile next. Smiled when the whimsical music began to play and the tiny knit animals went around and around.

Back at the dresser, she opened the top drawers, which were filled with nighties and soft cotton T-shirts. When she looked up, she caught a glimpse of her reflection in the mirror. She'd been eating good and taking better care of herself since she learned she was pregnant. Her face was filling out again. Her cheekbones were less prominent, and the haunted expression was finally disappearing. She laid the palms of her hands on her growing belly, felt her baby kick, not once, but twice. It was still hard for her to believe Jared's baby was growing inside her.

She picked up the photo Jessica had snuck into the room as a surprise before they all left. She knew it was Jessica because she was the one who had run back into the house at the last minute, telling everyone she'd forgotten her cell phone. The picture was of Lizzy and Jared, taken a few years ago on an exceptionally beautiful day with nothing but blue skies in the background. They were holding hands, both smiling. Jessica had taken the picture without their knowledge.

A lump caught in her throat.

She was having their baby. A baby made in love. Their child would grow up hearing stories about his or her daddy. How brave his or her daddy was. How handsome, too.

"What a touching moment."

Her head snapped up.

A sickening jolt of awareness lit up her insides. Wayne Bennett was standing in the doorway of the baby's room. He wore a boot on his bad leg, but apparently he no longer needed crutches. He'd lost a considerable amount of weight. His face was a mess.

"You honestly thought you could do what you did and all would be forgiven? I thought you were smarter than that, Lizzy Gardner."

She put the picture down, her fingers feeling around the top of the dresser for the screwdriver.

Where the hell is it?

She found it. With screwdriver in hand, she took a slow backward step toward the crib, her gaze never leaving the man in the doorway. "How did you find me?"

He tried to flash his trademark grin, but his upper lip was twisted because of a thick keloid scar that now ran across his face; his attempt to smile failed miserably. The scar ran diagonally across his face, starting at his lip and across his nose and one eye, ending at his hairline.

"I have my ways," he said as he stepped closer. "And you must have known I never overlook unfinished business."

"Was Miriam Walters unfinished business?"

"What do you think?"

"What did you do with her body?"

"The same thing I'm going to do with yours. Nobody will ever find you. Just think—you'll be sparing your friends and family the price of an expensive coffin." His eyes lit up. "And if there is an afterlife, you and Jared will be together again." He looked at the crib beside her. "All three of you, in fact. How sweet it will be. I have a place ready for you—a nice, deep grave beneath rich, dark soil."

He took another step toward her.

She jabbed the screwdriver in the shrinking space between them.

He chuckled. "Put that away. You'll just hurt yourself."

Another step toward her. He pulled a knife from his pocket and opened its short blade.

Pinned in the corner between the crib and the wall with a lousy screwdriver for a weapon, Lizzy had no illusions about her chances. Still, there was nothing for her to do but strike first. Just as he began to take his last closing step, Lizzy swept the tangled, glittering mobile hard into his face with one hand and drove the screwdriver into his arm with the other, ramming him with her shoulder as he bellowed and running past him before he could inflict any damage of his own.

The bellowing went silent as she raced for the front door. Whether the silence was good or bad she didn't know, but she had her answer as she fought to free the door of its chain and felt a sharp, searing pain between her shoulder blades. His knife went deep. Her hands fell away from the chain and went flat against the door. An immense whoosh of breath left her as she felt him pull the knife from her flesh.

Bennett released a long satisfied sigh, like a lover might, and then she felt him begin to move again.

Her baby. She must save the baby. Dropping and wheeling, she pushed herself from the door and rolled to one side as he struck again. The blade struck hard, impaling the wood.

She found her feet and staggered away, her body already growing numb.

A weapon. She needed a weapon.

Gun and holster had been locked away. She'd made the mistake of thinking her life could be a simple one, but she'd been wrong. *Evil never dies.* Zachary Tucker's words.

She could hear Bennett on her heels again.

As she passed the decorative cabinet in her living area, she grabbed the heavy iron statue—an elephant, its thick trunk reaching for the sky, a sign of good luck—and pivoted hard on her heels, swinging the elephant with every ounce of strength she could summon and making contact with Bennett's left shoulder, lifting a grunt from him and sending him staggering back, an expression of surprise on his face.

The heavy cut glass vase came next, but that one he ducked.

She ran past the couch, down the hallway, and to her bedroom. She planned to lock the door, call 911—but Bennett's reactions were faster than hers. He cut between a chair and the coffee table, dived for her, and stabbed her leg with his knife, bringing her to the ground with him.

He yanked the knife out, releasing a lance of pain from her leg and a low chuckle from Bennett. He sounded as though he was having the time of his life. He probably was, at least until she drew the knee of her good leg to her chest and kicked her heel into his chin, then delivered another swift kick to his groin.

He doubled over. Growled in pain.

All she could do was crawl away from him, leaving a bloody trail across the floor as she made her way to the kitchen.

She couldn't feel him coming after her, but she knew it wouldn't be long. She dragged herself across the floor, past the small wood dining table to the cabinets, straining every muscle as she tried to pull herself upward. Another inch and she could reach the top drawer where she kept the knives.

But he was coming.

She could hear him now.

She opened a different drawer instead. When he appeared, she threw everything she could at him: an apple slicer, serving spoons, and a rubber spatula.

It was no use.

Even with his bad leg, he had no problem maneuvering. He ducked and shuffled, easily dodged every utensil.

He was laughing again now, having fun with her.

With the meat tenderizer in her grasp, she caught sight of the broom leaning against the wall and the cabinets in the far corner of the kitchen.

She had explicitly told Kitally no weapons allowed in her house.

But Kitally had left the broom for her anyhow.

The girl knew about living alone. She was brilliant, and the love Lizzy felt for her in that moment was boundless.

Lizzy crawled that way, keeping the table between herself and Bennett, dragging her injured leg behind her. She must've made quite a picture, because he laughed again.

Keep laughing. Take your time. Toy with me, you bastard.

And he did. He let her reach the broom, let her maneuver herself until she was sitting upright on the floor, leaning against the wall for support and struggling to catch her breath. Shivering and weak, she knew she was losing the fight. Holding the broom with one hand, she placed the other on her belly and willed the baby to kick. There was no movement.

"Give it up, Gardner. It's over."

He stood near the sink, ten feet away.

This was it. All of her past training, everything she'd been through had brought her to this moment. She refused to be a victim. She needed to get to her feet. She had no choice. Using the broom and the wall for support, she pushed her body upward, grimacing in pain, until finally she stood tall. Their gazes never strayed from each other. "I will not let you harm my baby."

"You should have thought about that months ago." He cocked his head to one side, staring at her with a confused look in his eyes. "Who do you think you are?"

With both hands clutched tightly around the broomstick, she twisted the handle, trying to release the brush at the bottom as she talked to him, hoping to keep his attention on her words and away from the broom. "I'm just one person trying her best to get a little justice in the world." She twisted harder. Something clinked and came loose, but she kept her eyes on Bennett's.

He smiled. "Was it worth it?"

"I think so," she said.

He shook his head. "You've found yourself in a very tight corner, haven't you, Lizzy?"

"It appears so, but I have my broom and I will not lay down my weapon and give up."

"Your weapon?" He let out another throaty chuckle. "You're ridiculous, Lizzy Gardner, but you're a fighter. I'll give you that. I could see it in your eyes the day you and that reporter came to film me. That was your first mistake. That was the day I started watching you, Gardner. And I never had to go out of my way to find you because I have eyes and ears everywhere."

"So, why are you here? Why didn't you send one of your goons to do your dirty work?"

"Because *this* right here," he said, wagging a finger back and forth between the two of them, "means too much to me to hand it off to one of my 'goons,' as you say."

"Oh, I see. I'm special." Her thumb slid back and forth on the smooth wood as she searched for the button or lever Kitally had used to release the spear.

"I don't know if *special* is the word I would use."

"I have a word for you," she said, still searching for the damned lever. "But I don't think you deserve to know what that word is."

"Oh, you're a tease," he said. "Please, tell me now and spare me the suspense."

"Not until I'm standing over your cold, dead body," she said as she slid a hand to the top of the handle. "That's when I'll bend down on my knees and whisper it into your ear, so softly you'll think an angel is blowing you one last kiss before she boots your ass to the devil downstairs."

There. Her thumb made contact with the tiny switch that would cause a sharp spear to jut outward. She smiled.

"You do realize you're bleeding out, don't you?" Bennett asked her. "If I choose to stand here long enough, I could watch you die a slow, painful death, but I'm more compassionate than you think."

"I'm not the one who is going to die tonight," she said between ragged breaths.

"You never give up, do you?"

"Never."

"Well, Gardner, I'm a busy man." He started for her, his ugly and crooked smile twisting into a mask of rage right before he lunged for her.

She lifted the broom handle, pushed hard on the lever, and braced for impact.

The next few seconds were a crazy blur. Bennett had come at her so fast she never saw the tip of the spear before it sprang into place and disappeared within his chest.

His face paled.

Gripping the broom handle as tightly as she could, she yanked back and pulled the spear out of his chest, then slid slowly to the floor, her back against the wall.

Blood bloomed up through his shirt as he staggered backward, out of reach. A look of surprise touched his eyes before he toppled over, unmoving.

Within a minute, his chest no longer rose and fell with each breath. It was over. He would never hurt anyone else.

She closed her eyes, every breath a struggle. White light exploded around her. And then she saw Jared. He was smiling at her, and her spirit lifted at the sight of him. She reached for him. He leaned close to her ear and whispered three words.

Detective Chase was watching a football game and enjoying deep-fried tortellini when he got a call.

Officer Gary Johnson was on the line. "You called it, Detective. They found Miriam Walters's body less than a mile from Wayne Bennett's Lake Tahoe cabin."

Stunned, Chase picked up the remote and shut off the TV. "Where exactly was the body?"

"There's a trail that leads from Bennett's cabin to the lake. Her body was found half-buried just off the beaten path, so to speak."

All the air left him. Chase knew Bennett was bad news, but he'd never figured the man for a murderer.

"Are you still there?"

"I'm here," Chase said, trying to collect his thoughts.

"So it looks like Gardner was right. Bennett was lying through his teeth when he said he never met Miriam Walters."

"Where did you hear that?"

"It's on the tape that Gardner sent to the station, along with other evidence against Wayne Bennett before she announced her retirement from the PI business."

"Where is Bennett now? Have they brought him in for questioning?"

"We're trying to find him. He wasn't home, so I went to his work."

"He couldn't be back at work already. He can hardly walk."

"According to his secretary, he returned a few days ago. The last time he called in, he told her he had a dinner meeting. She hasn't heard from him since."

Detective Chase hung up on Johnson, grabbed his keys, and ran out of the house. He knew Lizzy was living in Loomis, but he had no idea what her new address was, so he called Jimmy Martin.

First time for everything.

After he explained what was going on, Jimmy's voice went tight. He gave Chase her address and told him to call him once he reached the house.

Detective Chase white-knuckled the steering wheel all the way to Loomis. Forty-five minutes never felt so long. By the time he arrived, it was dark, which didn't help matters, considering she lived in the middle of nowhere. There was a BMW parked in front of the house. He called in the license plate and didn't like the information he got back. The car belonged to Wayne Bennett.

He called for backup and then headed for the front door, listened, and quickly decided he didn't like what he heard.

The sound of nothing was seldom a good thing.

With his gun in one hand, he turned the doorknob with the other. The door was unlocked. There was blood everywhere. He could practically taste it.

Working his way to the right, he called out Lizzy's name as he went.

Paint. He could smell paint. He flipped on a light. The baby's room had just been painted. The lamp on the floor, broken. His pulse raced, adrenaline soaring as he exited the room and made his way through the living area and into the kitchen, where he found Bennett faceup on the floor in front of the sink. Pools of blood had formed on both sides of his body.

He knelt down. There was no pulse.

And then he saw Lizzy.

Her head was propped up against the wall at the far corner of the room. She wasn't moving.

His heart sank. Blood—so much blood.

Kneeling at her side, his fingers on her neck, he felt for a pulse.

He tried her wrist. Nothing.

"Lizzy Gardner. Don't you die on me."

And that's when he saw it.

A twitch of her finger.

He called Dispatch. "Where the hell is the ambulance? There's a live one here. Get someone here pronto, or I'm taking names!"

EPILOGUE

One Year Later

Nicholas Gardner Shayne had taken his first step at nine months, when he still looked way too young to walk. According to the pediatrician, he was average in height and weight. He had dark hair and dark eyes just like his father, Jared Shayne. He liked to do everything fast. He loved animals, although Hannah ran and hid every time Nicholas came too close. Nicholas also loved following Lizzy around the property.

Today Nicholas turned one, and at the moment, he was chasing after the new puppy Detective Chase had brought him—an Entlebucher Mountain Dog.

Chase had assured Lizzy the animal was smart, personable, and agile and would be devoted to Nicholas. He said they needed protection up here in the middle of nowhere. And Lizzy knew firsthand that he was right.

At the moment, Jessica and Magnus were sitting by the willow tree near the pond—Jessica on a bench and Magnus in his wheelchair, some off-road number he powered through the grass without much effort.

Jessica still worked for the FBI and was on the fast track to becoming one of the best criminal profilers in the world, spending most of her time working cold cases.

Magnus had quit working for the DEA. He and Jessica were talking marriage, but those two liked to take things slow. They were waiting to see if Jessica could get transferred to the Sacramento area. Although Magnus would never walk again, he had mastered the use of his wheelchair and he was getting on with life. From where Lizzy stood, she saw Magnus laughing as he watched Nicholas chase after the puppy.

Kitally hadn't changed a bit. She was energetic, always teetering on the wild side. She had followed through on her plans to buy Lizzy Gardner Investigations and had no plans to change the name, since she hoped Lizzy might decide to join her later down the road.

Not a chance.

In twelve months, Kitally had become one of the best damn insurance fraud investigators in Sacramento, and business was good. She had also started a new line for security weapons: bra with hidden dagger, broomstick with push-button spear, brass knuckles that delivered an electric shock, and her newest weapon—a wraparound leather-and-chain belt that doubled as a lethal whip.

Jimmy Martin had retired, just as he said he would, and a postcard had arrived yesterday wishing Nicholas a happy birthday. He and his wife had sold their house in California and were now traveling the world, spending months at a time in France, Mexico, Italy, and England.

Brittany and Cathy were the next to arrive, their arms loaded with birthday gifts for Nicholas. Cathy visited often, and the two of them would sit outside and enjoy long talks while Nicholas played close by. Lizzy had heard from Brittany that her sister was dating again, but apparently Cathy wasn't ready to introduce him, since she hadn't brought him to the party.

Brittany was a sophomore at Sac State. She'd grown another inch. With light-brown hair and a smile that didn't quit, she was beautiful.

"I told you we weren't going to spoil Nicholas," Lizzy said to the two of them. "No presents, remember?"

"Mom's fault," Brittany told her as she slid the gifts under the food table. "Where did that puppy come from?" She pointed toward the pond, where the dog barked at Kitally as she climbed into the kayak and pushed off.

"Detective Chase thought Nicholas and I needed additional protection."

"I think that's a good idea," Cathy said. Her face paled when she saw a Mercedes pull up and park alongside all the other cars in the gravelly parking area.

It was Jared's mom and dad.

Cathy turned to Lizzy. "Did you invite them?"

Lizzy nodded. "I thought it was time they met their grandson. You two make yourselves at home. I'm going to go get Nicholas and have him say hello to his grandparents."

A few minutes later, introductions were made. Jared's father became teary-eyed. Nicholas, being a perceptive little boy, took the old man's hand and dragged him off to see his new puppy.

"Is he going to be OK?" Lizzy asked Mrs. Shayne.

"He'll be fine. I think he's overwhelmed by how much Nicholas looks like Jared at that age. We have the pictures you've sent us, but seeing our grandson in person is quite a shock. I'm sorry it took us this long to come see him."

Lizzy didn't mind. Everyone had his or her own demons to deal with. She and Mrs. Shayne watched the two of them walk off—the tall man with the slow gait being led by a one-year-old who reminded them all so much of Jared.

Tommy was the last one to pull up the long drive and join the party. Everyone converged on his car, straining to see if he might have brought anyone else along for the ride, but he was alone.

After Hayley had made certain that Lizzy would survive Bennett's attack, she had left Sacramento. Tommy had begged her to stay. They all had. But there was no stopping her. Her mind was made up. And no one had seen Hayley since.

Tommy often stopped by to see how Lizzy and Nicholas were doing. He would play with Nicholas, do odd jobs around the house, and then Lizzy wouldn't hear from him until the next time he showed up unexpectedly.

Lizzy greeted Tommy as he climbed out of his car. "Any word from Hayley?"

"Not so far."

Watching Tommy jog down toward Nicholas, Lizzy wondered if he knew anything about the list that she, Kitally, and Hayley had put together so long ago. She'd probably never know the answer to that, since she had no intention of ever bringing up the subject. Far better to let it lie. As she watched, he picked up her son and twirled him about, making Nicholas laugh.

Hayley would come back eventually, Lizzy thought. She was certain of it.

Tommy had been driving for an hour on the highway when his phone rang. He hit Talk on the console.

"Where are you?" she asked.

"I'm on my way to your place. I'll be there in another thirty minutes."

"Did you see everyone?"

"I did. They're all good. Nicholas is a great kid. He's already so big. Lizzy looked happy."

"I'm glad."

After Hayley left Sacramento, six months had gone by without a word, but she finally made contact. Tommy had been certain she would, and he was right. He had seen her dozens of times since that first call. She had rented a tiny dilapidated cabin with a leaky roof in the Sierra Nevadas, a riverfront home on the South Yuba with turquoise water for miles and countless swimming holes.

He no longer tried to talk her into coming back to Sacramento. Although it had taken him a while, he finally understood she needed time to heal, time away from people and society.

Until she was ready, he would be the conduit between Hayley and the people she cared about. He would keep her updated, and he would spend as much time with her as she would allow. With Hayley, he would always be patient. All she had to do was call, and he would be there. She was sassy, maybe even badass, but she was loyal to the core, and she would always be his girl.

Lizzy put Nicholas to bed. Her son fell asleep the second his head hit the pillow, the puppy curled up next to him. No nighttime story necessary.

She walked out of the room and strolled out onto the front porch, where her gaze roamed over the area dotted with pines and oaks. She knew she would have to remain vigilant if she wanted to protect her son. Today had been a day of celebration, and Lizzy had felt about as carefree and relaxed as she ever would. She'd come to terms with knowing she would have to remain watchful and alert. Always.

Six months after Nicholas was born, Lizzy had received a letter from Zachary Tucker:

Dear Lizzy,

I was saddened to hear you quit the PI business. I haven't been able to stop thinking of you since we met at the gallery downtown and then again at my beautiful waterfront home. Your niece, Brittany, is lovely, and I find it to be such a delightful coincidence that your niece and I share a passion for art. As I have been on my best behavior since arriving at my new residence, I have been given full access to the prison library. I have done my research, and I must say I find your fondness for serial killers to be a charming trait. I only wish I had checked you out more thoroughly while I had the freedom to do so. It is for this reason I am writing to you now. I appeal to you to please find it in your heart to visit me here in prison. If I do not hear from you or see you in the coming months, I would like to take this moment to wish you and your son, Nicholas, much happiness. I have absolute faith I will meet him someday, and see you and your beautiful niece again.

Until then,
ZT

Lizzy went back into the house and walked around, making sure every window and door was secure. After the alarm was set, she went to her bedroom, where she unlocked the fireproof steel door she'd had installed where the closet used to be.

Since the Wayne Bennett incident, she had stockpiled a few weapons: a Maverick 88 twelve-gauge shotgun, a Mossberg 500 twenty-gauge high-capacity pump-action shotgun, a Smith & Wesson Governor stainless-steel revolver with rifle barrel, a GLOCK 19 nonthrill handgun—so easy to fire—and her new favorite, a KRISS Vector with low recoil and fast follow-up shots and a twenty-five-round extended magazine.

She did a lot of practice shooting on the property. She was running again, too, pushing Nicholas in the stroller, and staying in shape.

Zachary Tucker's letter was on the shelf next to the ammunition where she'd left it—her constant reminder that evil never dies.

She shut the solid steel door and then turned the dial, locking it tight.

"Come and visit me anytime, Zachary. I'll be ready for you."

NOTE FROM THE AUTHOR

After nearly twenty years, I decided to transition from writing romance to writing thrillers. I had always loved reading in the thriller genre, so I thought, why not give it a shot? After writing the first hundred pages of *Abducted*, I found myself unable to sleep well. Researching real-life serial killers was not, I realized, for the faint of heart. I put the book away and wrote *Having My Baby*, a contemporary romance, instead.

When I came back to *Abducted*, I found myself sucked into Lizzy's world. Suddenly, nothing could stop me from finishing that book. Getting a good night's sleep was no longer a problem because I realized my book wasn't about serial killers, or bad guys, or rapists. The book was about Lizzy Gardner. She is a survivor. Although traumatized by her past, Lizzy is determined to push on and find a way to heal while also helping others.

Months after finishing *Abducted*, since the book had yet to be submitted to publishers, I self-published my first thriller. I never intended for *Abducted* to become a series, let alone a bestselling novel. But more than one million readers later, I can tell you that's exactly what happened.

Evil Never Dies is the last book in this series (although you never know what might happen down the road). Lizzy and friends have been living in my head since 2009, and I have mixed emotions about saying good-bye to them. But I absolutely cannot move on to my next thriller series without saying thank you to my readers, every single one of you. You're the best!

ACKNOWLEDGMENTS

Many thanks to Alan Turkus, Jacque Ben-Zekry, and Tiffany Pokorny for their ongoing help and support.

Special thanks to Kjersti Egerdahl for reading the manuscript and helping me every step of the way.

Again, much gratitude to David Downing for making my scenes come alive. I think you're amazing!

Thanks and gratitude to my sister, Cathy, who continues to read every book I write. For more than twenty years, she has taken her red pen to all my manuscripts. She reads every page, over and over again, without complaint, always asking for more.

I must acknowledge Joe Ragan Sr. and Pat Ragan for their continued enthusiasm and support. Their belief in me throughout the years never wavered, not once.

All my love to Joe Ragan. I couldn't do it without you.

ABOUT THE AUTHOR

New York Times and *USA Today* bestselling author Theresa Ragan grew up with four sisters in Lafayette, California. She has garnered six Golden Heart nominations in Romance Writers of America's prestigious Golden Heart competition for her work. After writing for twenty years, Theresa self-published in March 2011 and went on to sell more than one million books. In 2012, she signed with Thomas & Mercer and is having the time of her life.

Besides writing thrillers under the name T.R. Ragan, Theresa also writes medieval time travels, contemporary romance, and romantic suspense. To learn more about Theresa, visit her website at www.theresaragan.com.

ABOUT THE AUTHOR